THE SWORD OF PHOXNAY

THE CYTHEREA SERIES
BOOK ONE

DIANA KRISTINE WELLS

The Sword of Phoxnay

Copyright © 2023 by Diana Kristine Wells

All rights reserved.

This book or any portion thereof may not be reproduced or used in any manner whatsoever without the express written permission of the publisher except for the use of brief quotations in a book review.

Portions of this book are works of fiction. Any references to historical events, real people, or real places are used fictitiously. Other names, characters, places and events are products of the author's imagination, and any resemblance to actual events or places or persons, living or dead, is entirely coincidental.

Editing by Rooted in Writing, www.RootedInWriting.com
Cover image by Christian Bentulan, www.CoversByChristian.com

ISBN hardcover: 979-8-9879165-2-0
ISBN paperback: 979-8-9879165-1-3
ISBN e-book: 979-8-9879165-0-6

www.DianaWells.com

THE SWORD OF PHOXNAY

I

Tarquin spread his arms, eyes closed and voice lowered. He began the story: *A calm rested over the land of Phoxnay, broken briefly by a horse and rider galloping past. As hooves met cobblestones, they rushed from the soft path of the grassy meadow on the final stretch of their journey. The castle lay ahead.*

"That's you, Tarquin!" Cytherea exclaimed, and grabbed the worn wooden arm of Tarquin's rocking chair to steady herself as she leaned forward with wide eyes.

Beside her, Kenric frowned. "Let him tell it, Cyth." The floor creaked beneath him as he rocked his chair backward.

Cytherea scrunched her nose and lifted her emerald-green eyes to her guardian. "The rider is you, isn't it, Tarquin?"

Tarquin smiled. Creases lined his eyes and gray streaked his once-dark hair. "Yes, child, the rider was me," he said. "Now let me continue."

Kenric grinned, his fair skin pink at the cheeks in the heat of the fire. "You know she'll interrupt you again."

Cytherea huffed. "I will not."

The nine-year-old's brown eyes gleamed. "Yes, you will."

"Just because you're three years older than me, Kenric Feydeau, doesn't mean you know everything," she shot back.

Tarquin shook his head. Fenia, his wife, darned a pair of Cytherea's breeches.

"This is the story about how you became my guardian, right?" Cytherea laid her hands on her knees and cocked her head.

"Shh," Kenric hissed.

Once Cytherea quieted and the only sound was the crackling fire, Tarquin continued the story: *Royal guards spotted the rider's approach and pushed back the massive iron gates to keep from slowing his progress. The horse and rider burst through the gates, and after the massive steed slowed to a halt, the rider dismounted and ran toward the immense doors that led inside the castle of Phoxnay.*

He entered the castle and rushed through the courtyard. When he reached the doors to the throne room, he stopped and waited with the courtier, who had also arrived at the request of King Edmond. Tension radiated through the hushed conversations. The rider's name was Tarquin, and he had—

"See, it was Tarquin," Cytherea interrupted. "And King Edmond is my father!"

Tarquin raised an eyebrow.

Cytherea wilted. "Sorry."

. . . and he had served his king and queen faithfully since childhood. Tarquin let out a long breath to calm himself before he entered the presence of the king.

Silence reigned beyond the thick mahogany doors, where the king waited to meet with them, making it impossible to determine His Majesty's mood. Before the messenger's patience was tested any longer, the doors slowly swung wide to expose the king's cavernous throne room.

Tarquin rushed ahead of the others. "Majesty!" His breathless cry echoed through the chamber, and one of the king's guards blocked his path with a saber. "I beg your forgiveness, Your Majesty," he stumbled on, "but the reports have been confirmed. The Dark Realm is marching toward Phoxnay!" Tarquin absently waved his hand, mimicking his words.

Cytherea clenched her riding breeches. *Not the Dark Realm.* Ailmar and his evil nation were the villain in most of Tarquin's stories. But unlike the rest of his tales, the Dark Realm wasn't make-believe.

Kenric leaned forward, jaw clenched.

Tarquin continued the story: *The king sat at a table with his back toward his courtier and his head slightly bowed. He motioned him forward. "How far?" King Edmond asked.*

The courtier responded with more reverence, "If they keep their current pace, Your Majesty, they could reach the edge of the kingdom in two days' time."

The king rose slowly, not even glancing at Tarquin. The news was not unexpected, as the rumors had been swirling for months, but the king had hoped they would prove false. Ailmar's army had been spotted mustering near Phoxnay. The king worried that his enemies were moving too swiftly.

Deep in thought, King Edmond reached the window and looked out to the garden below. Lisel, his queen, and their beautiful child were playing in the afternoon sun. The toddler princess reached for the gold ring her mother wore on a chain around her neck. It was a gift from the king of Klobyn, a longtime friend of Edmond, who had given it to them at the princess's birth three years prior. He had it encrusted with small emeralds to match the eyes of the princess.

"My eyes!" Cytherea squealed and jumped up in excitement. Her chair clattered to the floor. The green coloring of her eyes was a bright contrast to her skin, which was tanned a golden shade from all the time she spent outside with the horses.

Kenric rolled his eyes and stood to get a drink of water from the pail they kept next to the door of the small cottage.

"Let Tarquin tell his story," Fenia said gently.

Kenric and Cytherea settled back down in the child-sized chairs that Tarquin had made them. Tarquin continued.

King Edmond knew his kingdom was filled with families like his, and he would not let Ailmar destroy their peaceful lives. The king turned from the window. The others in the hallway made their way past the guards and entered the chamber behind Tarquin. As he waited, the king absently fingered the hilt of his sword, the renowned Sword of Phoxnay, and the jewel that was embedded there glimmered. Outside the farthest borders of the kingdom, evil was rising. Ailmar, the ruler of the Dark Realm, had turned his sights and his army toward Phoxnay and the destruction of the royal family.

"Why did Ailmar want to destroy Phoxnay and my family?" Cytherea furrowed her brows in worry. Fenia leaned forward in her rocking chair and reached down to lay a comforting hand on Cytherea's shoulder.

"Because he is evil," Kenric interjected before Tarquin could reply. "Isn't that right, Father?"

"Yes, Son."

"But why Phoxnay?" Cytherea probed further.

Tarquin smiled. "You certainly are full of questions today." Cytherea smiled up at him. "Even at just six years old, you are so much like your mother. She too wanted to understand everything around her." He sighed.

"I was just wondering why someone would want to destroy a place as beautiful as you say Phoxnay once was," she said. "You've never told us that part."

"You were never interested before. Ailmar wanted power, and Phoxnay was legendary in both its size and its wealth. Ailmar also had a history with King Edmond. When Edmond was a young king, he led a battle against Ailmar's father. During this battle, King Edmond killed Ailmar's father, the ruler of the Dark Realm. So it was both revenge and power that fueled Ailmar's hatred, and he would not stop until he had destroyed Phoxnay and King Edmond." Tarquin paused. "May I continue?"

"Yes," Cytherea said curtly.

"Your Majesty," the messenger urged, "the legions of the Dark Realm

are close at hand, and we must alert the kingdom. We can wait no more."

"He is right, Your Majesty," agreed Drake, the commander of Phoxnay's army. "We must allow the people time to ready themselves for what is to come and begin moving within the walls of the castle for safety." Drake and Edmond had been friends since childhood, and the king trusted him with his life. However, at this moment, he wished Drake was wrong.

King Edmond was silent as he weighed what his next command should be. The fate of the entire kingdom rested on his shoulders, and while he felt the weight of the responsibility, he did not shy away from it. He gripped his sword's hilt, drawing strength from its power.

"Your Majesty?" The messenger's voice broke into his thoughts.

"Send out the messengers," the king commanded his guards, his voice gaining volume as he spoke. "Announce that all are welcome within the walls. The time has come for war." He paused, then added, "Ask the queen to come to me." He then turned to Tarquin. "Help move the people to safety."

Everyone but the king's guards exited the room. Moments later, the rustle of the queen's multilayered silk gown preceded her into the throne room. He couldn't help but smile. She never much cared for dresses, but she knew as queen she couldn't be in riding breeches every day.

"Like me! Only I get to wear my riding breeches every day!" Cytherea said excitedly.

Tarquin chuckled and glanced at Fenia, who shook her head with a smile. She continued sewing a patch into a pair of Cytherea's breeches. "I wish I were sewing silk dresses for you instead, Cytherea. But I know they aren't comfortable, and they just get dirty and torn anyway."

Tarquin returned to his story: *Queen Lisel rushed through the door, her cheeks flushed with concern.*

"I was told it was urgent. My love, is something the matter?"

"The army of the Dark Realm approaches. We must prepare for war."

Her face darkened with the news, but she quickly recovered. "We will defeat them. Ailmar will never prevail."

The king nodded. "We must get Cytherea to safety, and soon." It took all his will to get the words out, but he knew that Cytherea's safety was the most important thing.

Cytherea shivered.

2

Fenia interrupted the story as she stood. "Why don't the three of you move closer to the fire while I clear the table. I don't want Cytherea to catch cold."

"Finish the story now, Tarquin, please," Cytherea pleaded. She and Kenric moved their chairs closer to the warmth of the fire.

Fenia smiled and watched her son set up Cytherea's chair for her before getting his own. His brown eyes were hidden behind a waterfall of blond hair, which he pushed away, only to have it fall back into his eyes. His appearance was that of a child at the cusp of turning into a young man, with the shape of muscles beginning to show through his shirt sleeves.

"I think it may be time for Tarquin to trim your hair, my son." Fenia laughed.

"Can I cut mine too, Fenia?" Cytherea's voice was hopeful. "I want my hair to look just like Kenric's."

Fire sparkled in Cytherea's eyes. Fenia sighed, and a slight smile crossed her lips. Cytherea wanted to be able to do everything Kenric did, but Fenia would draw a sharp line at cutting her long hair. "Maybe when you are older, Cytherea, but for now I will put it in a braid so it is out of your face." Cytherea frowned, but Fenia's compromise would have to do for now.

Fenia settled Cytherea in front of her rocking chair and divided Cytherea's hair into three parts to begin braiding it. Cytherea's hair was brown, but in the light of the sun or the fire, flecks of auburn and gold danced within its strands. It was thick with a slight wave that refused to be tamed. Fenia struggled to keep it confined within her hands.

Tarquin shifted in his own seat, and Kenric wiggled into place once again to hear the rest of the story. "It looks like you may be ready for a full-sized chair now, Kenric."

"Me too!" squealed Cytherea.

"You still have some room to grow yet, Cytherea," Tarquin replied. "All right, where did we leave off?"

"Mother and Father were sending me away." Cytherea's eyes began to fill with tears. "Why did they have to send me away, Tarquin?"

"You know how the story ends, Cyth," Kenric said impatiently.

Tarquin turned a harsh eye toward his son, and Kenric quieted once again. He gave his son a soft pat before responding gently to Cytherea.

"The king and queen couldn't leave the people of Phoxnay when they were needed the most. Your parents were sovereigns, and as such, they had a sworn duty to the people of their kingdom."

"But why?" Cytherea crossed her arms stubbornly, clearly trying to hold back her tears.

Tarquin reached out and rubbed her back. "They loved you very much, Cytherea, and that is why they asked Fenia and me—"

"And me!" Kenric reminded him, with his chest puffed out in pride.

"Yes, that is why they asked Fenia, Kenric, and me to take you away and keep you safe until you were able to return."

"We are going back?" Cytherea looked up, hope shining in her eyes.

"Not yet, child." Tarquin hesitated before continuing. "But when you are older and the time is right, you will return to take your rightful place as queen."

"Queen?" Kenric threw his head back and howled.

"Well, I am a princess, Kenric," Cytherea said, trying her best to look regal.

This made Kenric laugh even louder.

Fenia admonished him. "Kenric, despite her age, you should still show Cytherea respect. She is our sovereign."

"Fine," Kenric retorted, "but you forgot the part about Everard." Regret flashed across his face as soon as the words had left his mouth.

"Who's Everard?" Cytherea asked.

Kenric wilted at Tarquin's glare of disapproval. "Everard is a story for another day, Cytherea," Tarquin answered somberly. "Besides, I think it's time for bed now, children." His rocking chair groaned as he moved to stand.

Cytherea grabbed his rough hand before he could get up from his chair. "What about the rest of the story? The part where we escape and come here to the farm?"

Tarquin laughed. "You know the rest of the story better than I do. I don't need to tell it again." He stood and placed more wood on the fire, which lit up even the far corners of the room. The small family all turned at once at the loud crackles and pops from the fresh wood.

"Please, Tarquin! I promise I won't interrupt again." With her hair freshly braided, she returned to her seat by the fire, her expression as serious as she could make it.

"Very well. Where would you like me to start?" He sat back down in his chair, and Cytherea and Kenric did the same, while Fenia moved about the small kitchen to begin preparations for the next day's meals.

"The part where you and Fenia were getting ready to take me to safety!"

"I helped save you too, you know," Kenric chimed in.

Cytherea wrinkled her nose at him as Tarquin took up the story.

Queen Lisel knew that preparations for Cytherea's escape had to be done quickly and secretly because she couldn't be sure that there weren't spies for the Dark Realm nearby. She took a deep breath, smoothed out her skirts, and headed to the children's corridor.

When the queen entered Cytherea's room, she found Tarquin planning their route while his young son, Kenric, helped Fenia gather the items Cytherea would need for their journey. The queen smiled at Kenric as he helped his mother. Because of their positions, Tarquin and Fenia lived in the castle, and Queen Lisel made sure that Kenric had the best tutors and nurses, as if he were her own. Once Cytherea arrived, Kenric wanted nothing more than to help Fenia care for her, even though he was only three years old at the time of her birth. Now he was six years old, but Tarquin was already training him in all manner of fighting. He already showed a particular gift in swordsmanship.

"That's me, Cyth!" Kenric said. "I am a gifted swordsman!"

Cytherea rolled her eyes without responding.

Tarquin ignored them and continued: *The queen suddenly realized that they were watching her while she was lost in her thoughts. They had all stopped their preparations when their sovereign had entered, but they returned to their tasks after she gently waved them away from formalities.*

Cytherea was not in the room, so the queen took that moment to talk to Fenia quietly. "I need you to give me your word that if something happens to the king and me, you and Tarquin will raise Cytherea as your own. The bloodline of Phoxnay must be secured through her. Promise me that you will protect her and keep her from the hands of Ailmar."

"Please don't talk like that, my queen!" Fenia said. "This war will pass, and we will bring Cytherea back to you."

"Promise me!" commanded the queen, desperate for reassurance that her child would be safe.

"I promise, Your Majesty," Fenia replied quietly, bowing her head to hide the tears rolling down her cheeks.

Cytherea whimpered and scooted her chair closer to Kenric. "I hate this part of the story."

Kenric put a protective arm around her shoulders. Cytherea sniffled and leaned into him. "It's OK, Cyth," he said gently. "Your mother and father were brave and never failed in their duty as sovereigns."

"Being a sovereign is stupid."

"You shouldn't say that, Cytherea," Tarquin gently scolded. "That is who you are, and it is your destiny."

"Well, then my destiny is stupid!" she yelled, her arms crossed tightly. "Being a sovereign is stupid and duty is stupid too!" A small tear ran down her flushed cheek. Cytherea took a breath and changed the subject. "Tarquin, can you skip to the happy part?"

"Of course, my child," Tarquin said, without chastising her. "Fenia, Kenric, and I took you and escaped just as the Dark Realm began their attack on Phoxnay. And, after traveling for several days, we came here to our little cottage in Ceka and made it our home." He smiled broadly with outstretched arms. "The end!"

Cytherea looked around her at the warm fire, the cool stone walls, and the table where they often laughed over meals. "I never want to leave our cottage."

"You may have to one day, Cytherea." Tarquin furrowed his brows. "You have a duty as the princess of Phoxnay."

Fenia scooped her up, frowning at Tarquin and Kenric. "That time is a long way away, so don't you worry about that." She carried Cytherea to her room. "Duty and destiny can wait. Right now, it's bedtime."

3

TEN YEARS LATER

Cytherea grunted as she plunged her sword into the barn's main post. Her swordsmanship was accompanied by the sound of Aherne, her charger, munching on the oats she had put in his trough. He was utterly unconcerned with her imaginary battle against evil. He stood outside his stall, which always remained open so he could come and go freely to the paddock area attached to the barn.

Ready for a break from her drills, she pushed against his hindquarters to move him out of her way so she could sit on the bench next to his trough. He bobbed his head in defiance before eventually stepping aside. His head bobbing was a bad habit that she should correct, but she didn't want to squelch his spirit, so, as always, she didn't admonish him. Instead, she laughed.

Cytherea leaned back on the rough wood of Aherne's stall and watched the horses move about the barn. Eight neat stalls surrounded a wide-open area that was enough space to saddle several of the large steeds at once. The hard dirt floor muffled the sound of stomping hooves from the impatient horses who were always ready to get their rides started. Down the middle of the barn, three thick, sturdy posts held the roof far above them and made for worthy opponents in Cytherea's sword drills.

Looking down at her sword, she ran her hand carefully along the flat of the blade. The coolness of the steel seeped into her fingertips in an oddly comforting way that brought a smile to her lips. The blade had dulled and would need to be sharpened again soon, an act required frequently when training with wooden posts. She raised the sword in front of her, and a peaceful warmth washed down her arm and through her body. Cytherea had always felt an odd connection to swords from her early childhood. Tarquin had often told her she had a gift and encouraged her to train, despite Fenia's constant protests. Cytherea lowered the sword and rubbed Aherne's muzzle in response to his persistent nudges. Barn cats rustled through the hayloft above her, either in play or in chase after a mouse that was eluding capture.

A birdlike whistle pierced the air a moment before Kenric shouldered through the barn doors, a load of wood in his arms. Kenric had always loved birds and often imitated their various calls, but his favorite was that of a red swift. A red swift was a common bird and more of a nuisance than anything, especially if you asked Fenia, who spent much of her time shooing them from her little vegetable garden. You could always hear them whistling to each other in the treetops during the day, making it easy for Kenric to practice mimicking them. He practiced until even his family had trouble telling the difference between Kenric and an actual red swift.

His whistle always reminded Cytherea of playing hide-and-seek with him as a child. If she had trouble finding him and got frustrated, he would let out a quiet whistle to help her. But Kenric hadn't played hide-and-seek with her for years. She met his eye with a grin, twirling the blade in front of her. She got only a flat look in return. His stubbly jaw was set in a frown.

"Don't tell me you're practicing sword drills in here again, Cyth."

"Fine. I won't." She tossed her braided chestnut hair over one shoulder and turned away from him.

"You know my mother doesn't like you doing that," he admonished.

Cytherea tried unsuccessfully to stifle her laughter at Kenric's attempt to chastise her. "I know." Cytherea sighed. "She thinks it is unladylike and unbecoming of a princess, which is why I practice where she can't see me. I don't want to upset her, but I do love training. Besides, no one around here knows my past, so it seems silly for me to act like a princess."

"But you are a princess, Cytherea. Or at least you are supposed to be." His exasperation showed through his words. "Anyway, that horse is the only one that will ever see you fight. There's nothing for you to fight here, and my mother wouldn't let you even if there were."

Aherne bobbed his head, snorting almost indignantly, as if in protest. "Tarquin says I need to know how to protect myself *because* I'm a princess. I'll be sixteen tomorrow, and one day I'll have to leave the farm to start a family of my own. It is better if I am able to protect myself."

After setting the wood down, Kenric crossed the barn and sat next to Cytherea.

"There will be no talk of you leaving in front of Fenia, young lady." Cytherea hadn't noticed Tarquin enter the barn behind Kenric, and they both jumped when his voice echoed through the rafters. "You won't be going anywhere anytime soon, and I don't want you to upset her if she hears you talking about it." Tarquin strode toward her and gently laid a hand on her shoulder. "And when you do leave here, it will be with someone to protect you."

"I can protect myself, Tarquin," she countered, her gaze determined as she looked up at him. "You have trained me well."

"You are still a princess, Cytherea, and your life will not be like others. You have a destiny that cannot be ignored."

"What if I want a normal life? I don't understand what my destiny is or why that makes me different. I have no kingdom to be princess of, and I like my life on our farm in the country without some imaginary destiny to worry about."

"But the heart of a queen beats within you, Cytherea. As the sole remaining heir to the throne of Phoxnay, you will be ready when it is time for you to take on the burden of the kingdom's fate. Even if you don't feel ready now."

Her face flushed, she stomped out of the barn, sliding her sword into its sheath that hung at her hip. She struggled to avoid tripping on the scabbard. She attempted to adjust it, but it kept sliding toward her feet on the silk ribbons that Fenia insisted on sewing into her riding breeches. The ribbons encircled her waist and continued down the legs in an effort to make her breeches look more feminine, but they got in the way of her scabbard. Cytherea gave up and let the sword hang at an awkward angle. *I have to get Fenia to take these ribbons off!*

Tarquin's muffled laughter coming from the barn at her back infuriated her. She wouldn't stay mad at him for long, and their conversation faded behind her as she made her way up the path to the house.

"Stubborn girl," Kenric muttered.

Tarquin rested his hand on his son's shoulder. "Don't get upset with her, Kenric. Her heritage beats within her heart, but she is not yet equipped to understand it or to control it. She is meant for far greater than this."

"She doesn't even want anything greater! She just wants to hang out with the horses and practice sword drills! How can she be a princess if she doesn't want to be one?" Kenric snapped before he could gain control of his emotions. He took a breath, his nostrils flaring. "I apologize, Father, but she doesn't want to accept the truth of who she is. She was raised on a farm with horses, not in a castle as a princess."

Tarquin's smile broadened. "You know as well as I that her stubbornness and her resistance to her heritage is only proof that she knows the truth." Kenric dropped his gaze in defeat. "And her gifted swordsmanship is only proof of what is inside her. The reason Fenia worries about her training with her sword is because it reminds her that Cytherea has a destiny beyond our little farm, and she is afraid of losing her." Tarquin paused to look at Kenric. "And I think that scares you a little bit too."

Kenric's jaw tightened, and he muttered, "You really should try harder to convince her to act more like a princess." Then he shuffled away to finish his chores.

Laughing to himself, Tarquin strode out of the barn and to the river to draw water for the mutton Fenia was preparing for their evening meal.

When Tarquin returned, Cytherea was meandering across the pasture, petting and talking to every animal grazing there. She took extra time with the horses because they were her first love. Many of the horses Tarquin had were descendants of the mighty warhorses who were once in the service of the king of Phoxnay. At seventeen and a half hands high, their trunk-like legs and feathered hooves dwarfed Cytherea's slender frame. She wove field flowers into their thick, long black manes. The massive steeds seemed content to allow her to do it—they were like kittens in her hands.

Tarquin laughed and muttered, "They are not looking very mighty at the moment."

Some of the townspeople would ask about the breeding of his horses, but Tarquin was always vague in his replies. The chargers were really the only visible sign as to who was living on their small, unassuming farm. All other signs—armor, weapons, jewels, gold—were kept well hidden from everyone, including Cytherea.

Tarquin let out a long sigh as he watched Cytherea's easy, fluid motions. Once she accepted her destiny, she'd be driven to reclaim her kingdom from the hands of Ailmar. She would not turn away and deny her heritage forever. It was her manner to right the wrongs of this world, and Ailmar in Phoxnay was the worst of wrongs.

Tarquin shook off his thoughts at the sound of Fenia calling to him.

"Tarquin, I need that water if you want to eat by sundown!"

He chuckled under his breath. "I'm an old man, Fenia," he replied. "I do nothing quickly these days." Tarquin moved a bit faster.

Their little cottage wasn't much, but it was theirs and had been a happy home since they'd arrived in Ceka, which lay between what was once the kingdom of Phoxnay and the kingdom of Klobyn. Originally meant to be temporary, the farm became a permanent residence upon the death of the king and queen. The fall of Phoxnay had been devastating, but they'd focused on creating a safe place for Cytherea. Suddenly, the image of a green-eyed boy with a birthmark like Cytherea's surfaced, but Tarquin pushed it away. He had done everything he could to save Everard. The Phoxnay loyalists were now waiting in exile for their princess to grow up and reclaim her family's crown. That time had always seemed so far away, but it was suddenly here, and he wanted desperately to push it away.

"Watch where you are going, Tarquin!" His wife's voice jarred him from his thoughts again.

He had walked right into her vegetable garden, and the soft earth melted beneath his boots. "My apologies, my love. I was thinking about something."

"More like daydreaming, I'd say," she responded with a wink

and a laugh. "Now bring me that water so I can get this mutton going before we all starve."

Tarquin laughed while carefully tiptoeing around the carrots, potatoes, and other vegetables that were just beginning to peek out from beneath the rich soil before hurrying into the cottage. He was greeted by the warmth of the fire and the smell of Fenia's cooking. His stomach grumbled, and he hoped the food would cook quickly. Fenia followed him inside with her apron full of vegetables. Tarquin sat at the table watching her finalize the meal preparations. As she stirred the mutton that had begun to boil, Kenric came in from the barn.

"It smells marvelous, Mother! How long until we can eat? I'm hungry!" Kenric removed his barn boots at the door. A cool breeze from the open door fanned the fire, and it danced under the pot.

"The mutton still needs time to cook, but why don't you go fetch Cytherea from the pasture? It should be ready when you get back."

"Just a minute, Son," Tarquin said. "Before you go get Cytherea, I need to talk to you and your mother alone."

"What is it, Tarquin? You sound so serious." Fenia wiped her hands on her apron and came to sit with Tarquin and Kenric at the table.

"There was another raid a few days ago."

"I knew it!" Kenric jumped up from the table. "Ailmar will never stop taking young boys to torture and pad his army! We have to stop him, Father!"

"Kenric! Sit down. How do you propose the two of us fight the entire army of the Dark Realm?" Tarquin responded more harshly than he intended. Then he wilted, lowering his eyes. "I'm sorry, Son. I'm just as frustrated as you, but our duty is here, protecting Cytherea."

Kenric crossed his arms and sat back down next to his father.

"This most recent raid was only a two-day ride from here," Tarquin continued.

"They are expanding their raids beyond even Phoxnay's borders," Fenia stated, horrified.

"Exactly."

"How many did they take this time?" Kenric asked.

"Twenty young boys," Tarquin responded with his eyes on the floor. "And they killed nearly all of the men that were of fighting age."

Fenia gasped.

"Do you think they will find us? Do you think they will come for Cytherea?" Kenric asked.

"I don't know, but they are too close for my comfort. No one here knows who Cytherea is, but it wouldn't take much for any of the elders to figure it out. She is the exact image of her mother, and of course, she has her father's remarkable eyes."

"It is time that Cytherea accepts the truth of who she is," Fenia said reluctantly.

"Yes, it is." Tarquin sighed. "Let's allow her one more unburdened birthday celebration tomorrow, and then I'll sit her down and explain it all."

"Go fetch Cytherea to eat, Kenric." Fenia's voice wavered slightly. She stood and went back to tending to their meal.

4

Kenric found Cytherea leaving the pasture with Aherne and Kenric's charger, Tredan, trailing her. Aherne's long, wavy black mane was laced with bright wildflowers that seemed to dance as he moved. Tredan also had flowers braided into his shorter mane as well as his tail, and both held their heads high, as if making sure everyone saw their equine coifs.

"You treat those horses like little dogs," Kenric shouted from the top of the hill.

Cytherea looked up, surprise etched on her face. "Why didn't you whistle for me?"

"I wanted to talk to you alone." He was determined to tell her the truth even though his father wanted to wait. It was time. It was past time, in fact, for her to face her destiny.

"About what?"

"About Ailmar."

She sighed. "I don't like talking about him. Why would you even bring up his name on such a beautiful day?"

"We have to talk about him, Cyth. He is evil." He lowered his voice once she drew closer. "Do you know that he steals young boys from the villages?"

"I've heard those rumors in the marketplace too, but that is all they are—rumors."

"They are not rumors. They are real." He took her shoulders and turned her to face him. "When he gets those small boys back to his castle, do you know what he does to them?"

"Keep your foolish tales to yourself, Kenric!" Cytherea tried to turn away, but he had a firm hold on her shoulders. "I don't want to hear it."

"Well, you need to hear it," he continued. "He takes those boys and throws them into a dark cell in a cold dungeon. Away from their mothers, their homes, and their security. Once there, they are terrorized, tortured, starved, and deprived of sleep until one day, Ailmar gathers them together and forces them to bow to him using his dark magic."

"Stop!" Cytherea shouted through her tears.

"Listen, Cytherea! This is not a rumor or a stupid tale. They are real. The boys are real, the torture is real, and those he kills are real." Kenric paused and released her, wiping a tear from her face as he gazed at her. "You can't hide from it any longer. You are the only living sovereign of Phoxnay. It's your duty and your destiny to save them and protect our kingdom from Ailmar and the Dark Realm!"

Cytherea took a deep, steadying breath, pushed his hand from her cheek, wiped away her tears, and straightened. "I told you before. I am not a sovereign and I have no duty to the people of Phoxnay because there is no Phoxnay anymore." She met Kenric's eyes steadily. "My parents died fighting for Phoxnay, but it was for nothing. Ailmar still destroyed their kingdom and killed them in the process. I lost my parents for nothing because nothing can stop Ailmar, not my parents and certainly not me."

With that, she turned and walked toward the cottage, leaving Kenric alone, questioning whether Tarquin was right in believing Cytherea would follow her destiny when it was time.

All thought of the Dark Realm was pushed from their minds, at least momentarily, as they ate. After their evening meal, they remained sitting around the table. Fenia pushed back her chair with a grin. "Cytherea, I have a gift for you."

"But my birthday isn't until tomorrow." Cytherea feigned mock resistance.

"I know. Just wait here while I get it."

Cytherea wiggled in her chair, eyes sparkling in anticipation. Tarquin smiled, thinking she would always be a little girl inside despite her years.

Fenia returned with a small box in her hand. "Here we are!"

"What is it?" Cytherea giggled with glee.

"Why don't you open it and find out, Cyth," Kenric said sarcastically, which earned him a nudge from Tarquin under the table.

She took the box and opened it. Inside was a beautiful ring encrusted with emeralds on a golden chain. She took the ring in her hand, and a memory instantly flooded her mind: The ring hung from her mother's neck and glistened in the sun. She bent over and lifted Cytherea into the air, her mother's laughter tickling her ears.

"My mother's necklace!" she gasped.

"It is your necklace now," Fenia said. Kenric walked over to get a closer look at it. "It was given as a gift from Aldegunde, the king of Klobyn, at your birth. Your mother wore it around her neck every day until she placed it around your neck the day we left Phoxnay. Since you were such an active child and always playing with the animals, I was afraid you might lose it. I put it away and kept it safe until you were older."

Cytherea closed her eyes as she held the ring between her fingers. The smell of lavender filled her senses. She always thought she could smell lavender anytime she thought of her mother. Fenia said it was because Cytherea's mother had always worn a lavender perfume and that all of our senses held memories of our past. Cytherea opened her eyes, and a tear rolled down Fenia's cheek.

"Why are you crying?" She wiped the tear from Fenia's cheek.

"You have grown into the very image of your mother, and she would have been so proud to see you now."

"Will you put it on me?" Cytherea held the necklace out and lifted her thick hair out of the way. Fenia latched the delicate chain around her neck so it lay over her dragon-shaped birthmark.

Fenia turned her around and adjusted the ring. "It looks perfect!"

Cytherea beamed as she turned to show Kenric and Tarquin, who gave the required mutterings of approval.

"If I'm not mistaken, Fenia, I believe I saw a pie cooling on the windowsill earlier," Tarquin teased.

"Always thinking about food, aren't you, my love," Fenia teased back before turning to retrieve the requested pie.

Cytherea smiled. She loved how in love Tarquin and Fenia were and how safe she felt despite what had happened to her parents. Although, behind his smile, Tarquin's eyes looked tired and worried.

5

"Under the bed," Tarquin ordered.

"Why?" Cytherea whispered. She attempted to clear her head after the abrupt awakening while also obeying his command.

"Someone is approaching," he whispered, gesturing sharply for her to obey.

Visitors were uncommon at the cottage. Tarquin's sword glinted as he crept silently to the main room with Kenric right behind him. Cytherea shivered slightly on the bare wood floor beneath her bed, and she peered out. Tarquin looked out the window and then turned toward Kenric and Fenia with an expression that made Cytherea's breath catch in her throat. Without a word, all three began going through cabinets and pulling out weapons Cytherea had never seen before. The flurry of hushed motion and the muffled clang of metal left Cytherea confused. But before she had time to process any of it, Kenric rushed in, grabbed her by the hand, pulled her out from under her bed, and dragged her toward the back door.

The dirt path was cold beneath her bare feet. Kenric picked up the pace, leading her in the direction of the barn. Cytherea craned her neck to see what was happening inside their cottage.

Through the open door, she briefly saw Tarquin and Fenia frantically pulling up floorboards and retrieving weapons and other equipment from underneath. It left Cytherea feeling as if she were caught in a dream.

"Wait! What is happening?" said Cytherea, wrestling to get loose.

"Move!" barked Kenric in a voice that startled her into obedience.

Cytherea regained her feet and planted them to stop Kenric from pulling her. "Tell me what is happening!"

Kenric was bigger and stronger than Cytherea, so instead of arguing, he scooped her up and carried her. Loud voices Cytherea couldn't understand erupted from the cottage. Fenia screamed. Kenric's grip on Cytherea tightened, and he began to run.

She kicked. "Wait! Let go!"

His usually gentle voice boomed at her. "Hold still and be quiet or you will get us *all* killed!"

Startled, Cytherea held her tongue and allowed him to carry her farther from the cottage. Soon the shouting from inside the cottage grew louder, and the clang of metal hitting metal spilled out into the once-still night. Fear coursed through Cytherea, and her entire body began shaking.

Kenric set her on the ground. "Can you run?"

Without a word, Cytherea gathered up her nightgown and nodded.

"Go to the barn, to Aherne's stall, and hide under the hay." Kenric's voice was low but urgent. "Don't come out. Don't even look out until I whistle." Cytherea nodded numbly, and Kenric released her. "Now run!"

Cytherea did as she was told this time. Rocks on the dirt path tore her bare feet, and the chilled night air hurt her lungs as her breath quickened in her race to the barn. Her heart pounded frantically inside her chest, and her mind struggled through the fog, trying to comprehend what was happening.

Cytherea did not slow or look back. When she reached the barn, she was relieved but a little surprised to find Aherne in his stall because he disliked being in the confined space. It almost seemed as if he were waiting for her. His stall door was open like always, but he remained motionless. He stood at his full height with his ears up and directed toward the cottage. He did not greet her as he usually did but instead shifted slightly to allow her past him into his stall. Cytherea grabbed her riding boots that were next to his stall and stumbled into the pile of fresh hay in the back corner. If she needed to run again, at least she would have something on her feet. She shoved them into the boots before concealing herself under the hay. Aherne shifted his body until his hocks were almost touching her.

Is Aherne guarding me? Why does he seem to know what is happening? I don't even know what is happening. Cytherea's thoughts were spinning. Where did all those weapons come from? Who were they fighting, and why were they here? What was happening to Kenric, Tarquin, and Fenia? The questions churned through her mind with terror and guilt, but all she could do was stay hidden and wait. She had promised.

After ensuring that Cytherea made it to the barn, Kenric silently prayed that she would do as she was told for once. He then turned and raced back toward the cottage. When he ran through the door, he found his parents holding their own against four Dark Realm soldiers. Kenric scanned the room and grabbed two swords from the floor. He leaped into the fray, silently vowing that the soldiers would not make it past him to find Cytherea. His family had pledged to their king and queen that they would protect their child with their lives. All three were prepared to do just that.

Cytherea had been hiding in Aherne's stall for what seemed like a lifetime. Despite the distance to the cottage, the clashing of swords and muffled shouts still reached her ears.

She flinched at every sound, desperate to help her family somehow, but she was bound by her word to stay where she was. Besides, every time she shifted, Aherne would step directly in front of her, blocking her exit. He might not let her leave even if she tried.

Who are these people that have attacked my family? Cytherea wondered. Her mind was swirling. Did they come to rob them? That couldn't be it, because the cottage had nothing of any real value. Why did it seem like her family had been expecting them, why did they have all those weapons hidden, and why was she sent to hide?

"You are the only living sovereign of Phoxnay," Kenric had said.

Could this have something to do with my parents and Phoxnay?

I must find a way to help my family.

Her thoughts were interrupted by the screech of the barn door opening. Cytherea waited for Kenric's whistle so she could come out from under the hay, but instead Aherne let out a scream. The sound, high-pitched and terrible, froze Cytherea in place.

The footsteps moved farther into the barn. It wasn't Kenric, and her mind raced. The door to the equipment room squeaked open, and the sound of toppling buckets reverberated through the barn's stale air. Cytherea blinked through the hay and spotted Aherne's grooming bucket hanging on the back of his stall inches away. Could she reach it without the intruder noticing? Other horses shifted nervously in their stalls. She hadn't realized before now that they were all in the barn too. Why weren't they running away? Their stalls were open like Aherne's, yet they were not attempting to escape.

Cytherea listened intently, tracking the intruder moving through the barn. They continued to search the barn, knocking over more buckets as they moved through the unfamiliar darkness. The noise pierced the muffled silence and gave her the chance to reach up and lift the grooming bucket from the wall and bring it down into the hay with her unnoticed. She was relieved to find what she sought—the hoof pick and the sharp blade used to trim Aherne's mane. Cytherea froze again as the intruder moved closer to Aherne's stall; everything around her became still. With every footstep, Cytherea's fate and destiny became threatened. She could barely swallow without the fear of being discovered. Her heart pounded. Aherne shifted his weight from side to side. He now stood almost directly over her, and Cytherea could sense his body tense. The heavy footsteps stopped right outside Aherne's stall.

The barn was silent except for the horses' hooves shifting restlessly beneath them and the air blowing through their nostrils. Cytherea held her breath. She couldn't hear any movement, but she could feel someone peering into the stall where she lay hidden and unmoving under the hay.

Suddenly the intruder shouted, "Search the entire barn! The girl must be in here somewhere!"

Cytherea's gasp was drowned out by Aherne's and the other horses' ferocious screams followed by the thuds from more boots entering the barn. The horses' hooves shook the ground beneath her. The huffs and bizarre cries of fury escaping their throats intermingled with the shouts of strange men as the horses began an uncharacteristic assault.

Aherne remained standing sentry over her, and she could feel the power of his great hooves hitting the ground around her.

Cytherea fought her desire to stay hidden as a newfound strength took over. She had to do something. Pushing aside her fear, she gripped the grooming tools in both hands and rose to her knees. Before she had the chance to leave her concealment, Aherne knocked her over with his haunches and pawed a fresh pile of hay on top of her. Startled, she shrank back and listened helplessly to the men shrieking in fear and pain as the horses attacked with teeth and hooves.

Soon Cytherea felt a fresh wind lift the hay from her head, and the familiar sound of Kenric's boots joined the fray. She shifted, and the hay pricked her skin. She tried to see what was happening, but Aherne's trunk-like legs blocked her view. She gripped her makeshift weapons tighter and strained to hear voices, but the clang of metal deafened her. After a few minutes that felt like days, she was startled by one long, piercing scream followed by footsteps running out of the barn. The rhythmic thuds of giant hooves gave chase to those that ran out of the barn, the stirred-up dust choking Cytherea.

And then, silence. She held her breath, not knowing who had survived besides Aherne still standing guard directly over her. The only sound was Aherne's labored breathing, but soon the tension began to ease. She moved her legs, which were stiff, and tried to get up until another sound made her pause. Someone else was breathing heavily in the barn, and she strained to hear if she was safe or still in peril. A familiar whistle pierced the air.

Kenric is alive!

6

Aherne shifted, and Cytherea scrambled to her feet. Kenric stood outside the stall. His look of fear melted into one of relief when he spotted Cytherea brushing off the hay. Before she had the chance to walk out of the stall, Kenric lunged through the open door and threw his arms around her, breathing out a great sigh. Dirt, sweat, and blood ran down his face.

"You're bleeding—" Cytherea sputtered, gently pushing him away and frantically searching for an injury.

Blood dripped from the blade in Kenric's hand that now pointed toward a soldier lying on the barn floor. Even dead, he was frightening. His skin was unnaturally dark, like soot from a fire had been rubbed into his flesh. He wore a layer of light armor over his tunic, which was a deep black with an odd reflective quality. It was hard to turn away from its trance-inducing allure. Cytherea felt a dark cloud forming inside her.

Kenric gripped her arm. Cytherea shook off the feeling and forced herself to look away, turning her attention back to Kenric. She was thankful that the cuts he had would need attention but didn't look to be life-threatening. The other horses began to return to the barn, lathered and huffing after chasing away the remaining soldiers. Cytherea and Kenric gave them a quick inspection while the horses took long draws from the water trough. Two of them were spattered with blood, but thankfully not their own, and one mare had a minor cut. Nothing a little time wouldn't heal. Cytherea was relieved that they were all right but couldn't believe they had fought so valiantly against the terrifying soldiers.

"Why did they stay and fight?" Cytherea asked. "Horses are supposed to run from danger, not fight it."

"I'll explain later." He rushed out of the barn, pulling her along with him. "We have to get back to my father and mother."

"Tarquin and Fenia!" Cytherea exclaimed. She had been so relieved to see Kenric unharmed, she had momentarily forgotten about them. "Are they hurt?"

"They are hurt, but I don't know how badly." His words were muffled as he ran up the path. Cytherea kept pace. "When the soldiers all ran for the barn, we thought they had found you, and I got to you as quickly as I could. There were more of them than us, and Father is not as strong as he once was." His voice trailed off when they reached the cottage and walked through the open door.

Cytherea gasped at the scene before her. Tarquin's beautiful hand-carved furniture was broken and strewn about, and the cupboard doors were agape with their contents in shambles on the floor.

Fenia rushed from the main bedroom. "Cytherea!" she shouted, barely able to mask her panic. "You are alive!"

"I'm OK," Cytherea answered. "But what about you? Where's Tarquin?" She grabbed the disheveled Fenia's hands.

"Where's Father?" Kenric brushed past his mother toward the room where she had emerged.

Fenia's face turned ashen, and Cytherea lunged forward to wrap her arm around Fenia's waist before she crumpled to the ground. Cytherea's eyes darted, frantically searching for Tarquin while she helped Fenia to the back of the cottage.

Kenric was kneeling next to his father, who lay motionless while Kenric frantically tried to stop the bleeding. A sliver of the waning moon slipped through the broken window and glinted off the growing pool of blood beside the only father Cytherea had ever really known. Her breath caught. Tears began to sting the back of her throat.

"Father," Kenric whimpered. "I shouldn't have left you!"

Cytherea stood, stunned, unable to move. The scene before her unfolded as if she were somehow both there and far away at the same time. Salty tears splashed over her cheeks, flowing silently.

Fenia lowered herself next to her husband and wiped the blood from his face in an act of helpless futility. She tried to steady her voice. "You had no choice, Kenric." Kenric looked up as she drew in a shaky breath. "If you had not followed the soldiers to the barn, then we might have lost Cytherea. We pledged our lives to protect her. You must always remember that."

The room began to spin around Cytherea while a strange ringing in her ears drowned out all other sounds. *Is Tarquin dying because of me? Could I have somehow saved him? Is that why he pushed me to accept my legacy as the heir of Phoxnay? Could I have stopped these soldiers if I had accepted my destiny earlier?*

Kenric's firm hand grabbed Cytherea's arm more harshly than she was accustomed to. "Cytherea!" he shouted, jerking her from her altered state. "Cytherea! Don't be a frightened child! Go to the cupboard and get some rags and fill a bucket with water. Now!"

His outraged tone shocked Cytherea into movement. She did as she was told. By the time she returned to Tarquin's side, his eyes were barely open, and he struggled to speak. Fenia's muffled sobs mingled with the raspy sound of

Tarquin willing his lungs to fill. Kenric stood helpless over him.

Tarquin reached out a pale hand toward Cytherea, motioning for her to move closer. She leaned in to hear him better. "The time has come, my sweet child, for you to accept your great heritage," he whispered.

Cytherea was unable to speak, and she choked on the tears she tried to hold back.

Turning toward Fenia, Tarquin continued, "Go get the sword."

Fenia looked pained. "It's too soon," she pleaded. "She isn't ready yet."

"Fenia, my beloved." He paused, closed his eyes, and struggled to draw a breath in order to continue speaking. "You've known all along that you could not keep her from her destiny."

"She is just a child."

"It is time, Fenia. We can wait no longer."

Cytherea clutched Tarquin's hand. Kenric and Fenia hurried to the back of the room where Kenric pried up several floorboards before moving back and allowing Fenia to reach inside. She pulled out a worn scabbard from below the floor. Only the bejeweled hilt betrayed how valuable a weapon it really was. Fenia struggled slightly with its weight while walking back to kneel next to Cytherea.

Kenric stood directly behind his mother with a steady hand on her shoulder. Tarquin struggled to speak again, but he was so weak. Cytherea had to lean even closer to him, her ear almost touching his mouth, to hear his words.

"This is the Sword of Phoxnay," he whispered. "Take it."

Fenia held the scabbard and turned the hilt toward Cytherea. She hesitated, incredulous.

"Take it!" Kenric said, his face stern, belying the tears that brimmed in his eyes.

Cytherea stood and reached forward with shaking hands. The immense hilt required both of her hands to grasp it. Her fingers wrapped around the cold metal, and it grew hot, causing her to loosen her grip and look up at Fenia for reassurance.

"It's OK, child." She sighed through tears, conceding that she could not protect Cytherea from her fate any longer. "Tarquin is right. It is time."

Cytherea tightened her fingers again around the thick hilt, and this time it began to glow. The large gemstone set at the base of the hilt below her hands glimmered as if lit by some mystical fire. She pulled the majestic sword from its scabbard. The glow intensified until it filled the air around them, causing Kenric and Fenia to shield their eyes momentarily.

When her eyes adjusted, Cytherea fell to her knees beside Tarquin once again, who attempted a frail smile. A single tear fell from his eye before he turned to look toward his wife of many years.

"I love you," he whispered. His eyelids fluttered and closed for the final time.

7

The little cottage was still.

Cytherea stared at Tarquin's lifeless body, and the sword slipped from her hands. Numbness crept over her. She felt Kenric's hand grip her shoulder. It was warm despite the cold that seeped through her. Cytherea didn't want to move because when she did, it would be without Tarquin, and she wasn't sure she could continue without him. He had always been there, close by, helping her, protecting her, fixing anything that she messed up.

"It's my fault," she whispered. "They came for me. He died because of me." Kenric gripped her shoulder tighter. She gazed helplessly at Fenia lying across her husband's lifeless body, mournful sobs pouring from her very soul.

Cytherea stood, sucked in a deep breath, and retrieved the sword from the floor. She had to move, do something, but she didn't know what. Her entire world had abruptly ended. Everything she thought to be true swirled within her, threatening to overcome her entirely as she stood transfixed by the glowing sword in her hands. Last night, she was a farm girl dreaming about her horses. Now the Dark Realm had invaded her world,

Tarquin was dead, and she stood holding the Sword of Phoxnay. It was more than she could take in.

The thunder of galloping hooves on the road outside shook her back to reality. Kenric pulled his sword from his belt. He and Cytherea moved toward the door that hung limply by one hinge. Fenia, her eyes wide with fear and still brimming with tears, continued to cling to Tarquin's body.

Standing in the doorway of the cottage, Cytherea watched the horse and rider approach, sweat forming on her palms, making it more difficult for her shaking hands to grip the imposing and unfamiliar sword. She silently vowed that she would not allow another soldier to enter their home. Her anger burned for the Dark Realm soldiers, and the sword became warm in her hands. A sudden glow of the jeweled hilt startled her, but she quickly turned her eyes back toward the road. The sky was changing from black to a deep blue, though the sun had not yet risen, which left the rider's identity impossible to make out in the distance.

As he neared, she saw that he was not clad in the black armor of the Dark Realm soldiers, and soon Cytherea recognized Christian, one of Tarquin's furniture clients. Cytherea remembered thinking he must have a large home to fit all the furniture he bought from them every week. *Why is he here? He has never come to the cottage before.*

Christian leaped from his horse and ran toward them. Cytherea took a step behind Kenric but then rethought it and stepped forward instead.

"I came as soon as I heard," Christian said breathlessly. "Are the soldiers gone? Is anyone hurt? I sent word to the local healer before I set out. She should be close behind me."

Kenric examined the ground. "We've lost my father."

Christian's face twisted with anguish, and he laid his hand on Kenric's shoulder. "I'm so sorry. He was a good man and a mighty warrior."

Cytherea stood there, taking in yet another scene that did not fit into her reality. Words failed her. It was all too much for her to understand.

Christian turned his eyes to Cytherea. "So you wield the Sword of Phoxnay now."

Cytherea didn't acknowledge him. Her mind was a blur as she desperately tried to make sense of what was happening.

"Yes. Tarquin bestowed it on her with his dying breath." Kenric looked at her, his brows knit together. She stared forward blankly, his words buzzing in her ears. He turned back to Christian. "She will come out of it soon enough. She is stronger than she knows, and the heart of the Sainte-d'Agneaux line beats within her. I have seen it show itself on occasion in the past."

"Why are you two talking about me like I am not here?" Cytherea demanded after shaking the fog from her mind. "And why are you here, Christian?"

"There you are," Kenric said. A slight smile found its way onto his tearstained face.

"My name is Christian Rimeaux, and I have pledged my allegiance to the Phoxnay crown." Christian finished with his head bowed and his fist across his chest.

"I don't understand—" Cytherea was interrupted by the approach of another horse and rider. It was the healer, who, after dismounting, rushed toward the cottage with her saddlebags in her arms.

Cytherea had not had much exposure to healers in the past; they had all been healthy until today. A sadness pierced her heart anew at the thought of Tarquin. Healers had an innate ability to heal even mortal wounds or illnesses—if they could get there in time. They were experts in herbs, potions, and salves as well as in many physical procedures when needed, like amputation and surgery. It was believed that they also possessed some form of magic that aided them in their healing ability. *I wish she had gotten here sooner. Maybe Tarquin would have survived.* Cytherea shook the useless thought from her head when the healer approached.

"Who is injured? How may I assist?" she asked.

Christian stepped in to save Kenric from repeating the sad news himself. "Tarquin has been lost," he said. "Fenia is inside with him. Perhaps you should see about her."

"Of course." She turned toward Kenric and Cytherea. "I'm so sorry for you both." With that, she paused in front of Cytherea with a quick, awkward curtsy before running to Fenia's side.

Cytherea watched her go. Fenia's wails momentarily increased and then quieted again as the healer comforted her. Cytherea turned her gaze to Kenric. "Tell me what is going on, please."

"I don't have time to go into details," Kenric said, "but Christian is one of a secret group of those still loyal to the Phoxnay crown. They have a network of spies that have been keeping track of the movements of Ailmar and his soldiers for the king of Klobyn and our family."

"But why?" Cytherea asked.

Christian stepped in to answer. "For your protection."

"Why my protection?"

"You were so young when our king and queen were killed and when Tarquin and Fenia brought you here. We had to protect you and ensure that Ailmar could not find you. We wanted to give you time to grow up and prepare to take your place as our sovereign."

"How many others know who I am?"

Christian shifted uncomfortably. "We have all had to remain in hiding, so I can't tell you how many, but I assure you that others are out there." He gazed steadily into her eyes. "They are waiting for you to lead them."

Cytherea raised a hand to her head, trying to stop its spinning and to comprehend it all. When she did, she realized she was somehow still gripping the sword tightly in her sword hand. Her fingers had begun to tingle. Kenric watched her movements closely and wrapped his hand over hers to keep her from losing her grip and dropping it.

"I apologize. Your Highness and Kenric, I know you are grieving, but we must get you away from here before more soldiers come looking for you."

"But what about Fenia? And where are we supposed to go?" Cytherea stammered.

"I will take Fenia with me, and she will be safe." Christian's voice became more reverent. "And we will give Tarquin a proper burial. You have my word." He inclined his head toward Cytherea. "Your Highness, we can't wait any longer. Ailmar's evil influence is spreading beyond his borders, and he must be stopped. It is time for you to take your place as our sovereign. The people of Phoxnay need their rightful ruler."

"Stop calling me that!" Cytherea snapped. "I can't lead anyone."

"Where should we go, Christian?" Kenric asked, ignoring her.

"I will send word to Gregor. He currently leads one band of loyalists, and his village, Haight, is not far from the border of the Dark Realm but safer because there are more loyalists there that can help protect Cytherea. You will also be better informed of Ailmar's movements from there."

"Very well. We will gather some supplies and head out today."

"I will send a messenger ahead of you so they will be expecting you, but, Kenric," Christian said, "the journey to get there will be perilous. I can only assume that Ailmar's soldiers will be back for Cytherea, and when they find her gone, they will be searching the countryside for her."

"I can take care of myself," Cytherea chimed in. For proof, she grasped the sword with both hands, shaking off Kenric's hand that had been helping her keep it steady in one hand.

"I am sure you can, Your Highness. I was only preparing Kenric for what you might run into before you reach Gregor's village." He stepped toward the cottage door. "I will take care of Fenia and everything here. You have my word." With that, he hurried inside.

Kenric met Cytherea's gaze. "I know you have a lot of questions, and I promise I will try to answer them as best I can, but we have to leave now. Are you ready?"

Cytherea bit her lip, gazing blearily at the sword clenched in her fists. "Tarquin died protecting me—for *this*. So that I could take up the legacy of my parents." She lifted her eyes to Kenric. "For Tarquin, I will do whatever I can to end Ailmar's evil rule."

8

Cytherea made her way to the barn with the events of the last day swirling in her mind. Her body was still numb from Tarquin's death and saying goodbye to Fenia. The look of grief in Fenia's eyes was more than Cytherea could bear. She shook the vision from her mind and pushed open the barn door.

When she entered the barn, she saddled Tredan and Aherne and prepped them for their long journey. Kenric loaded supplies into the large saddlebags on the backs of the two chargers. The horses stomped their hooves, impatient, creating small clouds of dust that rose from the barn floor. The ground vibrated with their power, and Kenric rubbed their necks in an effort to calm their excitement.

"I know, boys," he soothed. "You have been resting in the pastures long enough. Your blood runs thick with your own legacy, and I imagine you are eager to get there. We have a long road ahead of us, but you will soon see the pastures of your grandsires."

Once the horses were ready, Kenric drew the Sword of Phoxnay from its scabbard on Aherne's saddle and gazed reverently at it. "The Sword of Phoxnay. My father used to tell me stories about it, although I was never sure it was real until it had been found and brought to him after we arrived on the farm. He once showed me where he had it hidden beneath the floor, but he never let me look at it." He studied it briefly. "It is exactly the way he described it."

"What kind of stories did he tell you about it?" she asked, looking over the sword. "What kind of magic does it possess?"

Kenric smiled wryly at her usual stream of questions. "I don't think my father knew the extent of its power. It looks like you'll have to figure that out yourself."

Cytherea examined the sword, taking in his words. "It's a lot of responsibility to hold this sword, and I don't even know what to do with it."

"You will figure it out. Of that, I am sure." He presented it to her in his outstretched arms.

Cytherea stared at the sword for several long seconds. She was not in the mood to practice her drills.

Kenric eyed her and said firmly, "Take it."

"Can we practice another time?" Her voice exposed her exhaustion. "I just don't feel like it right now. Besides, you said that we need to get going so we are able to get as much riding in as we can before nightfall."

"This is more important, Cytherea. You know how to spar, but it is time for you to learn to *fight*," Kenric urged. "This sword is unique, and you need to start getting comfortable with it before we leave. You must be able to defend yourself if I am unable."

His words hung heavy around her, weighed down by the sword. She grasped the massive hilt with both hands once again and lifted it from Kenric's grip. However, the memory of what Ailmar's soldiers could do strengthened her resolve. She stretched her arms before her. The thick blade threatened to pull her arms to the ground, but she resisted.

Kenric frowned. "You cannot fight effectively if you can only hold it with two hands. You have to also be able to use it with a single hand."

"I can't," Cytherea complained. "The hilt is too big for just one of my hands to hold, and its weight is more than one arm can bear."

Kenric held out his hand, and she relinquished the sword to him. "This sword was meant to be held by you, so just relax and allow yourself to feel the life within the sword. Take a deep breath and try to clear your mind."

Cytherea closed her eyes and drew in a long, deep breath. The scent of horses mingling with fresh hay helped slow her racing heart. The sound of the horses shifting restlessly combined with Kenric's voice counting her breaths cleared the chaos of her thoughts. Her body slowly relaxed.

"Now, with your eyes closed and your breathing steady, reach out again for the hilt with just one hand."

Cytherea obeyed. As her hand slid over the cold, hard metal, it began to warm again, and she could feel the glow of the gemstone on her face. She tightened her grip around the hilt. The metal seemed to meld to her palm until her single hand rested comfortably around it. She attempted to raise the sword again, expecting resistance, but this time it lifted effortlessly into the air.

Cytherea opened her eyes, gazing at her hand before turning her eyes up to Kenric. "It fits!" she said with a broad smile. "It's like it was made for me."

"In a way, it was. Your bloodline awakens the magic within it. I don't know the full magnitude of its powers, but I do know that it is the only thing powerful enough to defeat Ailmar."

Kenric guided her through some of her drills, and they sparred briefly. At first, Cytherea tried to force herself to wield the sword smoothly, but she wasn't used to the weight and feel of it yet. Her first attempt to lunge forward landed the blade clum-sily on top of the nearest stall door. The horses all shifted noticeably backward while Kenric struggled unsuccessfully to stifle a smile.

Gathering himself, he stopped her. "You're trying too hard, Cytherea. Close your eyes and center yourself and then try again."

Cytherea did as she was told. This time when she swung the sword, she felt a vibration through her arm, like a silent hum. She sliced through the air, nimbly executing each move like a seasoned swordswoman. She beamed with pride, and Kenric watched approvingly.

Her exhaustion was all but forgotten as a renewed energy coursed through her body. Returning her sword to its scabbard on the saddle, she and Kenric led the horses outside. He gave Cytherea a boost onto Aherne's broad back before mounting Tredan, and they headed toward the road beyond. Before leaving their beloved farm and heading onto the road beyond, Cytherea stopped and turned around momentarily. She studied the cottage behind her in the distance, trying to seal it in her mind because she wasn't sure when or if she would be back there again.

She turned back around and gently urged Aherne forward. The horses trekked down the familiar farm road, and she took it all in one last time. The scent of moss mixed with the fragrance of wildflowers and the chatter of the birds overhead seemed to be wishing them well on their journey. She breathed deeply and smiled before leaving it behind her. Cytherea loved this place, but her destiny lay before her.

Thus, her journey began.

As the day wore on, the surroundings and the path became less familiar, and apprehension rose within Cytherea's belly. She had never been away from the cottage she called home—at least, not that she remembered. She felt vulnerable in the foreign surroundings, which brought forth thoughts of Ailmar's soldiers. *How far away might they be? Will they find me again? Could they even be watching me now?* Her fear grew as her thoughts raced to dark places.

Sensing his rider's uneasiness, Aherne tossed his head and let out a soft whinny, breaking into Cytherea's frightening thoughts. She leaned forward and scratched his smooth neck, shifting her focus off the strange surroundings and back onto the safe and familiar rhythm of her stallion beneath her.

9

Shadows crawled across the path as the sun sank lower in the sky. The horses often carried Tarquin and Kenric from Ceka to other villages for supplies or to sell Tarquin's furniture, so they were used to long days of travel on the market road. Cytherea, however, was not. Kenric watched as Cytherea desperately tried to hide how tired she was, physically and emotionally.

Kenric slowed, and Cytherea frowned at him. "What's the matter?"

"It's nearly dusk. I want to find a place to stop for the night," he replied, wisely omitting that he thought she was too tired to keep going. "There's a path into the forest up here that leads to a small pond. It's not commonly traveled, and it's far enough from nearby towns and any attention you and our horses might attract. It will be a safe place for us to stay tonight."

"Can Ailmar's soldiers find us this far from the Dark Realm?"

"They found our home." Kenric hesitated briefly, but realizing there was no point in hiding the truth from her anymore, he continued. "They will likely try."

Cytherea and Kenric slid off their horses, and they walked

beside them into the forest, allowing their legs to stretch after a long day of riding. Cytherea slowed to trail behind Aherne so he could go ahead of her to tamp down some of the underbrush and push through the bushes and tree limbs that threatened to take over the narrow path, saving her a few extra scratches. Before long, the trees thinned, and the small group found themselves in a beautiful clearing. Cytherea gasped.

Lush grass surrounded a small spring-fed pond. The forest encircled it as if guarding its beauty against the rest of the world. The setting sun cast strokes of pink and orange across the glass-like surface of the water. Birds and other small creatures scurried in the distance as they gathered for a final drink before returning to their homes for the night.

Cytherea unsaddled and began rubbing Aherne down, her wide eyes soaking in the scene around them. Kenric worked in silence as he watched Cytherea's eyes slowly clear and brighten, her shoulders relaxing as she settled into her chores. She left her sword with her saddle, and he absently reached down to ensure he had his close at hand.

When Aherne was glossy and unladen, Cytherea smiled at Kenric. "This place is beautiful. I wish we could stay here forever."

His face relaxed; he was thankful to see the sparkle returning to her eyes that had dimmed with Tarquin's last breath. "I'm glad you approve."

~

Later, the fire was warm on Cytherea's face as they finished their meal of smoked meat and bread that Fenia had packed for them. Though not cold, the night air held a slight chill on the breeze that felt pleasant paired with the warmth of the flames. The horses snuffled and munched grass behind them before settling into position for sleep. The sparkle of the moon replaced the colors of the sunset on the water's surface, and the night felt almost perfect. Almost, because despite the peace and beauty around her, Cytherea could not keep thoughts of Tarquin and the recent events from her mind for long.

"I can't believe he is gone," Cytherea sobbed suddenly.

Kenric moved closer to her and wrapped his arm around her shoulders. Tears rolled down his cheeks. "Neither can I." After a few moments, Kenric wiped his eyes with his sleeve and turned to face Cytherea. "We will take time to properly mourn my father in due time, but now we must focus on getting to Gregor."

"What are we going to do once we reach Gregor's village? Wait, what was it called?" She wiped her tears.

"The village is Haight. Gregor will have information on Ailmar's activities as well as those of the loyalists," Kenric said. "We will need to get some idea of how many would be willing to fight with us. And with that information, we will plan how best to attack Ailmar and his soldiers."

"There are a lot of unknowns in that plan. We may be defeated before we even begin."

"Never lose hope, Cytherea," Kenric reminded her. "I think you'll be surprised how many people are willing to fight with you. Ailmar has held his evil over the people of this land for too long, and they are waiting for you to lead them."

"Who exactly are the loyalists?"

"As part of my father's effort to keep you safe, he received word of Ailmar's activities regularly through a network of loyalists who are still devoted to the Phoxnay crown. And you," he added with a glance at her. "They are either soldiers of Phoxnay that survived Ailmar's attack or villagers that had managed to escape Ailmar's grasp."

He stirred the fire before continuing. "In the years following Phoxnay's fall, they gradually found one another and began adding to their numbers. The loyalists operate with the help of

King Aldegunde of Klobyn. He also uses them to train his men in the hope that his army will be prepared for any possible attack and escape the same fate as Phoxnay."

"What about Christian?" she asked.

"Christian was my father's connection in our village who would secretly relay information to him of the movements of Ailmar and the soldiers of the Dark Realm. My father wanted to know if they ever discovered you or if they started patrolling close to Ceka. In fact, the day before the attack on our cottage, my father told me that Christian had given him news that Ailmar's soldiers had raided another village close to Ceka. Much closer than any previous attacks. But my father had no idea that they knew where you were until the Dark Realm soldiers attacked last night."

Cytherea pondered all this for a while before shifting her thoughts to a more pleasant time. "Did you and Tarquin stop here when you traveled to buy supplies?"

Kenric gazed at the pond. "We did. This was one of his favorite spots. Sometimes we would stay for more than one night to enjoy it for a bit longer." He glanced back at her and smiled. "But then he would start missing you and Fenia so much that we would rush home the next day." He reached over and gently wiped away the fresh tears that rolled down her face. "He loved you like a daughter. To him and my mother, you were like their own child."

"I should have done something to save him," she whispered.

"What could you have done? If anyone is to blame, it's me. I should have protected him."

"Kenric, I'm the one who is supposed to somehow stop Ailmar and his soldiers. If I had not wasted so much time avoiding what Tarquin said was my destiny, then maybe he would still be alive!" She stood abruptly and moved quickly toward the water's edge, her face hot with anger against the cool air.

Kenric stood and walked up beside her. "Cytherea, no one

blames you for any of this. Ailmar is to blame. His soldiers killed my father, and *his* evil has been poisoning this land and its people. Places like this"—Kenric gestured sharply to their surroundings—"won't be here much longer; his dark cloud of evil will eventually destroy them. If he is not stopped, there will be nothing of beauty left in our world or no one left to enjoy it. The stories that Christian and other loyalists brought us are things of nightmares. Ailmar and his soldiers are either killing or torturing and brainwashing entire generations." He spun Cytherea toward him and took her hand. "You have to focus your anger on him, not on yourself. You should also prepare yourself for the things we'll discover when we get closer to the Dark Realm."

Cytherea turned her eyes from his. "I feel so small compared to Ailmar and his soldiers."

"You are not alone, Cyth," Kenric said gently. "You've got more people behind you than you know. Don't lose heart. You also have more strength inside you than you realize."

Cytherea huffed. "I can't even defend myself. How in the world can I take on Ailmar and the armies of the Dark Realm?"

"You have something that no one else still living possesses."

"Do you mean my sword? It's just a sword." She flipped her free hand in the direction of their belongings near the fire.

"I'm not talking about something you can hold in your hands. I'm talking about something inside of you. Something you can't see or touch. It is in your blood and your heart." Kenric tapped her chest.

"You keep saying things like that, but I don't know what that means," Cytherea huffed. "Stop speaking in riddles."

"I'm not speaking in riddles. I am speaking as plainly as I am able."

"Well, then you are wrong. I don't feel anything 'inside me.' I'm not any different than anyone else."

"I'm not wrong. You will find it when you need it, but trust me, you have a greater destiny than either of us can understand."

Cytherea tossed her long hair over her shoulder and turned away from Kenric, trying to make sense of everything he was telling her. She needed to calm herself again. She didn't want to argue with him, but she desperately wanted to understand how she was supposed to fight Ailmar and his army and find the destiny Kenric and Tarquin both seemed so sure about. She took a few deep breaths to soothe her mind, which had started reeling again.

Before she could fully relax, she was startled by the rustling of branches in the trees beside them. Her breath caught. Kenric drew his sword, but Cytherea was too far away to reach her weapon. A dark shadow sprang into the once-peaceful meadow. Kenric stepped in front of her and readied himself for the attack. The woods came alive with movement as more shadows emerged. Terror shot through Cytherea's body. She suppressed a scream just before the shadowy figures moved into the moonlight, the silvery rays illuminating them. Kenric lowered his sword, and Cytherea let out a long breath. Elk. It was a herd of elk that had been spooked out of their cover in the trees.

Kenric and Cytherea stayed rooted in place to avoid being run over while the large herd thundered past and disappeared into the trees on the opposite side of the meadow. The thundering hoofbeats eventually faded until the air was once again quiet.

"What do you think frightened them?" Cytherea looked around nervously.

"I don't know, but it was likely a predator of some kind."

"Like Dark Realm soldiers?"

"No. Even if they saw a soldier, or any human for that matter, it would not cause them to stampede like that." Kenric appeared thoughtful for a moment. "My father and I saw some wolves running scared like that not long ago. We thought it odd but didn't think much more about it. But now I'm wondering if there is something causing an unnatural discord within the wild animals."

"Ailmar?"

"I don't know how he could have anything to do with it, although no one really understands the type of power he has."

They fell silent and stood there for a few moments more. The wind moved across the pond, distorting the reflection of the moon passing over. Soon the long day of travel caught up to Cytherea, and her eyes became heavy. Kenric had made a simple shelter for her in a copse of trees, and she made her way there to sleep, taking her sword from her saddle and laying it next to her in the soft grass. Thoughts of Phoxnay ran through her mind. She absently reached up and cradled the emerald-encrusted ring that hung around her neck. She allowed her thoughts to drift to the stories Tarquin had told her about her parents and her childhood. In her mind, she reached up to grasp this same ring as it hung around her mother's soft neck. She could almost hear her mother's laughter. Tarquin and Fenia had retold the stories so many times that Cytherea was not sure if she remembered the stories or if they were actual memories of her time with her parents. She was still lost in thoughts about her mother when her eyes closed in sleep.

Cytherea saw a woman's familiar face. The woman's sparkling eyes, full of laughter, studied her. "You are such a pretty little girl, Cytherea."

The warmth of the woman's voice flowed over Cytherea. She looked around and discovered she was sitting on the woman's lap. She touched the shimmering skirts that seemed to surround her. They felt like butter —soft and smooth. The woman's gentle hands ran through Cytherea's hair, and her own hand, pudgy and small, reached toward the woman's neck to grab one of the two rings hanging there on a golden chain.

My mother!

Cytherea tried to force herself to look around, but she didn't seem to have control over what she saw.

Is my father here too?

When her eyes did turn, she was looking at a small boy playing in the grass next to her mother. She didn't recognize him. When he looked up at her, she gasped. He had emerald eyes!

IO

The next morning, Cytherea strolled along the pond's edge, stopping occasionally to bend down and pull up wildflowers from the dewy grass to feed the horses. The dream from the night before had faded except for the face of her mother, and she wanted to try and hold it in her memory forever. The sunlight revealed flecks of auburn and gold within the waves of her brown hair, which blew in the breeze as she tried unsuccessfully to keep it out of her eyes. She turned and caught Kenric watching her intently. He jumped with a start and went back to readying their horses, doggedly ignoring her gaze as he fidgeted with Tredan's saddle.

Cytherea couldn't hide her smile as she walked over, fed the wildflowers to the horses, and took Aherne's reins from Kenric. He always worried about her, maybe even more so than his parents. She had caught him looking at her like that before. Like he was worried about something he wasn't telling her. *What is he holding back?* She discarded the thought. Maybe she was imagining things.

"The horses are ready," he said. "We can head out whenever you like."

Cytherea obliged him by adjusting a few straps on Aherne's saddle while both horses munched on the wildflowers. "I am ready."

"I think it's best if we avoid the main road and keep to the forest, so we won't have to worry about passing anyone or being seen."

"Very well."

Kenric boosted Cytherea into Aherne's saddle before mounting Tredan and leading them slowly past the pond to a small trail that wove through the trees on the other side. The elks' prints from the night before were still imprinted in the dirt ahead of them.

"It's beautiful here," Cytherea said. She took one last look at the water and sky before urging her stallion into the tree line. "I wish we could stay and hide from Ailmar and his soldiers."

"I wish that too, Cytherea," Kenric responded, "but Ailmar must be stopped and Phoxnay must be restored. You are the only one who can do that."

"Tell me what Phoxnay looked like."

He shrugged. "I don't remember much. I was very young when we left. My father's stories told you more than I ever could."

"I know the stories, but I want to know what you remember, Kenric."

"I remember your father had a booming laugh that could often be heard throughout the castle. And I remember what it sounded like when your mother entered the room. It was like the trill of little birds whistling."

"Birds whistling? That's a funny way to remember my mother."

"Well, it's the way a young boy remembers her." He laughed. "Her dresses were made of silk and had many layers. When she moved, all those layers sounded like birds whistling to me." He pulled Tredan to a stop and looked at her. "I'm not going to tell you any more of my memories if you're going to make fun of them."

"I'm sorry." She fought to wipe the grin from her face. "You have my word that I will not make fun of them anymore." She laid her fist across her chest the way she remembered Christian had done at the cottage.

"Ah, the word of a princess is as good as gold." Kenric relented and started moving once more. "Really, that is mostly what I remember. Sounds, feelings, that sort of thing. No detailed memories. I do remember being happy though. That is the main thing that always comes through when I think back. Everything felt happy. That is, until that last day."

"What do you remember from the last day?" she asked. "I know the stories Tarquin told us, but what about the rest? Did you ever hear what happened that day after we escaped?"

Kenric stiffened in his saddle, and his voice was softer when he spoke. "Christian met a man who was there that day and managed to escape. He saw it all, and it was awful. I'm not sure you want to hear it."

"I want to know what happened to my parents," she said firmly, gripping her reins to anchor her. "If I am supposed to fulfill a destiny they left for me, I need to know what happened."

"All right. I'll tell you what I know and what I've heard. Beyond that, you will have to ask Gregor and others when we reach Haight."

While they rode side by side, Kenric began telling her what happened on their last day in Phoxnay. "We rode from the castle into the safety of the dense woods beyond the walls, and then we started up the mountain pass. Before we entered the trees, my father looked back toward Phoxnay one final time. He gasped, which made me turn to look, but I wish I hadn't. From our vantage point, we could see that the army of the Dark Realm was already nearing the castle gates."

"What did they look like?"

"I only saw them from a distance, but much like the ones that attacked us at the cottage. Only, instead of three, to me as a child, it looked like a sea of black waves pouring over the castle walls." Kenric's eyes darkened. "I noticed a thick black cloud—but not really a cloud, more like a blackness—that seemed to hover over their army, and the reflection it caused on their black mirrored armor scared me."

He hesitated, but Cytherea gave him a grim nod, encouraging him to tell her. He took a breath and went on. "The sounds I heard that day were worse than what I saw. The screaming and shouting. There was one particular sound that I can't ever forget." He clenched his jaw. "The piercing scream of a baby that was abruptly cut short. I can only imagine what must have happened to him. It haunted my dreams for months after that, but I never told anyone until now."

Tears welled in her eyes, threatening to spill over. Cytherea couldn't imagine such cruelty. She met Kenric's gaze when he glanced over at her, her sadness and anger reflected on his face.

"I'm sorry. I shouldn't have told you."

"No, no. I'm glad you did," Cytherea said, clearing her throat and wiping her eyes with the back of her hand. "What a terrible thing for a young boy to carry with him."

Kenric shrugged it off. "Anyway, that is the last memory I have of Phoxnay. The rest I have heard through my father, Christian, and other loyalists throughout the years."

"Did any of them tell you what happened to my parents?"

"They did, but I'm not sure you want to hear that part. You always wanted to skip the sad parts when my father told us his stories."

"I was a child then, Kenric. I no longer have the luxury of skipping over the sad parts."

"Very well." Kenric drew up his reins, slowing Tredan to a

more comfortable pace. "Not long after we left, Phoxnay's army became overwhelmed by the sheer power and ruthlessness of Ailmar's army and had retreated within the walls of the castle proper. King Edmond, your father, rushed to his commanders, and your mother went to be with the villagers huddled in the courtyards and lawns of the castle while the battle raged on. The sounds of fighting and the screams of dying men surrounded them, and the people of Phoxnay were terrified. They all knew there was nothing they could do to save themselves. They were waiting helplessly, knowing that this evil force was coming for them and that there was nowhere left to hide."

Cytherea's face was stony. She couldn't believe what she was hearing. Kenric searched her eyes, and she blinked back tears. No, she needed to hear this, to hear what Ailmar was capable of. "Go on," she whispered.

Kenric dipped his head. "By nightfall, they could see the flickering of firelight from the other side of the walls. As the smoke drifted over those left within the castle of Phoxnay, the smell made them realize that Ailmar was throwing the dead on the fires as fuel. Your mother tried desperately to comfort those around her, but it was useless. They could only cover their ears to block the screams of those not yet dead being tossed onto the burning flames. The smoke hung thick over the castle. By morning, it eclipsed the rising of the sun."

"How could someone be so vile?" Cytherea asked quietly.

"Do you want me to stop?"

"No. Tell me." Her gut churned, dreading what had happened next. "I need to know."

"That day, the Dark Realm breached the walls of the castle grounds. The remaining men of Phoxnay fought valiantly, along with any women who could wield whatever makeshift weapon they found, fighting to the end. And in the middle of it all stood your father, not hiding in a secret chamber or retreating to the safe haven of a nearby land. He was not even hiding behind his guards. Instead, he was protecting those around him. The Sword of Phoxnay shone brightly each time he bravely swung it. It was believed by many that it would protect the king from harm as long as he held it."

"Then how did he die, if it was supposed to protect him?"

"Because on that day, as your father swung his sword at an oncoming soldier, he was caught on the wrist by his opponent's blade. It sliced his hand from his arm, and his mighty sword fell helplessly to the ground next to him." Kenric paused to catch his breath before continuing. "As the story was told to me, your father fell to his knees with blood spewing from his severed arm, and he raised his eyes toward his adversary and tried to speak. However, before any words could come, your father fell lifelessly to the ground, the great sword hidden beneath his body, while the evil knight stood over him and laughed."

Cytherea emitted a choked sob, and Aherne's ears flicked back toward her. "What about my mother? Do you know what happened to her?"

Kenric nodded. "All the stories I've been told say that your mother fought too, and she witnessed the fatal blow to her beloved husband. They say that fury washed over her when the soldier laughed over the slain king, and she hurtled toward him. The Dark Realm knight turned his laughter toward her as she approached him.

"The story goes that a look of surprise crossed his face when he realized he had been impaled by her blade. Unfortunately, in her anger and grief, your mother had swung wildly, and her blow did little more than anger him. As the battle raged around her, the queen continued her futile efforts to slay the vile knight. Exhausted, she ceased her blows and looked defiantly into his eyes. With one swift blow, the Dark Realm soldier's sword pierced her side, and she fell to the ground next to your father.

The man who told me this story was the king's young page at the time and was hiding behind a wall in fear. He saw that soldier remove his helmet. He stood over the bodies of your mother and father, shouting in victory. The page believes that the rider who killed your mother and your father was Ailmar."

II

Kenric looked over again at Cytherea, but she refused to meet his gaze. Heat stung her cheeks. After a few moments, she responded, "Ailmar has killed almost everyone that I love and destroyed my home, and he has done the same to the people of Phoxnay. I must find a way to destroy him, exact revenge for all that our people have lost, and return them to their home." She looked at Kenric. "It is what my parents would want me to do."

He smiled at her with pride and nodded, adjusting his hands on Tredan's reins.

They rode in silence for the rest of the morning. Cytherea's mind replayed the story of her parents' death over and over despite her attempts to stop it. She stroked Aherne's neck with one hand. She needed to ground herself in the present, and connecting with Aherne helped her do that.

"We need to be on guard even more going forward," Kenric said quietly. "Ailmar's soldiers regularly patrol what was once the kingdom of Phoxnay, even beyond the outer border, which we should cross tomorrow. The closer we get to the Dark Realm, the more dangerous it will be."

Cytherea nodded silently, and a chill ran through her.

After several hours had passed, Cytherea's stomach grumbled, and she knew the horses likely needed a rest. The trails through the forest had become narrow, so they could not ride next to each other, which made talking difficult.

So, when Cytherea spoke, the sound of her voice shattered the silence. "Could we stop for a while to eat and rest the horses?"

"We have made good time. A break won't hurt."

A few minutes later, they found a small clearing by a stream where they could rest and refill their waterskins. The sound of the horses munching on bits of grass mixed with the flowing stream helped to calm Cytherea's racing thoughts. She brushed down the horses where she could around the saddles. Kenric lay back and studied the rough map Christian had given him. Cytherea tried to relax. The trees of the forest provided some protection, but even there, she knew she could be found. She had felt safe on the farm, far away from Ailmar, but if they'd found her there, they could find her anywhere.

To take her mind off Ailmar and soldiers, Cytherea decided to tell Kenric about the dream she'd had last night. "I dreamed about my mother last night."

Cytherea had never before mentioned dreaming about her past to him. Sure enough, Kenric perked up with interest, the map he'd been studying discarded beside him. "Really? What was she doing?"

"We were sitting in the grass, and she was smiling at me. I could feel the silk of her dress that I was sitting on, and she told me I was pretty."

"I remember her sitting with you in her lap a lot. Especially after I finished my lessons and was allowed to go out and play with you and—and play with you for a while."

Cytherea looked at him for a moment and then resumed brushing the horses. The earlier feeling that Kenric was hiding something from her rose in her chest. It shook loose a part of her dream she'd almost forgotten. She continued carefully, "Someone else was there in my dream. A little boy about my age. He was too young to have been you. Do you know who he was?"

Kenric looked down as he picked up the map again and didn't answer her.

She set the brush down and leaned against Aherne. "Answer me, Kenric. Do you know who that little boy was? His eyes were the same color as mine. Who was he?"

"Cytherea, I . . ." Kenric faltered.

Her voice started to raise to a level that threatened to crack, but she lowered it, remembering where she was. "You said you would tell me everything I wanted to know. Who was that little boy?"

"Your brother," Kenric finally answered, so softly she wasn't sure she heard him correctly.

"What?" Her voice was calm in the dangerous way that sounded like it was holding back a firestorm.

Kenric cleared his throat and slowly looked up at her. "He was your twin brother, Cytherea. I told my father that he should tell you about—"

"I have a brother?" Cytherea almost shouted, and the words weakened her knees. Aherne's solid presence kept her standing. "What do you mean I have a brother? Where is he? Why have I never heard about him before? Tell me, Kenric! Tell me everything!"

"All right, but you need to calm down first."

"Calm down? You want me to *calm down*? When you and Tarquin and Fenia have been hiding the fact that I have a brother my entire life? And not just a brother, a *twin* brother! I am nowhere near calming down. Start talking!"

"All right. You should have been told from the beginning, but I was just a child myself," Kenric tried to explain. "I was told not to ever mention Everard, so I never did."

"Everard? Is that his name?" It was vaguely familiar.

"Yes."

"I remember that name. You said it a few times, but Tarquin always stopped you."

"Yes. He did, but you have to understand that my father didn't do it to be mean or cruel."

"Why did he feel the need to hide the fact that I have a twin brother?"

"He was ashamed, Cytherea, OK?" She watched Kenric struggle to keep his frustration in check. Although she was angry at Tarquin, he was dead. She understood Kenric wouldn't want to malign his father. "He believed that he had failed in his duty to his king and queen, and he couldn't bear to hurt you or expose his shame to you. Although he never spoke about him, I know he thought about him a lot. I believe it ate at him."

"Why was he ashamed? What happened to my brother?"

"I'll tell you the whole story, but please sit down and lower your voice. We don't know who is in these woods."

Cytherea glanced around uneasily and then obeyed.

"The day after we escaped," Kenric said, "we were overtaken by a small regiment of Ailmar's soldiers who were looking for you and Everard. My parents had tried to disguise our little group as a merchant caravan as much as they could, but the horses of Phoxnay were hard to hide. It was also hard to conceal the identity of you and your brother because twins are rare, and then there is the unique eye color you both have. And that dragon birthmark on your neck? Everard has it too."

"We have the same birthmark?"

"Yes. And, except for your eye color, which comes from your father, I have been told that you are both the exact image of your mother."

Cytherea slowly let the air escape her lungs as she took in this information. Her mother suddenly had a face, and it was her own.

"Anyway, my mother told me that what they assumed happened is that someone we passed along the way must have been suspicious of us and alerted the soldiers, either out of fear or misplaced loyalty to Ailmar." Kenric frowned.

Cytherea waited patiently while he organized his thoughts.

"The soldiers appeared out of the cover of the forest and were on us before anyone could react. The queen's guard, who was traveling with us, tried to warn us seconds before they appeared, but then the horses leaped into a full gallop with the wagons careening dangerously behind them. I was riding beside the wagons on my horse, and I remember trying to hang on when he bolted. But the horses pulling wagons, even the horses of Phoxnay, were no match for the swift Dark Realm riders." Kenric turned toward Cytherea, who was staring back at him with wide eyes.

"When the soldiers caught up to us, two of them jumped onto the wagons while the other two leaped on the backs of the horses to try and slow them. The horses were not going to allow the soldiers to control them, and they continued at a full gallop. The queen's guard fought off a soldier on one wagon. My father stayed with you and Everard and tried to get the other soldiers off your wagon while my mother jumped in back with you both as a last line of defense.

"My horse took off into the tree line, instinctively trying to get me to safety. Then a soldier called out, 'They are here!' My heart sank because I knew that they had found you and your brother." Tears welled in Kenric's eyes. Cytherea fought the sting she felt herself.

"All I heard after that was the sound of the wagons slowing and lots of yelling. Eventually I heard my mother scream, and I tried to turn back to help, but my horse would not stop. It was trained to protect me, so it just kept moving me farther away." Kenric looked at Cytherea with pleading eyes. "I tried to go back and help. I did."

Cytherea fixed her eyes on the space between them and didn't say a word. Her mind swirled, trying to take in this new information and the emotions that accompanied it. She had just discovered she had a brother, and then he had been taken away from her, all at once, and she wasn't sure if she should feel sad or angry or both. She also knew that if Ailmar had her brother, then they must rescue him. Her destiny was not just to save the kingdom of Phoxnay. Now it was also to save her brother, Everard.

After a moment, Kenric continued. "I asked my mother about it once when my father was traveling to buy supplies, and she told me what had happened on the wagons. She said that someone managed to stop the horses. She didn't remember who or how, but the wagons suddenly came to a halt. My father and the guard fought off the soldiers, and my father managed to kill one of them after tumbling from the wagon onto the ground beside it. That was when another soldier hit my mother on the side of the head so hard that she blacked out momentarily. She must have been thrown or knocked off the wagon because she ended up on the ground near my father and the dying soldier. It was then that she heard you scream.

"My father frantically struggled back onto the wagon to help the queen's guard protect you, but as he did so, the remaining three soldiers unexpectedly rode away. My mother thought the guard had fought them off, and you were both safe. However, when she climbed into the back of the wagon, she saw you there still screaming, but the guard was lying dead on top of you. That's when my father realized that the soldiers had taken Everard."

"Why didn't he go after them?" Cytherea pressed.

"He did! He tried," Kenric answered. "The Dark Realm soldiers had a head start, and he lost them in the thick forest. He heard other soldiers shouting not far from where he was, so he knew he had no choice but to return to you and Fenia and make sure you were safe." He reached out to put a hand on her shoulder, but Cytherea shrugged him off.

"He just let the Dark Realm soldiers take my brother?"

"There was an unknown number of Dark Realm soldiers

nearby. He couldn't fight them all off alone, and he needed to keep you out of their hands. He had no choice."

"Of course he had a choice. He had a choice to keep chasing them until he caught them and rescued my brother!"

"Cytherea, please try to understand," Kenric pleaded. "What was he supposed to do—leave you and my mother alone on the road? Since your mother's guard had been killed, he had to make the choice to protect you and then try to rescue Everard once you were safe and he had more men to help him."

"So my brother was a sacrifice."

"No." Kenric clenched his fists. "My father died for you! You know that he was a good and noble man."

Cytherea's eyes brimmed with hot tears. "I also thought that you and Tarquin would never lie to me."

"We never lied. We just hadn't told you about Everard yet."

"A lie by omission is still a lie, Kenric."

He groaned. "Cytherea, let me finish. Tarquin whistled for my horse to return, which it did, and then he took you, me, and my mother to safety in a nearby farmhouse. He knew the family there because they had been a regular vendor at the palace, and he trusted them. As soon as he knew you were safe, he headed out to find help and get Everard back."

Cytherea glared at Kenric with a pained expression.

"My father searched for him day and night but couldn't find any sign of Everard. He had to assume that he had been killed, and my father had no choice but to go back and get you to real safety."

"So my brother is dead?" Her tears threatened to escape.

"He's gone, Cyth. Ailmar certainly had him killed so that Everard would not be a threat to his rule. And he wants to do the same to you." Kenric suddenly grew uneasy. "We should start moving." He bent down and picked up the map he had been studying earlier.

"I'm not finished, Kenric," she said with more anger than she intended.

"We need to move. We will finish this conversation later."

"We will finish it now!" she demanded.

Kenric suddenly clapped his hand over her mouth. She jerked away, turning, but he pulled her behind a clump of bushes that kept the horses in sight. Aherne was bobbing his head and Tredan was restless. Kenric froze. Cytherea's eyes flashed toward Kenric, trying to read his face as her heartbeat thundered in her ears. His face was turned away from her, and he slowly began walking backward. The horses sidled up next to them soundlessly. Kenric put a finger to his lips for her to remain silent. She leaned forward and listened intently until she heard it.

Something, or someone, was moving just beyond them in the forest.

Without looking at Kenric, she grasped Aherne's bridle, fumbled with the stirrup, and pulled herself onto the saddle. He turned without prompting. Kenric was right behind her on Tredan.

12

They rode down the trail in silence, straining to hear any indication that someone might be following them. After only a short distance, Tredan and Aherne tensed and raised their heads. Kenric scanned the trees all around them, his head swiveling. Cytherea was motionless, a hand clutching her sword's hilt.

The horses' ears pricked, and Cytherea thought she heard rustling nearby.

Her eyes darted to the branches overhead and then at Kenric. He was peering into the trees, trying to make out anything that didn't belong. When she faced forward again, Aherne shifted, and a deep growl sent chills down her spine. A black form flashed in the corner of her eye. Aherne whinnied and reared. She let go of the hilt of her sword and gripped Aherne's mane as he danced wildly beneath her.

Kenric shouted. In that same instant, an eerie howl filled the air around her.

Aherne continued to plunge and whirl, which kept Cytherea focused on staying in the saddle. When he reared again, Cytherea felt a thud as his hooves hit something solid.

Aherne's mane blinded her as he reared and leaped. Kenric

shouted again, but she couldn't make out what he was saying. She felt another thud, and Aherne, at last, lowered his front legs back to the ground and kept them there. His breath huffed from the exertion. Once again balanced in her saddle, Cytherea swiftly drew her sword.

A familiar whistle pierced through the blood pounding in her ears, and she turned toward the sound. There stood Kenric, pulling his blade from the side of a large black panther.

Kenric's eyes met hers. "I wanted to make sure you knew where I was while you waved that thing around." He gestured to her sword with a slight smile.

Shakily, she slid her weapon back into its scabbard. "I wouldn't have hurt you. I do know how to use it." Her voice was still angry.

"It was just a panther." He looked down at its lifeless form. "It is odd for it to attack without provocation, but this is not the first I've heard of it happening. I wonder if this is what spooked the elk last night."

"Do you think this panther is what you heard earlier when we were stopped?"

"I can't be sure, but most likely, yes. Panthers are known to track their prey for a time, waiting for an opportunity to attack. Perhaps he was following us."

"Is it dead?" Sorrow tightened Cytherea's throat.

"Yes, unfortunately. Although it would have likely killed us if Aherne had not kicked him. He smashed its skull, but the animal was slow to die, so I wanted to put it out of its misery." Kenric wiped the blood from his blade.

He grunted slightly as he hauled the panther's lifeless body off the trail and into some bushes. It had been a beautiful creature, and Cytherea was sorry it had to be killed. She scanned the woods around her warily while Kenric worked. The incident had shaken her, and she was ready to be moving again.

Kenric paused next to Aherne before he remounted Tredan. "Are you OK?"

"Yes, I'm fine. I just want to start moving again. It doesn't feel safe sitting here on the trail." Her tone was still cool but her anger had dissipated.

Kenric looked relieved at her softened tone. But Cytherea knew forgiveness for not telling her about Everard would take time, maybe a lot of time. As she watched Kenric pull himself into his saddle, she realized that they had never really been angry with each other. They had fought the kind of petty fights of siblings, but never anything serious. This was new territory for them, and she did not like the disconnected feeling.

"Cytherea, I'm sorry I didn't tell you about Everard sooner," Kenric began cautiously. "I was told not to ever bring it up, and when I did, the hurt I saw in my father's eyes would keep me from pushing further. I think he wanted to tell you, but he just couldn't."

"Why couldn't he?" Cytherea challenged. "Everard was my *brother*. That is a pretty big thing not to tell someone."

"My mother told me once that it was the type of pain that time doesn't heal. My father's duty to his king was more important to him than even life itself, and if he could have died in Everard's place, he would have done so willingly. The shame of failing to protect your brother overwhelmed him."

"Why didn't Fenia tell me? There were many times when we were alone while you and Tarquin were traveling. Why didn't she tell me then?"

"I don't know, Cyth." He sighed. "Perhaps she didn't want you to ask my father about it and bring up the pain for him."

"Didn't I have a right to know? I had a right to know," Cytherea said quietly to herself.

"I'm sorry." Kenric's voice was strained.

He couldn't fix it. Not this time.

They rode in silence for the rest of the day, and Cytherea kept to herself even after they stopped for the night. She stayed physically close to Kenric, but she kept her back to him, making sure he knew she was not interested in any conversation. Instead, Cytherea stared into the distance, seeing nothing, her head swimming.

She shook off her thoughts long enough to pull together a small meal. After Kenric fed and cared for the horses, he lowered himself next to her. She thrust a piece of bread toward him, which he gently took from her hands. Cytherea turned away from him once again and sighed, a tear escaping down her cheek. She desperately wanted life to go back to the way it had been. The four of them had been so happy in their little cottage, and life had been so simple. Now, it seemed every day revealed new details about her life that were so hard to understand and accept. Everything about her life had changed in a single day, a single moment, and it was almost more than she could withstand. She forced herself to eat a few bites before lying down on the cool grass, her head propped up on Aherne's saddle, and gazing up at the stars through the canopy of trees. When she finally fell asleep that night, she dreamed again of her mother and Everard.

The following morning, Cytherea and Kenric readied the horses for another day without speaking, and she watched him when he wasn't looking. She missed their fun banter. It had helped ease the tension and distract her from Ailmar and the soldiers of the Dark Realm. But she didn't know how to get past her anger and hurt.

They lied to me, she thought, her heart aching. What had Everard been like? What would her life have been like if he had lived?

Kenric caught her looking at him. "Are you ready?" he asked flatly.

"Yes." She smiled, trying to lighten the heavy mood that had been hanging over them.

He brushed past her to check Aherne's girth straps. He always double-checked everything before Cytherea rode, and she usually complained about it. She was capable of putting on and checking her own tack. Still, she held her tongue today. If he noticed, he didn't let it show and simply completed his checks before mounting Tredan. They traveled again in silence until they stopped for a midday meal.

"There is a small village beyond the forest on the other side of the trail," Kenric said as they finished eating. "I will walk there after we eat."

"What village? Why?"

"Christian told me that a loyalist who could give us information on the movements of the Dark Realm soldiers, so we can hopefully avoid them. Besides, we could use a few more supplies. I can pick those up while I am there."

"Why can't we go together? And why would you walk instead of ride?" Cytherea suddenly felt very vulnerable being alone in this unfamiliar place.

"I will not raise suspicion because I look like any other traveler stopping for supplies." He gestured toward the horses. "The horses always call attention to themselves because of their size, and you, well, you can't hide the color of your eyes or your face."

She looked down automatically in an attempt to shield her eyes, but she knew he was right. She toyed with the hem of her tunic. Then she took a deep breath and rested a hand on her sword hilt. "OK, but hurry, please."

"I will." He stood. "You are well hidden by the trees here, and you have both horses, who will help protect you. This is an old trail, and it is unlikely anyone would use it with a much larger road beyond, but if you hear anything at all, take the horses deeper into the forest and hide. I'll find you." He met her eyes. "If necessary, use your sword."

13

Before Cytherea could respond, Kenric darted through the trees. Sunshine fell on him when he exited the shaded forest and headed toward the village. From where she stood, she was only able to watch him for a short time before he disappeared behind the trees. As soon as she lost sight of him, her heart thrummed faster. Aherne and Tredan must have sensed her fear because they shifted to a more alert stance, which helped calm her slightly. The forest suddenly felt more sinister, and she imagined Dark Realm soldiers hiding behind every tree. Cytherea tried to convince herself that it was just her imagination, but that didn't work. She hoped Kenric would return quickly.

She stood silently and allowed the birds chattering above her to distract her mind. She needed to stay put so Kenric could find her easily when he returned, and the horses would welcome a few hours of rest. Cytherea patted Aherne's neck before she lowered herself to the ground next to him.

Within minutes, she felt Aherne stiffen beside her, and she held her breath. The birds fell silent, their cheerful chirping replaced by the soft plodding of other horses moving toward them in the distance. She stood and quietly guided her horses deeper into the forest, away from the trail. She resisted the urge to hurry as the horses trod silently on top of the thick underbrush. Soon, the steady plodding of the interlopers grew closer. Cytherea quickened her pace. The trees closed in around them, and she winced when a branch scratched her side and momentarily stuck on her tunic. The strangers were even closer, so Cytherea stopped moving and held her breath, but the forest was quiet. She strained to listen, and the horses' ears twitched. They stood among the thick tree branches, but there was only a suffocating silence.

Hunters, probably, she tried unsuccessfully to convince herself. After a time, a soft rustling suggested the horses and riders were moving away, but Cytherea remained still, wishing Kenric would come back. When the sounds faded, she began to relax a little until she felt Aherne and Tredan tense again.

"There is someone over here!" a gruff male voice yelled, so close that Cytherea instinctively jumped.

Another voice shouted farther away. Horses crashed through the underbrush, breaking off branches with loud snaps as they went. Aherne stamped his hoof, startling her into action. Cytherea had little room to mount, but she braced herself against a small tree anyway, its branches digging deep into her back. She clamored up the side of the saddle and flung herself ungracefully onto Aherne's back, pinching her ribs against the leather as she righted herself. The stallion snorted, and twigs snapped somewhere behind them. Aherne bobbed his head frantically, and she urged him forward with Tredan close behind, his reins held firmly in one hand. Ignoring the branches that pressed in on her legs, she remained flattened against Aherne's neck to avoid being knocked off by the larger branches above them. Space between the trees widened slightly, and the horses eased into a canter.

Cytherea gave Aherne his head and hoped he knew where to go. She could still hear pounding hoofbeats and shouting men behind them. She was not going to outrun them in the thick of the forest, but maybe she could hide.

But where?

Cytherea's mind raced frantically. Aherne thundered ahead, seemingly oblivious to the tree limbs that relentlessly struck his sides and legs. He let out three loud huffs.

You hurt, boy?

Aherne surged heedlessly on, but Tredan let out a loud whinny and jerked his reins from her hand.

"No," she hissed, looking back long enough to see, to her horror, Tredan turning around and running headlong into her pursuers. She gasped. Tredan rammed into the horses of two men wearing the mirrored black armor of Dark Realm soldiers. She could see more soldiers weaving between the trees beyond.

Cytherea urged her stallion to turn, but Aherne was not slowing, and she knew he would not stop. His job was to protect her. Behind them, Tredan bellowed like a soldier rushing into battle. Cytherea shook off the thought and concentrated on not getting knocked off Aherne's back. He was her only hope now.

With one final stride, Aherne shot into a small clearing, only to plunge back into more trees a few strides away. Even though the soldiers were no longer behind them, Aherne never slowed his frenetic pace, and Cytherea held on. *Will he ever stop?* He effortlessly jumped a small stream before he adjusted his gait and charged into more rugged and uneven terrain.

The wind nipped her face nearly raw, and she wiped her eyes for the hundredth time. When she scanned the area just ahead of them, a cave's maw opened on the side of a hill. Aherne headed straight for it. When they reached the hill, instead of stopping as Cytherea expected, Aherne slowed to a trot and entered the large cave. The clip-clop of his hooves on stone reverberated all around them. Only when daylight faded behind them and they were well within the natural tunnel inside the deep cave did Aherne finally slow to a walk.

He shook his head, breathing heavily. After they rounded a bend, the tunnel suddenly opened to a cavern that sheltered a natural spring. Cytherea slid from Aherne's back when he at last came to a stop and lowered his head to get a well-deserved drink from the spring. The cave was dark except for a shaft of light flooding in from someplace above the pool of water.

While Aherne took in the cool water and slowed his breathing, Cytherea drew her sword. The familiar warmth spread through her hand, causing the gem to glow brightly enough to fully light the cavern around her. A few bats screeched and fluttered around overhead in response to the light intruding on their resting place, but otherwise, there was nothing else there. Every so often, a draft would blow into the mouth of the cave, cooling the sweat still running down Cytherea's body and causing her to shiver.

She walked toward the saddlebags to retrieve her cloak, but then she used the Sword of Phoxnay's light to check Aherne for any wounds. Blood dripped from multiple cuts on both sides of his body, but only two looked severe. She washed them off with the spring water and found some of the salves in the beaten and torn saddlebag that the healer had given them before they'd left the cottage. Aherne flinched slightly but allowed her to cover the deeper wounds with it. She was not a healer, but healer's salves always worked surprisingly quickly.

Aherne was still breathing hard, but he was settling. As he began to relax, so did Cytherea, until a thought shot through her mind—*How is Kenric going to find us?*

Ice gripped her heart. He had no idea where they were. *She* had no idea where they were.

14

Unable to do anything about finding Kenric with Dark Realm soldiers nearby, Cytherea occupied herself by exploring the cavern, using the glow of her sword to cut through the shadows. The area could accommodate her, the small pond, Aherne, and a few bats that fluttered and squealed above her whenever the light moved too close, but not much else. The walls were cold and damp, as was the floor, with bits of moss growing on everything. The stalactite-riddled roof rose above her until it narrowed into a small opening, which allowed the shaft of light to sneak in. She assumed the bats came and went that way to avoid flying down into the cavern. Cytherea was still shivering from the cold despite her cloak, but she didn't dare start a fire for fear the soldiers might still be in the woods looking for her. She couldn't help but dwell on the fact that she would be trapped in here if they did manage to find her because, she had not found another way out.

She hadn't had much time to notice details upon their frantic arrival, but she remembered the mouth of the cave was on the side of a hill. She assumed that meant that they were in the foothills, which should be near the trail that lead to the mountain pass to Haight.

She finished the brief tour of her surroundings and walked to the water to clean up some of her own scratches and scrapes. The water was ice-cold, escalating her shivering as it ran over her arms and legs. Several cuts were deep enough that she applied the healer's salve to them before she looked through what supplies had survived her escape from the soldiers.

Cytherea pulled out some oats to feed Aherne and a piece of bread and dried meat for herself. Her waterskin had been torn off the saddle, so she used her hands to drink from the pond. After she ate her simple meal, she sat down, set her sword beside her, and stared into the darkness. She wondered what she should do next, understanding that she was hopelessly lost in the vast forest and that Kenric had no idea where she was.

She rested her eyes on Aherne, who appeared like a large shadow in front of her. She listened for any sound that might warn of the soldiers nearby, but she assumed she was well insulated from outside sounds in here.

She reached forward to rub one of Aherne's legs. "Where's Tredan?" she wondered aloud, and the sound of that name made Aherne nicker softly. "Could you get me back to where Kenric left us?"

Aherne nickered again. She always marveled at the way he always seemed to understand what she said. She was beginning to understand why Kenric always said that Aherne was "not just an ordinary horse."

She smiled, thinking about the easy conversations she had with Kenric. "I shouldn't have gotten so angry with him," she told Aherne.

What mattered now was that she knew about Everard. If there was any chance that he was alive, she had to find him. That was, if she could get out of here and find Kenric before the soldiers discovered their hiding place.

The darkness in the cavern around her deepened as the light outside faded. Aherne wasn't even a shadow before her now, his black coat blending seamlessly with the night; all she could see was blackness. Her lids grew heavy as the long day caught up with her.

Aherne snored.

"No time for a nap," she admonished him gently, yawning. "We have to figure out a way to find Kenric."

She walked over to the edge of the water and looked up. The gap at the top of the cave blended with the night sky and was no longer visible. She followed the rough walls to the other side. Unsure what she was even searching for, she gave up and returned to Aherne's side to rest. She had to figure out what to do next, but the darkness and the deep breaths of a sleeping Aherne made it hard to keep her eyes from closing. Despite her intentions, she fell into a restless sleep.

Cytherea was unable to see through the darkness around her, and she wondered briefly if her eyes were actually open.

Somewhere, the clang of armor echoed through the cave.

"Find her!" a sharp voice shouted, and she jumped. "We know she is in here somewhere. Those large hoofprints led right to this cave. Hurry! Ailmar wants her captured before dawn."

Cytherea froze. She groped her side, her fingers searching for her father's sword. It was gone. She ran her hands frantically over the damp stone floor, but it wasn't there. Confused, she crawled along the cave wall, moving deeper into the shadows, away from the cavern's entrance. Each of the soldiers' movements echoed off the walls, making it sound like they were all around her. Where is Aherne? she wondered frantically. She tried to peer into the dark to find him, but it was no use. She quietly moved along the wall, and an icy chill encased her right hand when it slipped into the water. There was nowhere to go.

She was trapped.

The soldiers' footsteps grew louder, and the deep shadows in the cavern began to dance and flee before the glow of their torches. She searched the area desperately, trying to find somewhere to hide. But the cave was surrounded by solid rock walls, and there was nothing that might conceal her.

She huddled against the wall and watched helplessly as the soldiers rounded the corner and entered the cavern. She was exposed. The light from the torch's flame blinded her. She looked at the ground and blinked as her eyes tried to adjust. A soldier's boots suddenly appeared in front of her. Turning her face from the gleaming boots upward, she shrank back at the sight of the soldier in full armor.

"I've found her!" he shouted behind him. When his face turned back toward her, Cytherea gasped.

His eyes were the same bright green as hers, and he held the Sword of Phoxnay.

Cytherea sat up, gasping for air, pressing her face against the damp rock. Aherne shifted next to her, and with a trembling hand, she touched the steed's reassuring warmth.

A flood of relief washed through her when she realized it had only been a dream. Her outstretched fingers moved to grasp her sword's hilt.

Even so, she sat still for a while longer and listened. Bat wings flapped above her. A fresh breeze blew in from the mouth of the cave and washed over her. She let herself breathe again and tried to slow the rhythm of her heart before lying back down. It was unlikely that she would fall asleep again, and she wasn't sure she wanted to risk having another dream like that one anyway.

Instead, she lay with her hand on her sword, looking up toward the slit at the top of the cavern, watching for daylight, hoping that Kenric and Tredan were OK. She remained on the cold, hard floor of the cavern until a gray light began to pierce the darkness above her, interrupted periodically by the bats returning from a night of hunting. They wriggled and flew about as they settled in for the day.

What should I do now?

Cytherea thought back to another time she had gotten lost, years ago when she was much younger. Tarquin, Fenia, and Kenric had been busy with something; she couldn't remember what. But with everyone else occupied, she'd decided to take herself exploring. Assuming she was with the horses, no one had noticed she was missing for a few minutes. Cytherea had gone into the woods and was unable to find her way home. She remembered the fear and panic that had set in and how hard she'd cried.

She'd been so relieved and happy when Kenric, whose face had mirrored her relief, had found her after a short time, and she never forgot what he'd told her that day. He'd said that if she ever got lost again, then she should stay in one place. The fact that she'd kept walking around the woods that day had made it harder for him to find her.

Cytherea reflected on that day. Should she stay where she was and wait for Kenric to find her? But what if the soldiers captured or hurt Kenric? She had no way of knowing if he was even looking for her. She abruptly grabbed her sword and stood. She needed to do something. She needed to try to get her bearings, and since she was unable to stop the shivering, she also needed to find a way to get warm. She crept down the passage to the mouth of the cave with Aherne following right behind her, hoping to reach the warmth of the sun's rays and not Dark Realm soldiers.

The interior of the cave became brighter as she neared the entrance, and soon she could see trees framed by the walls of the cave. While she moved closer, she flattened herself against the wall and stopped from time to time to listen for any sounds of soldiers in the forest beyond. Aherne hung back in the shadows but stayed close by. She strained her ears, but the only sounds she heard were birds singing and the wind rustling through the leaves. Everything else was quiet. She took a few hesitant steps into the sunlight and looked around. No one was there.

She stood for a few moments, letting the rays of the sun soak into her skin and permeate the cold. She stretched her stiff body in the open air and, as she did, she felt her cuts tug at the new movement. She clicked her tongue quietly to let Aherne know it was OK to come out with her. He trotted out into the filtered light and stopped at the first spot of grass he found on the forest floor.

Cytherea climbed up the gradual incline of the hillside, using the trees to pull herself along. She wanted to get a more unobstructed view of where she was or, at least, get her bearings on which direction was north. She was taking in her surroundings from her new vantage point when Aherne's ears pricked. She slid behind the nearest tree, her hand gripped tightly around her sword hilt. She strained to figure out what he heard, but all she could hear were the birds.

Aherne's ears pricked again, and he brought his head up, alert.

Wait—

Cytherea's free hand gripped the rough tree bark, and she carefully poked her head around to look. A faint whistle met her ear.

There it is again!

Aherne shifted and let out a low whinny. When the familiar whistle sounded again, there was no mistaking it. *Kenric!*

15

To Cytherea's delight, Kenric's familiar whistle repeatedly pierced the morning air. She hadn't realized how tense her entire body had been until it relaxed at the sound. She lowered her sword and picked her way down the hill until she was once again next to Aherne. He gave a low whinny each time Kenric whistled. It seemed to take forever for the sound to move closer, and fresh relief washed over her when another whinny followed Kenric's whistles. He had found Tredan!

After a few more long minutes, Cytherea caught sight of Kenric's blond hair through the tree branches. Tears welled up in her eyes when Kenric rode into the small clearing in front of the cave. Aherne's body shifted and his muscles lost some tension. Kenric's smile was broad as he leaped from Tredan's back, and Cytherea thought she might have seen a tear or two escape his eyes before he blinked them away.

"You found me!"

Kenric opened his arms but then immediately lowered them again.

Conflicting emotions flashed across his face, so she ran and threw her arms around him. He sighed in relief and encircled her with a giant bear hug. When he eventually let go, Cytherea stepped back, and Kenric's smile disappeared.

"You're hurt!" he said.

Cytherea realized how haggard she probably looked. "Only some cuts and scratches, nothing major. Aherne took the brunt of the tree limbs." She walked toward Aherne.

"Some of those look fairly deep," Kenric said, his brow wrinkling.

"I used the salve that the healer gave us before we left the farm. They will heal quickly enough." She surveyed her tunic and riding breeches. "But I'm afraid nothing can save these."

Kenric smiled. "Maybe we could pick you up a new dress in the next village, since Fenia isn't here to make you any new riding breeches."

"You won't get me in a dress that easily," she teased. "I'm sure Fenia packed a few extra pairs of breeches in my saddlebags."

Kenric's familiar smile crossed his face as if they were out for an afternoon picnic and he hadn't a care in the world. Cytherea knew it was partially to help keep her calm, and she appreciated it. However, his eyes belied worry and sadness.

"How did you find me?" she asked.

"It wasn't easy," he answered with a sigh. "Did you stay in that cave last night?"

"Yes. Aherne found it, or we stumbled upon it. I'm not sure which, but either way, I'm thankful we did."

"Let's get inside," he said, glancing around. "I don't think anyone followed me, but I don't feel safe out in the open."

Cytherea led Kenric into the cave and around the turn into the cavern. Both horses followed. She held out her sword to add some light while he looked around. They sat down on the cool floor of the cave while the horses got a drink and settled in for a rest.

"These horses never cease to amaze me," he said. "The fact that Aherne brought you here is one thing. The fact that they are both inside a cavern is quite another. A cave is not the type of place an ordinary horse would want to be."

"You told me that they are not ordinary horses."

"They certainly are not."

"So how did you find Tredan?" she asked.

"I met with Christian's contact, who told me that Dark Realm soldiers had been patrolling the area. He also said they were asking about a girl around the age of sixteen with green eyes."

Cytherea looked down instinctively to shield her eyes.

"After hearing that, I tried to leave and get back to you, but when I stepped back onto the road, a group of Dark Realm soldiers rode into the village." He paused, staring blankly forward. "They went from house to house, breaking things, throwing people out into the street, and yelling for money and young boys. The mothers' screams were horrific, Cyth.

"One woman wouldn't let go of her son. He couldn't have been more than five or six years old at the most. The soldiers slapped her and demanded she give him to them, but she wouldn't let him go. When she refused, one soldier got off his horse, walked right up to her as she begged, and ran his sword straight through her. She dropped to the ground, still clinging to her wailing son. When her arms fell lifelessly beside her, the soldier grabbed the child, threw the screaming boy over his shoulder, and rode out of town." He stopped, his expression pained and haunted.

Cytherea remained silent, unable to speak.

"It was awful." He looked at her. "These soldiers—they have no souls. They are ruthless and the very embodiment of evil."

She reached out and wrapped her hand around his.

"I left to find you as soon as I could. When I was leaving town, I saw the soldiers up on the road and panicked. I thought they had found you. I knew I couldn't run to where you were for fear that they would follow me, if they hadn't found you already." His hand tightened around hers. "So I walked down the road in the opposite direction until I was out of their sight. Then I doubled back inside the tree line, and eventually, I made it back to the spot where you should have been. But you weren't there."

Cytherea's chest tightened. She understood how frightening that moment must have been—to not know whether someone you cared for was alive.

Kenric continued, "I tried to determine which way you went, but another group of soldiers came through the trees. I hid and strained to hear what they were saying. All I heard was what sounded like 'We'll have to tell them she got away' when they rode past me to join the soldiers still waiting on the road below. Once I was sure they weren't coming back, I ran in the direction they had come. I followed the trail of the underbrush that had been trodden upon, and after a mile or so, I started whistling." He stopped to catch his breath.

"Before long, Tredan appeared out of the trees, which made me hopeful that you were close by. We continued looking even after it got dark, but we were forced to stop when we could no longer see the ground in front of us. We began again this morning at first light. I kept whistling, hoping you would hear me." He eyed her, gauging her reaction.

"Your magnificent whistle! I was relieved to hear it." Cytherea beamed and squeezed his hand. "I'm not sure what I would have done if you hadn't found me. Yesterday, I remembered you once told me that if I ever got lost, I should stay in one place."

"I'm glad you listened to something I taught you." He smiled before turning serious again. "We need to figure out how to get to Gregor's village now that we know the Dark Realm soldiers know you are here. They will be patrolling the forest and back trails as well as the main roads."

"Do you have any ideas?"

Kenric nodded. "I do. The only way we can feel certain about avoiding another run-in with soldiers is to travel at night."

"But no one travels through the forest at night." Traveling in the dark was dangerous—not just from the unpredictable terrain but also because night was when many of the animal predators came out to hunt.

"Which is exactly why we need to," Kenric replied definitively. "We can use your sword for light, and beyond that, we will have to rely on the instincts of Aherne and Tredan."

"I've never traveled at night," Cytherea said hesitantly.

"I have a couple of times with my father, but only along roads we were familiar with, not through the forest. And"—he gave her a solemn look—"I have to warn you, the mountain pass will be the most dangerous section of our journey."

"Why?"

"Because we will not be able to stay in the cover of trees. The drop-offs are too risky, so we will have to travel through the pass on the road."

"And what do we do if we see more soldiers?" She wasn't sure she wanted to hear the answer.

"Let's hope we don't." Kenric's eyes focused on the ground in front of him. He raised his head with a smile and deftly changed the subject. "But on the other side of the mountain pass, you will see where the castle of Phoxnay once stood."

"Is there anything left of it?" Cytherea hadn't considered that she might see the place where her parents had lived and died on their way to see Gregor. The concept chilled and excited her.

"I haven't been back since the day we left all those years ago, but I've been told there are parts of it still standing. It's been a long time, so don't expect to see much."

Cytherea nodded. "I want to see whatever is left. I want to see what was once my home."

16

Kenric and Cytherea settled into the cavern to wait for nightfall and to try and rest. Cytherea was grateful that Tredan and Aherne would have another day for their wounds to heal a bit more. Kenric ran his hands methodically across the bodies of both horses, making sure they didn't have any more serious injuries after their wild flight from the soldiers the day before. The healer's salve worked quickly, and the deepest wounds were now merely scars.

After Kenric was satisfied that the horses were healthy, he walked over to Tredan's saddlebags, pulled out a blanket, and wrapped it around Cytherea's shivering body.

"Thank you." She smiled up at him.

He went back, pulled out some bread and cheese, tore it, and handed her half of each. "You must be hungry."

"I had some bread last night, but I saved most of it, just in case we were separated for some time."

"I'm glad that I was able to find you before the soldiers did."

"I am too." She tried to smile at him again, but it morphed into more of a grimace at that thought.

Kenric chewed his own bread thoughtfully, studying her with

soft but wary eyes. She sensed that he didn't know where he stood with her, and she could feel his hesitation when he spoke. She didn't want to be mad at him anymore, but she also didn't want to have another conversation about it. She wanted to move forward and get back to the way they'd been before her hurt and anger.

Cytherea kept her eyes lowered but sensed Kenric examining her face and trying to read her mood. "I was so happy to see you that I didn't even ask," she said, trying to sound friendly. "Did you get any other news from Christian's contact in the village?"

"I didn't stay to ask any other questions once they told me that the Dark Realm soldiers were active in the area, but of course, I think you already knew that bit of news." He emitted a choked laugh, which would have helped Cytherea relax another time. His brows furrowed. "Now that we're settled, I'm going to go out onto the hill above the mouth of the cave and keep watch while you get some rest. If I found you, then there is a chance Ailmar's soldiers can too."

Cytherea shivered, but this time it was not from the cold. "Why don't you rest and I'll keep watch for a while?"

"I wouldn't be able to sleep worrying about you out there." He took his sword from his saddle and strapped it around his waist. "You will have plenty of time to return the favor later." He grinned at her before turning and heading back down the passage, not giving Cytherea a chance to argue.

She watched him disappear into the darkness before lying down and closing her eyes. Her mind swirled with all that had happened since that first attack at the farm, and she couldn't be still. She got up to brush the horses. The rhythmic sound of the brush strokes and the feel of the horses' soft coats under her hands slowed her chaotic thoughts. She braided their manes and pondered what her future held. *What does it mean to follow my destiny? How can I lead an army against Ailmar? Where will that army even come from?*

The questions ran through her head until she couldn't think about it anymore. She shook the unanswered questions from her head and sat with her back against the cave wall, listening to the bats flutter overhead.

"Cytherea."

Cytherea's eyes flew open to find Kenric standing over her. She hadn't realized that she had fallen asleep.

"The sun is setting. It is time to ready the horses."

"Of course." She forced herself fully awake as she stood. "Did you see any signs of soldiers in the forest?"

"No. I'm hoping they will be gone for a while, taking their captives back to Ailmar's castle."

"Do you think there are more out there?" she asked, lifting her saddle onto Aherne's back and starting to secure it.

"I'm sure there are, but we will move only at night for the rest of our journey."

"How do we know there aren't soldiers patrolling at night?"

"We don't, but all the information I have received so far is that they have only been seen during the day. They have no fear of being met with any kind of resistance, so they have no reason to patrol at night. The villagers' numbers are too small, and their spirits have been broken. They have given in to their fate and won't rise up against them." He walked over and checked Aherne's girth straps, and she let him with only a small huff. "The only time the loyalists have heard of them striking at night was when they attacked our farm. It is believed that they were worried that you had the Sword of Phoxnay."

"We did have it and didn't use it." Cytherea's grief and pain seeped into her voice.

Kenric squeezed her shoulder, pain lacing his words as well. "We didn't use it because we didn't know if you were ready yet, but it works in our favor now. Since the soldiers didn't see it that night, that likely means they think you don't have it. The element of surprise is key in any battle."

"How do you know I'm ready?" Cytherea asked. Her hand moved over the hilt of the great sword, and the gem glowed slightly.

"You're ready. The sword makes you ready. You just don't realize it yet." With that, Kenric took Tredan's reins, and they led the horses out of the cave.

17

It was a clear night. The light from the moon filtered through the branches above them, brightening small patches of the darkness, which helped guide them around more considerable obstacles. The horses navigated the minor obstructions like rocks and low-lying plants reasonably well as they slowly picked their way through the dim forest, heading toward the mountain pass. Aherne stumbled once when he misjudged the terrain ahead of him, so Cytherea kept a sharp lookout for any other hindrances on the trail. The wind blew the shadows around, making the forest dance eerily. The movement played tricks on Cytherea's eyes, and shadows became the crouched shapes of Dark Realm soldiers hiding in the moonlight. A small branch brushed against her leg, and Cytherea flinched. She was on edge, watching and listening for anything that might be out of place.

Kenric and Cytherea traveled in silence, vigilant and alert. They needed to safely navigate the unpredictable terrain and avoid the animal predators. She remembered the panther that attacked them in the daylight and wondered why. It had been unusual because panthers were usually nocturnal.

"Why do you think the animals have been acting so oddly lately? Both the panther and those elk seemed to be running in fear from something more than a predator," she whispered.

Kenric took a moment to respond. "They may have been spooked by either soldiers or hunters who had traveled off the well-worn path and deeper into the forest." He hesitated. "With all the soldiers patrolling, there is a lot more animal activity in the normally serene woods."

Cytherea peered around her cautiously. The foothills were the animals' territory, and in the dark, predators had the upper hand.

From that first night under the hay in Aherne's stall, she'd felt hunted. Both the panther and the Dark Realm soldiers had driven her into a panic like a rabbit. It occurred to her that the soldiers were predators too, and once she and Kenric reached the Dark Realm, they would be in their territory and the soldiers would have the upper hand. Cytherea's heart skipped a beat at the thought. Kenric must have sensed her unease.

"What's wrong?" he whispered.

"Nothing. I am just jumpy." She tried to give him a confident smile but realized he couldn't see it in the dark anyway.

Travel through the forest was slow and arduous. In the daylight, the journey to the mountain pass would have taken a short time, but the moon was high overhead before the terrain became noticeably steeper. Kenric raised his hand, and Cytherea brought Aherne to a stop. Kenric then waved her forward until she was alongside him. The hills rose into steep jagged slopes on either side of the road ahead of them.

"Here we are—the mountain pass. We must travel on the road until we reach the other side."

"Won't we be seen?" Her heart began to pound.

"We will stick as close to the tree line as we can, but there are too many drop-offs and cliffs that we won't be able to see until it's too late, if we stay in the trees." He put his hand on her shoulder, likely to reassure her. "There won't be anyone traveling this way in the middle of the night. It's too dangerous. We should be the only ones on the road."

"'Should' be?"

"We *will* be." He corrected himself, but she wasn't convinced by his act of confidence.

"How long will it take to get to the other side?"

"My contact in the last town said we should be able to reach the other side of the pass well before first light."

"That is still a long time to be fully exposed on the road."

"Yes, but with the moon out tonight, we should be able to move at a faster pace once we clear the trees."

They carefully directed the horses toward the road, and before stepping out of the trees, Kenric checked to be sure no one was coming. Once on the road, Cytherea felt uneasy, and she was constantly turning, watching, and listening. Even at night, Cytherea could tell the landscape was beautiful. In different circumstances, she would want to slow down and enjoy all of nature's beauty around her, but for now, she wanted to get through the pass as quickly as possible.

Time moved as if through a bog, and Cytherea hoped they were nearing the other side. They neared a bend in the road when Kenric raised his hand and signaled her to stop short of the bend. She held her breath and listened. In the distance, she heard it—the sound of a horse on the road ahead.

Kenric turned toward Cytherea with a frantic movement. *Hide!* her mind screamed. Trees loomed beside the road, but there was no way of knowing whether there was a cliff beyond. But they had no choice.

Cytherea swiftly dismounted and led Aherne toward the trees. Kenric followed. Beneath the trees, she wrapped her fingers around her sword so that the gem glowed just enough to show her the solid ground between the trees, and then she quickly released her grip, letting it go dark again. She and Kenric guided the horses carefully behind the first set of trees and became still. They listened to the sound of the horse and rider getting closer. Whoever it was, they were moving fast and were soon passing directly across from their hiding place, but the rider's eyes were trained on the road ahead. Thankfully they never looked to either side as they hurried past.

Kenric and Cytherea stood silently for a few moments more to make sure the rider was alone and would not double back.

"I'm going to check around that bend to make sure no one else is coming before we continue down the road. Stay here and don't move," Kenric said.

Cytherea shook her head. "Leaving me alone *didn't* work out very well last time."

Kenric's voice was tight. "Fine. Come on."

Within a few minutes, they were back in their saddles and creeping out of the underbrush on the side of the road.

Once they were moving again, she whispered, "Who do you think that was?"

"Likely just a messenger with an urgent message for someone in one of the villages, back the way we came." He paused, then added, "There is also the chance that it was a loyalist. They have been known to travel at night to avoid detection by the Dark Realm."

They both became quiet again, and Cytherea thought about what Christian had said. *I assure you that others are out there who are on our side.* First Christian, then Kenric's contact in the village, and now this lone horseman. Perhaps she wasn't a rabbit, hunted and alone. Perhaps she was a predator with a pack at her back, even if she couldn't see or feel them all the time. She was beginning to believe that the loyalists were real and that Ailmar wasn't going to have her without a fight. Even though Kenric had told her about the loyalists, they had just seemed like characters from one of Tarquin's stories until this horseman in the dark of night brought them to life for her. She thought about them, and about Tarquin and Fenia, and about home. Lost in her thoughts, she failed to notice that the steep incline of the road had slowly begun to smooth out until Kenric began leading her back into the forest and off the hard-packed road.

They had made it through the mountain pass!

18

"What do you mean you couldn't find her?" Ailmar asked.

The spear-like tip of the ebony staff struck the stone floor with such force that the soldiers had to take a step to steady themselves against the vibrations that shot across the floor.

"You had been watching her for days! You knew she was there." Ailmar stepped within inches of his war-hardened soldiers, and the blood drained from their faces. "How can you tell me you *couldn't find her?*"

The soldiers winced but did not move.

"We will find her, Your Majesty," one soldier said, his voice cracking. "We received word that another regiment found a girl alone in the forest close to the mountain pass and—"

"What does a girl in the forest mean to me? It could have been any of a thousand different girls. Did they see her eyes? That's what I need to know! Did she have *green* eyes?"

Ailmar's own eyes were blazing as he spoke, and the black orb at the top of his staff began to emit an ominous glow. The soldiers leaned back as if attempting to increase the distance between themselves and the staff. They had all heard the stories about its powers. It was believed that it could kill with a single touch, but whether the power came from the staff itself or Ailmar, no one knew.

"Answer me, fools!" His voice boomed, and he smacked the ground again with the staff. This time the vibration was enough to knock the soldiers off-balance. "Did the girl in the forest have the right eyes?"

"I . . . I don't know, Your Majesty. But the report was that she had those horses with her," the soldier said.

"What do you mean you don't know? Where is this girl?" Ailmar demanded.

"Your Majesty, they were unable to capture her," the soldier responded quietly. He bowed low in an act of humility, likely as a means to assuage Ailmar's anger.

"What did you say?" Ailmar reached forward with his staff and caught the soldier under the chin to pull him back up.

"They were not successful in capturing the girl in the forest."

Ailmar swung around and began pacing in small circles, his staff landing on the floor with an ominous thud at each step. A little wisp of darkness escaped the black orb each time the staff hit the ground.

When Ailmar stopped pacing, he turned back toward the soldiers. His voice became menacingly calm. "So, you are telling me that two different regiments of my best soldiers were unable to capture a young girl?" Ailmar stalked toward them.

The soldiers' eyes were wide, and they seemed unable to answer.

"Answer me!" he growled and struck the floor again. The staff's blackness swirled around his head.

The piercing screams of the soldiers could be heard throughout most of the castle as their fates were sealed. Upon exiting the throne room, Ailmar stormed down the passageway and rushed past other cowering soldiers, shouting at them, "Find that girl and bring her to me!"

19

As dawn neared, the forest began to thin.

Kenric pulled Tredan to a stop. Cytherea rode up next to him.

"We are almost there." He looked at her expectantly.

"Where?"

"Just ahead, the forest will open into a meadow that will lead to a cobblestone path, which will lead to—"

"The castle of Phoxnay!" Cytherea interrupted, recognizing the description from Tarquin's stories.

Kenric smiled at her childlike excitement. "That's right. You've come home, Cyth. We can't stay long because we need to get to Gregor's in Haight, but I promise you will come back here to stay one day."

Cytherea's exhaustion vanished, and she urged Aherne into a trot.

Astride Tredan, Kenric blocked her path. "Wait. We can't just go galloping through the front gate—if there's even a front gate left."

Disappointment swirled within her.

"I will take you there, but we have to be careful. Ailmar's

forces are likely patrolling this area. It makes sense that they might expect you to come here after leaving the farm."

"I need to see it, Kenric. I need to touch the walls and walk where my parents walked. If I'm going to lead their—my—people, I need to feel them with me."

"I understand, but my first concern is keeping you safe."

She nodded in agreement.

"If we keep on straight, we'll have to cross the large open meadow where we will be too visible. However, if we circle around along the edge of the forest toward the back of the castle, there is a section that has less open space between the forest and the castle. It's the way we left on the day of the attack. It will take us a bit longer to get there, but we will have less chance of being spotted that way."

Cytherea sighed. "I wish I could let Aherne gallop across the meadow and up to the castle. I have heard so many stories about this place. I want to travel the same path Tarquin traveled in the stories he told. I feel a physical pull, and I want to let it draw me in."

"I know, and you will get there, just by a more roundabout way."

Kenric clucked, and Tredan turned. Cytherea followed as they made their way along the edge of the forest. Cytherea tried to catch a glimpse of the castle through the trees, but in the dimness of the early dawn, she couldn't see anything. By the time Kenric slowed their pace, the sun had risen into the sky and the forest was alive with birds and other creatures starting their day. Cytherea was distracted by a pair of wild hares scampering across their path and didn't initially notice that Kenric had come to a stop. She raised her eyes toward him and followed his hand where he pointed through the trees ahead.

A wall of gray stone stood a short distance beyond the trees. Despite the distance, Cytherea knew instantly what it was. They had reached the outer wall of Phoxnay.

Kenric encouraged Tredan forward, and Aherne, with Cytherea, followed. As they moved farther out of the tree line, more of the crumbling castle wall came into view.

They progressed slowly toward the wall, and Cytherea searched her surroundings for something familiar from her time there. The overgrown landscape and fallen boulders from the wall didn't give her even a glimmer of any memory of her mother, father, or her past life. Kenric kept quiet, leaving her to her thoughts. He searched for a way into the castle grounds and found a jagged opening easily because the wall had deteriorated considerably.

They rode cautiously into the village that once surrounded the castle proper, and Cytherea realized that she had little hope of finding familiarity there. Any memories she might have had of this place had been destroyed by Ailmar's army. The magnificent castle of Phoxnay from Tarquin's and Fenia's stories was in ruins and inhabited only by wild creatures and overgrown vegetation.

The once-bustling market within the castle walls had been long since silenced. The shopkeepers' canopies were torn down, burned, and rotting—silent reminders of the Dark Realm's destructive powers. Cytherea slid off Aherne and stepped carefully over the shattered cobblestone streets. *What had become of those shopkeepers and their families?* Tarquin's tales had sometimes had stories of others escaping the battle on that final day, but they were all scattered throughout the kingdom. *How many of Phoxnay's people are alive today? How many loyalists are out there, waiting?*

Cytherea recounted the stories that she had heard throughout her childhood from Tarquin and Fenia about the beauty and prosperity that once made Phoxnay great. The battle that had ended the lives of her parents, destroyed this beautiful castle, and sent her into exile had once been just a story, a thrilling bedtime tale. But now, as the cracked castle walls towered above her, grief choked her throat. The inhabitants of Phoxnay were not characters in her imagination. They had been flesh and blood, and they had lost their lives here in a horrific and bloody battle. As she led Aherne farther down the dilapidated streets, Cytherea's heart broke for the people of Phoxnay—*her* people.

The destruction worsened the closer they got to the castle proper. Cytherea began to lose hope of finding anything recognizable that might trigger her memories of this place or her parents, who sacrificed themselves so that she might live. She realized she would likely never remember her life here, and tears flowed down her cheeks.

Kenric dismounted and walked alongside Cytherea. Periodically, he bent forward to pick through the rubble while Tredan and Aherne grazed on the wild grasses growing through the rocks and debris. Cytherea gazed at the contrast of the green grass forcing its way between the cold, gray stone, and a glimmer of hope flickered in her chest. Perhaps this once beautiful kingdom could be brought back from these ruins. The vibrant grass had found a way where it seemed impossible, and maybe so could she.

Inspired, she began tossing pieces of broken stone from one area into a pile a short distance away.

Kenric stopped. "What are you doing?"

"I'm cleaning up this mess."

A grin spread across Kenric's face. He looked around at the massive piles of broken stones and boulders as far as his eyes could see. "Really? All of it? By yourself?"

She rolled her eyes. "Well, apparently, since you are just standing there."

Kenric's smile widened. "Would you like some help?"

"Take those stones from there and put them all in one pile here." She pointed at the two locations.

Cytherea saw Kenric's wry grin before he managed to stifle it.

The two worked on clearing the small area until Kenric talked her into taking a break. They had traveled all night and needed to rest. Besides, he was not comfortable being out in the open of the village ruins. While there was enough of the wall left that they were not visible from the road, he still felt exposed.

"We'll be much more concealed in the castle," he said.

Cytherea agreed, and they led the horses inside. She traced the ridged wood of one of the massive doors still hanging askew from its hinges as they passed. It felt cold and rough beneath her fingers. The other door lay on the ground next to it, disguised by years of vegetation growing through and across it.

Once inside, Kenric pointed to their left and said, "I think the dining hall is this way."

They carefully picked their way through the ruins, passing broken furniture and torn tapestries until they came to a vast room. Nature had taken over the inside of the castle as well. Grass and vines grew wild throughout the room, but there were still hints of its previous life. An immense table, still intact, spanned the majority of the room. The beauty of the ebony wood could not be hidden even by years of neglect, and though many of the chairs lay broken and scattered, Kenric managed to find two that were usable. He made a futile effort to clean them off before offering one to Cytherea.

She looked around the room in silence and tried to imagine what it had looked like when her parents had been alive. She imagined bright tapestries hanging from the walls in place of the vines. There would have been enormous candelabras spanning the center of the great table, with food covering every empty space between them. She could almost hear her father's laughter echoing through the room over the excited chatter of his guests around him. She imagined the rustling of the silk dresses as the women moved about the chamber, eating and talking and sharing in the feast.

Cytherea smiled at the sight of the guests currently gathered around the great table. She chuckled, breaking the silence. "I bet this is the first time horses have eaten at this table."

"I don't know." Kenric laughed. "You get your love of horses from your father, so he probably tried to include them in a family meal at some point."

Cytherea smiled at the thought that she and her father had a shared passion. "I'll get something out for these two"—she gestured toward Aherne and Tredan—"while you get ours ready."

She approached the table where the saddlebags now rested. Tredan shifted to move in front of Kenric while he rifled through one of them.

"No treats, boy." Kenric pushed Tredan's head out of the way. Cytherea glanced at Aherne. Both horses had moved together and were looking directly at her and Kenric, not at the food. Aherne pawed the ground impatiently.

Something was wrong.

Kenric's eyes lifted.

Cytherea looked to Aherne. "Where?"

Aherne's massive head turned to look behind them in response, and he danced closer to her. Grabbing the saddlebags and hurriedly replacing their contents, Kenric jumped onto Tredan's back. Cytherea mounted Aherne. The horses needed no prodding, and they moved deeper into the castle.

She strained her ears, trying to hear what had spooked them. Thinking it may have been the wind or a wild animal, she started to speak, but Kenric signaled her to stay silent. Aherne bobbed his head impatiently again. She loosened her grip on the reins and gave Aherne his head. Both horses moved methodically over the stone floors and stepped over the stones that littered the ground. Cytherea knew they were trying to keep their giant hooves muffled.

They soon reached a small chamber deeper within the castle, where they dismounted to pass through the doorway. They stopped to listen. Moments passed before Kenric and Cytherea heard what had alarmed the horses.

Voices.

The acoustics of the castle made it difficult to determine where they were, or even in which direction.

"You think they're in the dining hall now?" Cytherea guessed.

"They probably came through the courtyard," Kenric agreed.

However, there was no way to know for sure, and this wasn't the time to take any chances. Kenric gave inaudible commands to the horses, and they stood motionless. Kenric and Cytherea strained to make out what the interlopers were saying.

"So what is this place anyway?" a male voice asked. "And why does His Majesty want us to patrol it? It is just a bunch of ruins."

"His Majesty despises this place," replied another voice. "It's the remnant of the kingdom of Phoxnay, and he wants to make sure none of the survivors—if there were any—try to return and rebuild it."

"I have heard stories of Phoxnay. But I never knew it actually existed."

"It doesn't exist—at least, not anymore. King Ailmar made sure of that. He killed everyone and everything that lived here in battle." The voice stopped and then continued, muffled as if around a mouthful of food. "He was victorious. He killed both the king and queen, and once their sovereigns were dead, the inhabitants that were still alive lost heart and either surrendered or ran away like dogs."

Wood scraped across stone, which confirmed that the voices were coming from the dining hall using the chairs that they had just vacated.

Dark Realm soldiers, Kenric mouthed.

Cytherea nodded, eyes wide. They were likely resting there before continuing their patrol.

"Do you think that Phoxnay girl will ever turn up?" the second soldier asked. "I heard they tracked her to a farm—some small village somewhere between what used to be the border of Phoxnay and Klobyn. But when they got there, the girl was gone."

The first soldier hesitated, presumably to take a bite of his meal, because his mouth was full when he spoke. "Bah, Felix's patrol probably saw some hunter's daughter in the woods, and he got killed for it. Don't believe the rumors."

"I was away on patrol at the time." The second soldier's voice sounded pained. "Someone said that their screams could be heard across the entire castle."

"I hope I never displease His Majesty like that."

"How did the king miss the girl in the first place?"

"Idiot, keep your voice down. Never speak against His Majesty. No matter how far from him you think you may be. No one knows what he is capable of, or what his magic . . ." The men lowered their voices, and Cytherea couldn't make out their words for a few minutes.

She and Kenric crouched in silence until they heard the first soldier say, "Finish eating. We should get back out on patrol. I don't want to miss our check-in and have to go before His Majesty."

Kenric motioned for Cytherea to move away from the door in case the soldiers decided to look through the castle before leaving. They sat quietly until the distant thud of the remaining castle door closing traveled through the building. The soldiers were leaving. Silence fell, and after several long minutes, they relaxed slightly. They were able to finally eat something and then took turns sleeping while they waited for nightfall.

20

Cytherea slept restlessly, and even then, she was haunted by dreams meshed with blurred memories. When she opened her eyes, she saw that the chamber had dimmed as the day wore on. She heard Kenric move nearby, and she turned to find him talking in low tones to Tredan and rubbing the stallion's neck. She got up and went to the waterskin to splash some water on her face. Lack of sleep and the long days of their journey had made her groggy. As she dried her face on her cloak, Kenric's footsteps sounded behind her. She turned to him.

"No movement or voices from any more soldiers," he whispered. "And our horses are still relaxed, so they haven't sensed any movement either."

"Well, we don't want to be here if they decide to come back for the night."

"Agreed." Kenric shifted to peer through an opening in the wall. "It is still fairly light outside, so we should wait a bit longer before continuing on to Gregor's village."

Cytherea gave the horses some grain and water, and as she did, she felt the ring moving along its chain on her neck. She absently reached up to rub it between her fingers, a habit she'd taken up during their journey.

I might be standing where my mother used to stand, she thought. Maybe even where she had reached up to play with the ring when her mother had still worn it. Cytherea smiled at the possibility.

"What are you thinking about?" Kenric asked with a smile.

"That we might be standing where my mother and father once stood."

"I'm sure you are. It is likely that they were in every room of this castle at some point," he said with his arms outstretched. "And I know that we were all in the dining hall almost daily."

"You remember that?"

"I do. I remember sitting at that big table. To me back then, it seemed like it stretched for miles. I was so small that they had to put blankets under me so I could see over the top of the table to eat."

Cytherea laughed, and it felt good. It seemed like it had been a long time since she and Kenric had been able to laugh. Grim terror and the weight of her responsibility hadn't made her feel much like laughing. However, just as quickly, her thoughts turned dark again. Her smile vanished, and her brows knit together.

"What's wrong?" Kenric studied her face.

"I was thinking about how much Ailmar has taken from us and from all of the people of Phoxnay." She tilted her head quizzically. "Why hasn't anyone tried to stop Ailmar before? There are other kingdoms nearby, like Klobyn, that surely want him gone."

"They do. And they've tried. Unfortunately, those attacks only resulted in more lives lost."

"Why do you think I will have any better luck?"

"No one quite understands the magic that Ailmar wields. Its source is unclear, as is how much control he has over it. But people believe that the only thing that can defeat Ailmar is the Sword of Phoxnay. That is what you have in your favor. The power of your sword is no small thing, even though I believe we have only seen a hint of what it can do."

"Why do people believe that? It didn't help my father."

"Ailmar knows that the magic of your sword is powerful, but it can only be used by an heir to the throne of Phoxnay. That is why Ailmar severed your father's hand from his body before his death," Kenric said it without thinking, and Cytherea winced. "It separated your father from the power of the sword and, at the same time, made the sword's magic useless."

"So they are waiting for the sword, not me."

"They are waiting for both, Cyth." He walked over and put his hands on her shoulders. "Your family has ruled Phoxnay for generations. Your ancestors are revered by all, including the neighboring kingdoms. Your father and those before him have always dealt fairly and kindly with others. King Edmond was always willing to defend and protect the people of Phoxnay and all her allies, and now they are ready to return the favor—but they need you to lead them."

All the anxieties and fears she had stifled in the days following Tarquin's death bubbled to the surface, and tears rolled down her cheeks. "But they don't know me. How do we know that anyone will actually follow me against Ailmar?"

"You are right. They don't know you. But they know your bloodline and the connection between that and the powers of the Sword of Phoxnay." He tilted her face to look at him and wiped her tears. "When you tap into the power of the sword and call on them to follow you, they will follow. I'm certain of that."

Cytherea didn't have much time to dwell on Kenric's words because the horses shifted restlessly. Aherne bobbed his head nervously, his bridle jingling.

"The soldiers must be returning for the night," Kenric said.

It made sense that the soldiers would choose to camp indoors when they had the option. Cytherea drew the great sword, and they led the horses out of the chamber and down the passage in the opposite direction of the dining hall.

"The back of the castle has some doorways that lead outside."

Cytherea hoped Kenric could find one before the soldiers discovered them. After a few minutes, Kenric and Cytherea exited the castle undetected. The sky had darkened, providing some safety, but they still had a small open glade to cross before they would be concealed within the trees beyond. Kenric scouted ahead, and Cytherea's eyes nervously followed him until he disappeared around the corner of the wall. They hadn't heard the soldiers as they made their way out of the castle, so they could be anywhere.

You couldn't hide from someone if you didn't know where they were.

After what seemed like an eternity, Kenric reappeared and beckoned to her. "The soldiers have made camp for the night," he said. "We need to get to the tree line before they start their nightly patrols."

Cytherea relaxed slightly and placed her father's sword back into her scabbard. She mounted Aherne. Before long, she was following Kenric into the trees, and they began another night's journey.

The night's travel was thankfully uneventful, but even so, after spending hours creeping through the brush, over fallen trees, and circumventing other hazards of the woods, the horses and their riders were exhausted. None of them were accustomed to long, hard traveling, especially at the quick pace they tried to maintain. However, they didn't slow down. Kenric was impatient to get Cytherea to the relative safety of Haight and out of the well-patrolled forest and surrounding roads.

As the night wore on, Kenric noticed the silhouette of Cytherea's body beginning to slump forward from exhaustion. "It will be dawn soon. Let's find a place to stop for the day."

She didn't argue.

Once they found an area with enough trees and brush to keep them hidden, they both dismounted and landed on the ground with audible relief. Immediately, Cytherea put together a simple meal while Kenric fed and watered the horses. None of them had eaten since leaving the castle. Their only focus had been getting as far as they could before daylight.

Crouching to join Cytherea for their meal, Kenric frowned.

"What?" she asked.

Still staring at the ground, Kenric replied quietly, "Our water is running low since your waterskin was lost when you escaped the soldiers. We will have to find a river this evening for the horses, at least, before we can continue."

"What if we can't find one?"

"We will. We have to. We can't expect the horses to continue without enough water. Besides, we will need more water by then as well. Once Tredan and Aherne are well watered, we should be able to make it to Haight by daybreak tomorrow. At least, that is my hope."

Cytherea nodded, holding out a piece of salted meat. "I hope so too. But for now, please eat. You can't do anything if you don't keep up your strength."

Kenric eyed the meat for a moment before taking it. "Do you still want to . . . try to find Everard?" he asked.

"Of course. He's my brother. He has the same blood as me as well as the same legacy." Cytherea swallowed a mouthful of meat. "My hope is that if he is still alive, we can find him. And maybe he'll join us in our fight against Ailmar."

"He does have your blood and your heritage," Kenric conceded, but he frowned, worried.

"You think that if he is alive, my twin brother has been completely changed by Ailmar."

Kenric braced his arms on his knees, tearing a bite from his scant meal. "From the stories I've heard, Ailmar has considerable success brainwashing his victims. Oftentimes permanently. We don't know exactly what he is capable of."

"Are you prepared for the fact that, if he is alive, Everard might actually be on our side?" Cytherea's voice was sharp.

"*If* he is alive, then of course I am, Cyth. And if that's the case, I will protect and defend him as I do you."

"Then we will wait and see."

"Very well." Kenric shoved the rest of his food into his mouth, ready to end the conversation, but he couldn't shake the uneasy feeling he had whenever they spoke about Everard.

21

Cytherea woke from another fitful sleep to the sound of the horses grazing quietly near her head. Birds chirped, and the sun still shone brightly through the branches overhead. Rolling over, she saw Kenric staring into the sky, although he didn't seem to be looking at anything. Instead, he appeared to be deep in thought.

"If I close my eyes," Cytherea said softly, "I can imagine that I'm lying in the meadow back home without a care in the world. But when I open them again, it is just a memory." She sat up and gently rubbed Aherne's soft nose. "I can't imagine how I was ever carefree with so much evil all around us."

Kenric turned to face her, blinking as if freeing himself from his thoughts. "That's the way my father wanted it. He tried to keep the evil of the world away from you. He wanted your life to be carefree for as long as possible."

"That was not very realistic."

"Maybe not, but it was love. He dedicated his entire life to protecting you. And not just out of duty to your parents. He did it out of love for you. You were his daughter in every way except blood."

"And he was like a father to me." She swallowed hard against the knot of grief that formed in her throat.

Kenric got to his feet, bringing Cytherea back to the present. "We have a few hours before dark. I'm going to walk into the forest and see if I can find water close by. I won't go far."

Cytherea pulled her sword out from under her blanket as Kenric prepared to leave.

Kenric then left to find water, and Cytherea remained seated, watching and listening until he returned without water.

They waited for nightfall before they broke their camp, loaded their things on the horses, and continued in the direction of Haight, hoping their trail would lead to a river. They traveled for a time in silence, listening intently for any sounds of soldiers. The last thing they wanted was to come upon a patrol's camp accidentally. The night deepened, and Kenric slowed.

Cytherea remained silent, trying to figure out what had caught his attention. He pointed in one direction, and they headed that way. Cytherea's heart pulsed like thunder in her ears. Had they come upon an encampment of soldiers?

Then suddenly, she heard it, and she allowed her body to relax.

Above the rustling wind was the faint trickle of water. A river. However, her relief was tempered by the knowledge that soldiers might have found it too and may have camped there for the night.

The sound of the river grew louder, and the branches and brush underneath their feet thinned. Cytherea peered toward the sky, and shafts of moonlight fell on her face. Her eyes lowered to a small river that seemed to sparkle in the distance. Kenric halted and dismounted Tredan. Cytherea waited while he made sure that it was safe for them to emerge from their wooded cover.

His investigation found both footprints and hoofprints that led to the water's edge, emerged on the other side of the river, and disappeared into the woods beyond. Someone, likely soldiers, had been there, but it looked as though they had moved on. To be safe, Kenric kept Cytherea and the horses hidden from view as he went to and from the safety of the tree line to give Cytherea a drink and then to fill up the waterskin. They had only been traveling for a short time that night, but Cytherea was already tired. Despite that, Kenric remained optimistic about reaching Gregor's village by dawn.

When Kenric felt it was safe, they crept toward the river and allowed the horses a long drink before they continued their journey. As they crossed to the other side, the sound of horse hooves splashing through the river was deafening. They followed a narrow trail into the darkened canopy of the forest beyond, and Cytherea was relieved when they were back in the cover of the forest.

Kenric stopped, looking in all directions before he glanced over his shoulder at Cytherea. "The soldiers' trail by the river seems to disappear here," he whispered. "I can't find any sign of them."

Fear bubbled up inside Cytherea. "Soldiers and horses don't just disappear."

"It could mean that the underbrush is thick enough to hide their trail, or"—his eyes, shimmering with anxiety, locked on hers—"it could mean they know we are here."

Cytherea's heart skipped and she went numb.

Without another word, they hurried deeper into the forest. Cytherea jumped at every sound, and Kenric hunted for any sign of others on the trail. He kept them moving as quickly and as quietly as they could. The rest of the night was tense and their progress slow.

Cytherea was thankful when the sky above the trees began to change from black to dark blue. Dawn was not far away.

They had failed to make it to Haight before daylight, so they found a secluded thicket that provided a natural shelter for them to rest for the day. They didn't talk much. She was lost in her thoughts, and Kenric studied the map Christian had given him to confirm that they were close to Haight. Before long, Cytherea gave in to exhaustion and slept while Kenric kept watch.

The pressure of a hand across Cytherea's mouth startled her awake and she was momentarily blinded by a ray of sun filtering through the forest canopy above. Forcing her mind into consciousness, she stifled her scream when she recognized Kenric. He touched a finger to his lips, and her body stiffened again.

". . . and then he shot it right between the eyes!" Unseen soldiers laughed loudly.

"Proud day when your boy kills his first wild boar!"

"I'll be cooking it tonight. Why don't you come by and celebrate with us?"

"I would be honored." The voices faded away as the soldiers moved past Kenric and Cytherea's shelter.

Kenric released her mouth and slowly stood, peering after them. After a few minutes, he hurriedly broke camp, erasing any sign that they had been there while Cytherea readied the horses. Once Kenric was sure the soldiers were gone, they rode in the opposite direction.

Soon, Aherne's ears twitched. He began pulling at the reins and moving faster. Cytherea glanced back to find Tredan had also lengthened his stride. Kenric's face had become colorless.

We're being followed, he mouthed.

At that moment, to Cytherea's horror, two soldiers burst through the trees behind Kenric. Her eyes widened, and she pointed. With a cry, Kenric and Tredan spun to fight. She faced forward as Aherne broke into a gallop without waiting for her command.

Behind her, Kenric yelled, "Run!"

22

The trees were a blur. Cytherea gave Aherne his head and leaned over his neck, her body pressed against her saddle's pommel. She didn't dare look back, but she could hear the soldiers shouting behind her, and they sounded close. The sun was hot today, and Aherne's neck was damp beneath her hands. His breath expelled in short huffs as he kept up his wild pace.

She wondered if Kenric was still behind her, but before she could gather the courage to check, Aherne abruptly slid to a stop and reared to his full height, roaring. Off-balance and off-guard, Cytherea ended up on the ground behind his back hooves, gasping for breath. Her eyes shot up, and Aherne's front hooves struck the air, barely missing the soldier and horse who had cut them off. Hoofbeats grew louder behind her.

She was trapped!

In desperation, she rolled to her knees and crawled through some low bushes to hide, hoping neither soldier had seen her fall. A sharp thud—one of Aherne's hooves had hit its mark—and a soldier's scream echoed amid the trees.

"Get control of the beast!"

"I'm trying!"

"Kill him if you have to, just stop him!"

Cytherea clucked her tongue, desperate to drive Aherne away before he was roped and captured. *Please hear me, boy!* she thought, clucking again.

Aherne's front hooves landed on the ground with a thud. To her relief, he took off, galloping away from Cytherea with the soldiers in pursuit. The soldiers either hadn't noticed that there was no longer a rider on his back or would be back to get her, but either way, Aherne had led them away from her. For now.

Cytherea looked around frantically for a better place to hide, praying that Aherne would be OK. Rushing through the under-growth, she came to a small copse of trees a short distance away with low bushes growing within it. Half crawling and half walking, she tucked herself as far into as she could, and then held her breath. The forest was silent.

Where is Kenric?

She listened for the sound of his whistle, but she only heard birds. She was terrified, and she was alone. Tears flooded her cheeks. The fear immobilized her until she shook her head.

Get control of yourself!

She was supposed to lead an army against Ailmar, and yet here she was, a crying little girl hiding in some bushes. She had to come up with a plan. *What would Kenric do?*

Her sword was still attached to Aherne's saddle, but she had a dagger strapped to her leg. She pulled it from its sheath. She scanned her surroundings for something else she might use as a weapon, but all she saw were branches and leaves.

A branch will have to do.

She grasped the thickest dead bough she could find and gently pulled it down so that it broke unevenly, creating a jagged point on the broken end. With a weapon in each hand, she sat and listened, waiting for the sound of the soldiers' return.

She didn't have to wait long before she heard two horses coming toward her. She wondered briefly if it might be Kenric and Aherne looking for her, but she quickly dismissed the thought. Kenric would be whistling if it was him, so she focused on what had to be the soldiers and waited breathlessly for them to get closer.

"You're sure she wasn't on that horse?"

"I cut through that wild horse's leg! When he fell, his saddle was empty. I know what I saw."

Cytherea's eyes filled with tears, but she blinked them away. A rage began building inside her.

"It is unlikely she could have survived a fall at the speed he was going. Look carefully. If she's dead, we will still need to take her body to show Ailmar."

Cytherea involuntarily sucked in a quick breath at Ailmar's name but did not lose focus. A thump indicated at least one of the soldiers had dismounted. She still didn't have a plan, but she was done letting them take away everyone and everything she loved.

First her parents and her brother, then Tarquin, and now Aherne.

The snap of a twig a few paces away alerted her, and she released the boiling fury inside. In her blind rage, she sprang from her hiding place and lunged toward the closest soldier with her dagger. Her small blade bounced off the soldier's armor.

The soldiers reeled back as Cytherea lunged toward them again. They saw that she only held a small dagger and a broken branch, and they laughed.

Their laughter only fueled Cytherea's wrath. When she lashed out again, her blade caught the hand of the soldier closest to her. His laughter morphed into a cry of pain, and his companion drew his sword. Cytherea stumbled back, fear dispelling her rage and giving her clarity. Her recklessness had put her in a dire situation.

"You stupid girl!" the wounded soldier yelled.

The other soldier advanced on her menacingly, his sword gleaming in the sunlight.

Cytherea glanced from her tiny dagger to the men looming over her, terror seizing her heart.

She wasn't sure if she should fight or run or lay down her meager weapon and surrender. Before she could act, the armed soldier, with one swift movement, flicked his sword tip and sent the dagger flying from her hands.

"Ailmar will like this prize even more than the horse you took down," the soldier snarled to his companion. He grabbed Cytherea by the arms.

She struggled against the soldier, who began dragging her toward his horse. Her mind raced.

"Let me go!" She squirmed to escape the soldier's grip, but he smashed the hilt of his sword against her temple. Cytherea stumbled, and stars exploded in her eyes. She was dazed and barely conscious.

The soldier sheathed his sword and tossed her over his shoulder. Once to the horses, he dropped her on the ground and tied her hands and feet. Through the haze, she tried to fight back by kicking and hitting him, but it was of little use. The blow to her head had left her too disoriented to fight anymore. She was soon bound and thrown facedown across the back of one of the horses.

As they rode off, she let her tears flow and felt the saddle's cantle bore into the side of her ribs from her unnatural position behind one of the soldiers. When they emerged from the trees, the sun was hot on her back, but all she could see were the legs of the horse that carried her and the dirt and grass of the path they were on. With every step, she moved farther from Kenric, and she wondered what had happened to him. Was Aherne really dead? If he wasn't and Kenric didn't find him soon to treat his wound, he would certainly die. She wept for her beloved Aherne. She could only hope that they had survived and she might see them again one day.

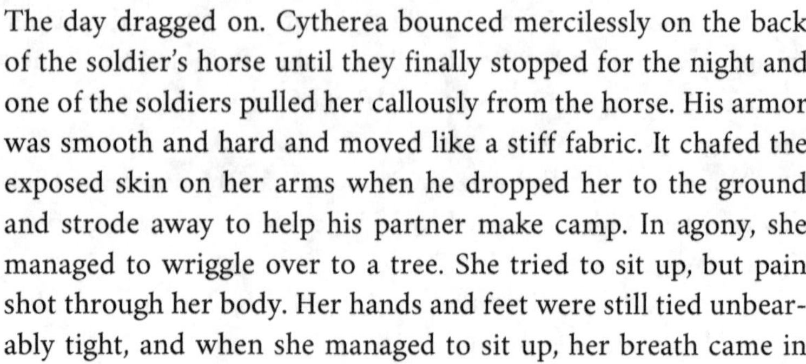

The day dragged on. Cytherea bounced mercilessly on the back of the soldier's horse until they finally stopped for the night and one of the soldiers pulled her callously from the horse. His armor was smooth and hard and moved like a stiff fabric. It chafed the exposed skin on her arms when he dropped her to the ground and strode away to help his partner make camp. In agony, she managed to wriggle over to a tree. She tried to sit up, but pain shot through her body. Her hands and feet were still tied unbearably tight, and when she managed to sit up, her breath came in short gasps and sweat ran down her face.

The soldiers didn't speak, not even to each other. They merely grunted and gestured to one another as they prepared to eat. Cytherea's stomach growled despite her lack of appetite, and one of the soldiers threw a piece of bread toward her. It landed on the ground near her legs. The soldiers laughed as she struggled and failed to pick it up.

Ignoring the bread, she studied the soldiers. They both had dark, soot-colored skin like the soldier Kenric had killed at the farm. Although they were dressed identically, they weren't wearing traditional armor like those that had attacked their home. Instead, they wore what looked like thick black tunics with riding breeches, and both had pieces of armor sewn into them. Their eyes were both dark-colored. It seemed their hair was the only thing about them that didn't match; one had blond hair and the other brown. Otherwise, it would have been difficult to find any difference between the two.

"Where are you taking me?" Cytherea blurted.

They merely glanced at her without saying a word before returning to their meal. She knew where they were taking her, but she thought they might seem less terrifying if they would talk to her. Once they finished eating, one of the soldiers walked toward her, picked up the dirty piece of bread he had thrown at her, and smashed it into her mouth. She bit down, and the excess fell onto her lap. She attempted to swallow the small, dry piece still in her mouth. The soldiers stayed up for a while longer before the one with the blond hair lay down to sleep and the brown-haired one remained awake, apparently assigned to keep watch.

The ropes on her wrists bit into her skin, making every move painful. She couldn't see them, but she thought she felt blood running from her wrists and down her hands. The bark of the tree she was leaning against prodded her back, but she was thankful she was not on the back of the horse. Her ribs screamed with every breath from the day's trip. She tried to get as comfortable as she could, too tired to think of escape. Even as her eyes grew heavy, she listened for a whistle in the distance.

23

Kenric awoke on the forest floor, his head screaming.

Tredan stood over him. Kenric could only assume he had hit his head on a branch and been knocked out in the melee when he tried to stop the soldiers from chasing Cytherea.

Cytherea!

He bolted to his feet and frantically scanned the trees, but his vision began to blur. He laid a hand on a tree to steady himself and tried to stay conscious. He let out a long whistle.

Silence.

He whistled again. Still nothing.

"Come on, boy," he said quietly to Tredan. "Let's go find her."

He mounted and started in the direction Cytherea and Aherne had fled. Kenric let out a whistle every so often, hoping she would emerge from a nearby hiding place.

With every whistle that went unanswered, the panic rose higher in the pit of his stomach. He had no idea which way she might have gone, so he gave Tredan his head and let him lead. The sun was descending toward afternoon. Kenric reached up absently to feel his pounding head and wipe blood from his eyes that dripped from an unseen wound. Then Tredan's ears perked up and twitched.

Hope swelled within Kenric and his heart beat faster. Ignoring his aching head, he let out a long whistle and then listened. Tredan's walking pace increased while Kenric alternated between whistling and listening for a response. Until finally, Kenric heard it.

A low whinny in the distance.

He had found Aherne and desperately hoped that Cytherea was with him. He urged Tredan into a trot and followed Aherne's whinnies. When Kenric came through the trees and found the stallion, he gasped. Aherne stood in an odd stance in a thicket with his head down. He was alone.

Kenric's heart dropped. Cytherea was not there.

He leaped off Tredan and ran over to Aherne. Kenric searched the area, but all he found was Cytherea's small dagger discarded on the ground near Aherne's hooves.

The air caught in his lungs. She had been captured.

Defeated, he bent down to retrieve the dagger and noticed blood running from a gash in Aherne's leg. "Aherne! You're hurt!"

The charger bobbed his head in agitation and shuffled, struggling to put weight on his injured leg. Kenric gently wiped the blood away, and he determined that the gash was likely caused by a sword.

"Faithful, brave Aherne," he said, his throat tight with tears as he imagined the fight Aherne had put up trying to protect Cytherea. He only hoped that Cytherea was still alive.

Kenric hurried to Tredan's saddlebags to get what he needed to tend to Aherne.

Running a hand down Aherne's wounded leg, Kenric applied some of the healer's salve to the gash and wrapped it securely with cloth torn from his cloak. Then he sat and waited restlessly, hoping the salve worked as quickly on horses as it did on humans.

"I need to get you someplace safe," he whispered to the stallion, "where you can heal fully while I find Cytherea."

Aherne bobbed his head again, and Kenric stood to check the stallion's girth straps. In doing so, his fingers brushed against the scabbard still attached to Aherne's saddle. He looked closer and discovered that Cytherea's sword was still inside. She hadn't even had a chance to draw it.

He lifted his eyes to the jeweled hilt still secured in Cytherea's scabbard. At least Ailmar would never get his hands on that sword. However, if Kenric didn't rescue Cytherea, all their hopes —sword or no—would be for nothing.

Have I lost Phoxnay's heir, and with her, all hope? His heart ached. Kenric shook the thought away, forcing his head to clear. A check of the map revealed that he was close to Haight. However, they would need to travel at a slow walk to accommodate Aherne's injury, even with the healer's salve. The journey would take a few days longer than normal.

Once Aherne was able to gently limp on his injured leg, Kenric mounted Tredan so he could lead Aherne to safety.

"To Gregor's village," he said to the horses while his mind spun. *How will I rescue Cytherea?*

24

That night, Cytherea's dreams were filled with dark figures chasing her through dark tunnels until she was awoken abruptly by the brown-haired soldier kicking her.

"Shut up." He grunted.

Had she been calling out in her sleep? He stalked back to their small campfire, and Cytherea laid her head back against the knotted tree. Stars peered between the tree branches overhead, and she tried to think of happy things to escape the nightmare she was living. She felt the ring lying on her skin where it still hung around her neck, hidden beneath her tunic. As she struggled to stay awake, the ring gave her strength, even though she could not hold it in her hand. She hoped that the soldiers wouldn't find it.

When Cytherea opened her eyes again, the soldiers were breaking camp and readying the horses. Cytherea dreaded another day spent draped across the back of a horse.

"Will you please allow me to sit up on the horse this time?" she asked.

Neither soldier responded.

"You only have to untie my feet. I can ride without my hands."

They hesitated and looked at her, then each other, so she pushed a little more. "Even if I managed to get away, I can't outrun your horses. Besides, if I'm sitting up, you will be able to move faster because you won't have to worry about me falling off."

They looked at each other again, and the blond-haired soldier nodded to the other one.

The brown-haired soldier came over and cut the ropes from her ankles. After they fell away, Cytherea looked down at her bloodied ankles and winced. She steeled herself against the pain, grateful she wouldn't have to spend another day lying across the horse on her stomach. Sitting up also meant that she would be able to see where they were going, which would help her find her way back if she ever managed to escape.

At the end of another long day's ride, the trees receded at a bend in the road, and Cytherea's breath caught. The air around her felt thick and dark, despite the sun trying to pass through the scattered, dark clouds overhead. Open pastures stretched in front of them, and on the far side stood blackened walls that clawed their way into the sky. Dark specks along the base of the walls were presumably sentries, and she imagined that additional guards lined the battlements and hid behind the arrow slits set at regular intervals slightly higher in the wall. Archers could easily fire onto the open field below, leaving anyone attempting to approach the castle without an invitation vulnerable. In the center of the massive wall, a drawbridge spanned an immense moat where even more soldiers guarded the castle's entry gate.

The soldier sitting in front of her urged his horse into a canter, forcing Cytherea to tighten her legs around the horse. Her muscles were weak from the long ride, and at one point, she almost jostled off. She assumed that her abductors' impatience to get to the castle was because they anticipated some great reward for capturing her. For her, however, the closer they got, the deeper the pit of dread inside of her grew. She had been watching and waiting for an opportunity to escape, but none had ever arisen. She didn't have any chance of escape now.

Through her vision blurred by tears, Cytherea saw a line of merchants making their way through the castle walls in the distance. Would any of them help her? However, as her group neared the drawbridge, hopelessness threatened to swallow her completely. She forced herself to try slowing her heart, which pounded within her chest, but as the horses rushed toward the menacing gate, she thought it might explode. The soldiers at the gate looked at her curiously when she passed, as did all those within the village, which was within the walls but outside the castle proper. Cytherea wanted to survey her surroundings but chose to keep her eyes lowered so that no one could see their color.

The hustle and bustle of the market fell away, and the massive walls that formed Ailmar's castle soared beyond the clouds and darkened the world around her. The weight of her despair was heavy within her.

What lay in wait behind those frightening walls? She struggled to quell the terror rising within her.

Once inside the castle proper, the soldiers surrendered their weary horses to young, haggard-looking grooms. Both soldiers gripped her arms, and Cytherea was led through a maze of passageways and large chambers before descending a long stairway into the bowels of the castle.

The air was stale here, and the floor and walls were damp, adding to the chill that seemed to reach into her lungs and pores. The soldiers turned at the bottom of the stairs and headed down a long, dark passage with doors lining both sides. Behind the doors they passed, she could hear what sounded like the whimpering and sobbing of children.

Kenric had told her stories of how Ailmar created his dark army. These stories had been passed down from the few children who had miraculously escaped, and Kenric had heard them from villagers he had met during his travels with Tarquin. He'd learned that each one began as a young boy who Ailmar had either ripped from his mother's arms on his murderous raids to the villages in the surrounding kingdoms, found lost in the woods, or welcomed as a misfit that had come to him seeking the acceptance he lacked elsewhere.

Once Ailmar had the boys, he would leave them alone in these cells deep beneath his castle. He left them here to cry until they had no more tears. He left them with no light, no comfort, and no human contact of any kind. Even their bits of food were shoved through a small opening in the cell doors. He left them here until they broke. Once they were broken, he freed them from their cells and began his merciless training.

Cytherea's heart ached at the thought of a child alone in such a terrifying place. She had to find a way to get them back to their homes. However, she didn't have much time to think about it because her trio came to an open door, and the soldiers shoved her into a damp, windowless room. After the soldiers severed the rope that bound her wrists, the heavy door slammed shut, and the thud of the lock echoed through the murky air. Alone, she allowed the tears to run freely down her face, dropping onto the cold stone floor.

It took her eyes a few minutes to adjust to the almost total darkness, and when they did, she looked around. There wasn't much to see. It was a small, cave-like room, barely wide enough for her to lie down. It was unfurnished, completely empty except for the rat that scurried from one corner to the other.

She sat, shivering, unsure of what to do next. She drew in a shaky breath to steady herself, which made her remember Kenric teaching her how to calm her breathing to help her connect to the Sword of Phoxnay. She closed her eyes and focused on each breath. Her heart began to calm, and she clutched the ring at her neck. Gradually, strength returned to her limbs, and she slowly opened her eyes once more. In the silence, the cries of children haunted her; only this time, they were all around her. Unable to bear the sound, she stood and felt her way along the wall to the small opening that had been carved in the door.

"It's OK. You're not alone," she called out as loudly as she dared. The crying lessened, so she continued, "I will find a way to get you all out of here soon. Don't lose hope."

The wailing was more subdued for a time, but then it grew louder and more mournful. Cytherea began to sing. It was a simple tune Fenia had sung to her as a child, and it had always helped Cytherea fall asleep. The dungeon became quiet for a time, except for Cytherea's singing. Then it was interrupted.

"Shut up down there, girl!" a voice growled. She could hear footsteps moving closer until they stopped outside her door. "If you talk or sing or make any noise again, I'm going to bring one of these boys in there and kill him slowly while you watch."

Cytherea's mouth opened in a silent gasp of horror.

"Do you hear that, boys?" the voice shouted. "This lady is going to make me kill you, but His Majesty, King Ailmar, ruler of the Dark Realm, will one day rescue you, when you are ready." The man paused. "Is anyone ready to be rescued by His Majesty, King Ailmar?"

Silence answered him, and then the man cackled. It was an evil, otherworldly sound that could barely be called laughter. It eventually faded away as the man returned to wherever he had come from. Once he was gone, Cytherea slid down the wall until she was once again sitting on the cold, damp floor with tears running down her cheeks, but this time, they weren't tears of fear. No. This time, they were tears of rage.

The blackness surrounding her pressed one thought into her mind: *Ailmar must die.*

25

When Kenric rode into Haight late one morning, he felt eyes staring at Tredan and Aherne. Kenric was used to the attention they drew, although he was hoping to avoid any scrutiny from the villagers while he was here. To avoid any unwanted onlookers, he turned off the main road that led through the middle of town and, instead, took the smaller road behind the shops and houses that made up the village.

Kenric searched for the blacksmith. He peered between the cottages into the market beyond, and soon the sound of a hammer hitting an anvil told him he was near. He followed the sound until he found himself standing before a giant of a man shrouded in the steam that emanated from the hot metal he was quenching. The fire of his forge glowed behind him.

Kenric dismounted and stood there for a few minutes before the man glanced up and saw him. Gregor strode over and stopped before the horses. His hands were massive and covered in the ebony residue from the soot that he wiped on his apron.

Gregor examined the horses with admiration before he spoke. "From the looks of those chargers, you must be Kenric."

"I am. And you must be Gregor."

"I am." The man smiled, looking behind Kenric. "Christian said the girl would be with you. Where is she?"

Kenric lowered his head. "We were overcome by Dark Realm soldiers. I was knocked unconscious, and when I awoke, Cytherea was gone. I can only assume she was captured."

Gregor grunted.

"I need your help to get her back."

Gregor grunted again. "It will take more than the two of us to get her out of Ailmar's castle. It isn't open for just anyone to walk in, you know."

"I know, but if you can tell me how to get in there, then I will figure out how to rescue her."

"Brave man." Gregor raised his bushy eyebrows. "Willing to face Ailmar and his soldiers on your own?"

"I have pledged my life to protect her, and I failed." Kenric clenched his jaw. "I must do whatever is necessary to get her back."

"Put those horses of yours in my barn and out of sight" —Gregor nodded to the barn that was next to his shop—"and then go in and see Anna." He waved a giant hand toward the cottage across the small road. "She will get you fed, and I'll be there shortly. We'll figure out then what to do about the girl."

Kenric did as he was told. After getting the horses settled, he slid the Sword of Phoxnay under the saddlebags before he carried them across to Gregor's home. He didn't want anyone to know he had it yet, including Gregor.

The cottage's small door was opened by an even smaller woman whose bright eyes smiled up at him. She moved aside for him to enter. The warmth from the fire wrapped around Kenric when he stepped through the door, and the smell from the hearth made his empty stomach rumble.

"Welcome." Her voice had an almost singing nature that made it impossible not to smile. "You must be Kenric. I am Anna."

A young boy ran from another room to greet Kenric. "And I'm Brockton!"

"Brockton! Mind your manners," Anna chided gently and closed the door. "Let the man come in and sit down."

Kenric grinned at the boy. "And I am Kenric. It is nice to meet you, Brockton, and you, Anna."

"Kenric, please sit down and let me get you something to eat," Anna said. "Brockton, take his things and set them—"

"If you don't mind," Kenric interrupted, "I'd like to keep these with me for now."

Anna started to object but relented and gave her son new orders. "Go fetch our guest some fresh water so he can clean up a bit."

Kenric followed the boy out behind the cottage to quickly wash off some of the dirt he had collected during the journey. Then he hurried back in to wait for Gregor and start discussing a plan to rescue Cytherea.

While they ate a midday meal, Gregor went over what he knew of the layout of Ailmar's castle, the guards, and the other protections the castle had in place. "There are a lot of solid stone walls, a lot of soldiers, and a lot of weapons that will be aimed at you if you get caught."

Kenric set his jaw and met Gregor's dark eyes resolutely. "I have to get Cytherea out."

"I figured you would say as much." Gregor's gaze returned to the rough layout he had drawn for Kenric.

Together, they tried to find a possible weakness in the fortress, but the front gate was the only way in. They had to come up with some possible ways that Kenric might be able to get through the main entrance unnoticed.

"I've got it!" Gregor announced with a fist to the table, making

Anna and his young son jump where they sat across the room. "The next village over, Belmis, is also the last one before you enter the Dark Realm. It is filled mostly with merchants who do business within the castle walls. I know someone there that sells cloth. You can get through the gates with her."

"Thank you, Gregor!" Kenric exclaimed. He stood and began gathering his things. "I'll head there now."

"She is a loyalist and a widow, so she is slow to trust strangers. I'll send a messenger ahead of you so she will be expecting you."

With a nod from his father, Brockton got up and ran out of the house. Kenric assumed he was being sent to find the messenger. Gregor then described the woman who would help Kenric and shared the loyalist code phrase Brockton would pass along through the messenger.

"Won't you at least stay until tomorrow to rest a little before you go?" Anna asked quietly. She was clearly better at hospitality than Gregor.

"Thank you," Kenric replied with a polite bow in her direction. "But I must get Cytherea back before Ailmar has a chance to do her any harm."

Anna stood and began packing him some food to take. "You can leave any of your belongings that you don't need to take with you here. Travel light. The village is only a short distance from here, a few hours by horse."

"Thank you. I will leave a few things of Cytherea's that she will need when I return with her." Kenric checked to be sure her sword was still wrapped and unseen before he tucked it away where Anna indicated. Then he was out the door.

"Wait!" Gregor shouted after him, following him outside.

Kenric slowed, almost dancing with impatience. Gregor walked with him into the barn. Brockton ran up next to them, returning from his errand red-faced and panting.

"Take one of my horses," Gregor said. "Yours will draw too much attention. Plus, they could use the rest after such a long journey." He reached down and patted his son's head. "Brockton and I will take good care of Tredan and Aherne while you are gone. You have my word."

Brockton murmured gently as he rubbed the necks of the great horses that he had only heard about in stories. Aherne and Tredan both responded to the young boy with happy tail swishes and nickers.

"Very well," Kenric said, "here is some money for their care."

"I'm not doing it for money." Gregor lifted his hands to refuse. "I'm doing it to help get that girl back here safely. She's our only hope, Kenric."

"I know, but keep the money." He pushed the coins into Gregor's calloused hands with a brief smile. "These horses are spoiled, so you may need it." With that, he saddled Gregor's horse and galloped out of the city.

26

Kenric arrived in the small village of Belmis well before the merchants had returned from their day of selling in the castle. While he waited, he settled the horse in a stable and got something to eat at the small inn. He sat close to a window where he could watch the road for signs of their return, and after a time, he saw them in the distance. As they approached, he went outside and watched each one pass by, searching for the cloth seller, but he never saw the woman Gregor had described. Bewildered, Kenric wandered through the streets to see if he had just missed her, but by then, most of the vendors were already busy unloading and readying their wares for the next day. There was still no sign of her.

He walked to the edge of town to scan the road again, and that's when he saw her. She was much slower than the other merchants. Her gray hair fell in her face, and her back was hunched over her cart of brightly colored cloth. Her slender arms shook as she struggled into town. When she drew nearer, Kenric could see that her sunken eyes looked weary and her skin was loose on her arms. He advanced toward her cautiously, almost afraid of frightening her away.

"My lady!" Kenric called with a smile and a friendly wave. "I need to purchase some cloth from you for my wife." This was the phrase the messenger was to have given her to assure her that Kenric was safe.

The cloth merchant peered warily beyond him into town before answering haltingly, "It is not safe out in the open like this, my lord." She hurried past him, glancing anxiously around her.

Kenric followed, trying to appear casual. "I will give you three pieces of gold for all of your cloth and your cart." He smiled pleasantly.

The merchant stopped and examined the gold in Kenric's hand. "Why would you want to do that? That is enough to purchase three times this amount of cloth."

"You don't know the wrath of my wife!" he said with a wink, keeping up the ruse. Kenric was equally as anxious to be done with their transaction and out of the middle of the main road. "And I promise to return the unused cloth and cart to you in a few days, once my wife has made her selections. But you can keep the gold."

The merchant looked surprised at the offer but quickly agreed. "When Gregor's friend said I would have a visitor, I didn't expect you would need my cart, but I wouldn't mind a day off." She managed a hesitant smile as Kenric handed her the gold coins. Pocketing the money, she shuffled up the path toward her home.

As soon as her stooped figure disappeared around the bend in the road, Kenric hurriedly pushed the handcart back to the stable where Gregor's horse was and left it there, hidden from view for the night. Kenric then headed back to his room in the inn. Although he doubted he could sleep, he had no choice but to wait for morning, when the other merchants would head back to the castle. Every bit of him ached to get Cytherea out of Ailmar's hands. The waiting chafed his nerves, but one of his father's favorite sayings repeated in his mind.

A good swordsman knows that patience and planning always pay off.

Sleep eluded Kenric, so he spent the night trying to figure out how he was going to find and then rescue Cytherea. Getting through the main gate was just the first step, and he had no idea where to go once he was inside those walls. Very little was known about the construction of the castle to those outside of the Dark Realm; even Gregor's map of the castle grounds was rudimentary. In the end, Kenric hoped that he would be able to figure it out and find an opportunity once he got there.

Throughout the night, Kenric pushed down the fear rising inside him as he paced the floor, thinking. It was one thing to say he was going to rescue Cytherea, but quite another to waltz into Ailmar's castle uninvited. If he failed and was caught, it would mean death for both him and Cytherea—and a lost hope for the people of Phoxnay.

Kenric was ready at first light, dressed in the simple garments of a merchant. He looked in the mirror and grinned. "Interesting look," he said to himself and let out a weak laugh. His attempt to lighten his own mood was a failure.

He headed down to the barn, retrieved the handcart, and then waited anxiously for the other merchants in the caravan to head out for the day. Kenric shifted nervously when the merchants came out of their homes and gathered in the square before they finally began their slow progression out of town. The last cart rumbled past, and Kenric moved in behind them without a word. When he joined the end of the caravan, only a few of the merchants spared him uninterested glances, and their sad and hopeless looks unnerved him. He tried to picture them in happier times, smiling and laughing together in excitement as they took their wares to sell in the market.

Kenric remembered how excited Cytherea had always been on market days when she'd gone with Fenia. She'd brimmed over with laughter and unbridled enthusiasm. By contrast, this scene was one of drudgery. A gloomy, stifling air hung like a stench around everyone, and little conversation brightened the sullen silence. Kenric hoped that Cytherea could one day bring joy back to the people of Phoxnay, but to do that, he had to get her away from Ailmar. He just hoped it wasn't too late.

27

"Guards!" Ailmar shouted as he paced erratically around his throne room. Two guards rushed forward from their posts along the wall of the chamber and stood silently at attention before him. "Bring me the girl that was captured yesterday."

"Yes, Your Majesty," they replied in almost perfect unison, starting toward the doors.

"Wait!" Ailmar shouted again, and they rushed back to him, heads bowed. "Find out if the girl had any weapons on her when she was found."

"I didn't see any weapons on her when she was brought in, and no one checked any into the armory, Your Majesty."

"Check again!" Ailmar pounded his staff on the ground, and the guards fell to their knees. "Bring her to me and any weapons you find." He turned his back on the terrified guards.

"Yes, Your Majesty."

When the doors closed behind the guards, Ailmar continued pacing.

～

Cytherea was alerted by the sound of the lock in her door turning. The rat she had been observing skittered away at the interruption. Cytherea had no idea how much time had passed, but she steeled herself for whoever was on the other side of her tiny cell. She peered forward into the darkness, her body shaking as she waited to see who would be standing there. When the door grated across the floor, she saw the outline of soldiers. The dim light from the passage beyond them was blinding as it tore through the blackness. Shielding her eyes, she studied the two shadows looming before her. They were each at least double her size, with what looked like armor covering waves of muscles that ran down the length of their arms.

Dread washed through her body.

"Get up!" one of them shouted.

The harsh command startled her into action, and she stood almost against her will.

"Start walking!" he shouted again, retreating into the passageway.

"Where are you taking me?" she asked.

"Be silent and move!" the second guard commanded.

Cytherea did as she was told despite everything inside her that wanted to refuse, afraid they were leading her to her death.

She walked between the two soldiers as they made their way up the stairway and out of the dungeon. She kept her eyes focused on the ground ahead, but she could feel the stares of those they passed searing into her. She glanced around her periodically, trying to get her bearings inside the castle. After a time, the floors changed from bare wood to lush carpets. This didn't seem like the kind of place where they would take someone to be killed. At least, she hoped. *Where are they taking me?*

Eventually, they stopped in front of a pair of doors that seemed to grow larger as she slowly let her eyes follow them upward. Two guards flanked the imposing doors on each side, and they struck their iron spears on the ground with such force, Cytherea felt the vibrations move through her body.

"Enter!" came the response from the other side of the doors.

The guards strained as they pulled the doors open. Cytherea found herself staring into a vast chamber. Dim sunlight fell from a large window above, illuminating only a massive wooden table set in the middle of the room. She caught glimpses of a figure moving in the shadows just beyond the light.

The guards grabbed her arms and dragged her into the chamber. The great doors slammed behind her, the sound bouncing off the stone walls in deafening echoes. She could now see a second window above let in another beam of light, which fell on what looked to be a black throne.

Her heart began to race inside her chest. *Is that . . . ?*

The mysterious figure strode methodically toward the throne. As he neared the light, she could see that he was clad all in black and wore a long cloak that dragged along the ground behind him as he walked, making him look more like a shadow than a man. The guards continued to pull her across the floor toward the figure, who slowly turned to sit on the black throne. He lowered himself and was immediately swallowed by the blackness that surrounded him, leaving only his face visible. When Cytherea took it all in, she knew, and her heart stopped.

Ailmar!

"What is your name, girl?" His staff landed with a thud, reverberating through the vast hall.

A small wisp of thick smoke slid from the staff. Cytherea cringed. The orb on top gleamed with a sinister light, and she lowered her face to stare at the ground beneath her, shielding her eyes.

"Your name!" he growled.

She felt a sharp jab to her back. "Cytherea," she blurted, realizing too late that she should not have given her real name.

"An unusual name, isn't it?"

"I was named for my father's mother," she lied.

"And where do you come from, Cytherea?" Ailmar sneered, drawing out her name in derision.

She inadvertently shivered. "A small farm in Cowe," she replied with another lie.

"Interesting." His eyes moved up and down her body as he spoke, making her feel exposed. "And what is a farm girl from Cowe doing alone in the woods near my realm?"

"I wanted to find some wild mushrooms for my mother to cook, and I got lost."

"And while you were looking for your wild mushrooms, did you carry a sword for protection?"

Cytherea's mind swam. *He knows about the sword!* She swallowed, thinking about her dagger, unsure if he had the ability to see her thoughts. "Only a small dagger, m-my lord. My family could never afford to own a sword." Her voice shook uncontrollably, and she hoped that he did not see through her lies.

"Bring her closer."

The guards pressed their hands on her back. Cytherea resisted with all the strength she had, but she was no match for them. They effortlessly shoved her forward. Stumbling, she fell to the floor at Ailmar's feet.

Ailmar let out a guttural sound that Cytherea had never heard someone make. "It is fitting that you bow at my feet, farm girl." He sneered. "Now look up at me."

Cytherea lifted her head but tried to keep her eyes lowered.

"Look at me!" Ailmar roared.

Cytherea lifted her eyes, and as she did, her hatred for him boiled inside her. She glared defiantly at him.

Ailmar roared again, only this time, his black eyes glittered with some sort of grotesque laughter. "I've got you, *princess*!" He stood and walked past her back into the shadows. "Guards, take her back to the dungeon!"

The guards grabbed her violently—almost desperately—by her shoulders and dragged her out of the throne room.

Back down in the dungeon, they flung open her cell door. One guard paused before he tossed her inside, and Cytherea followed his eyes to her neck.

My ring!

In the process of being shoved around and dragged, the chain with her ring on it had slipped from inside her tunic. The guard had spotted it. She fumbled with the chain, attempting to tuck it back in, even though she knew it was too late. The guard reached forward, grabbed hold of the ring, and pulled so hard that the chain around Cytherea's neck gave way, pulling her to the ground as it did.

She cried out in pain and anguish. *No!*

The other guard kicked her across the floor and back into the blackness of her cell. The door closed once again. She scrambled to her feet and slammed her fists against the door. The sound of the lock engaging clanged through her cell. She reached her hand to her neck where her mother's ring had once hung, and her despair threatened to overwhelm her. She helplessly beat on the door, sobbing.

28

Kenric stayed close behind the line of merchants heading out of the village. After some time, they rounded a turn of the winding road, and Kenric came to a stop. He was taken aback by the sight of immense gray walls looming beyond a seemingly endless open field.

Ailmar's castle!

The air began to thicken. The sun, though just beginning its rise through the sky, was muted by the ghostly haze that seemed to ooze forth from the castle itself. Kenric gathered himself and resumed pushing his cart because he didn't want to attract the attention of the many guards that likely saw the merchants' sluggish procession, but as he did, he continued to take in and analyze what was before him. Soldiers came and went from the great gate that was heavily guarded. He could only imagine the number of soldiers hidden from sight that carefully watched anyone crossing the expansive field.

How am I going to get Cytherea out of there?

The merchants ahead of him moved painfully slowly until, finally, the sound of the carts rolling onto the wooden drawbridge broke the early morning stillness and covered the muted conversations of the soldiers passing by on their way out to patrol. Sweat beaded on Kenric's face despite the cool air as the walls of the castle rose above him. These soldiers' movements and interactions with those ahead of Kenric informed him that they had not been brainwashed but followed Ailmar willingly. That level of loyalty meant they would kill him instantly if his ruse was detected.

Kenric inhaled and released his breath slowly as the procession halted. The merchants at the head of the group were passing through the massive gates to the interior of the castle grounds. The carts squeaked forward unhurriedly, and Kenric eyed a group of soldiers that emerged from the gate and passed the caravan. The group walked across the crowded drawbridge, casually discussing the various wares and foods in each cart. When they approached Kenric's cart, he avoided their eyes.

Keep walking, he pleaded internally.

But they didn't. One soldier leaned over the cart and scanned the cloth. "I need new breeches," he grunted to the others. "I forgot to let the seamstress know. Maybe I have time to go back and order them quickly."

Another soldier came forward. "If the commander sees any of us going back, he will have all our heads. Keep moving!" He slapped the first soldier on the back, and they moved away from Kenric.

Kenric inched closer to the imposing gates. A few more minutes, and he would be inside the castle wall. He eased his cart along. His heart pounded, and he focused on controlling his breathing until it was his turn at last. He rolled the cart to the enormous arch of the gate, where one of the guards fingered through the stacks of cloth and then stopped, glancing up at Kenric.

"You are not the cloth woman," the guard snapped. "Where is she?"

"She's sick today," Kenric replied, pushing down the panic that rose inside him. "I am her nephew, selling for her until she is well."

The guard stared at him for a moment, his gaze unreadable. Suddenly he jerked his arm, pointing toward the gate. "Fine. Go on with you!"

Kenric pushed the cart rapidly onto the cobbled streets, thankful to have made it into the castle walls and one step closer to Cytherea. Following the others over the uneven cobbles, he eyed the small cottages and shops that made up the small village within the wall and just outside the castle proper. He found a hidden spot inside the frenzied area of the village market and parked his cart there. Once relieved of the cart, Kenric slipped behind the shops while the other merchants set up their wares for the day.

Kenric picked his way through the back streets of the miniature village on the castle grounds. Worn cottages outlined the village area, occupied primarily by soldiers and their families, bladesmiths, and a few other craftsmen. Because Kenric's clothing was that of a poor merchant, dirty and worn from traveling, he was sure he wouldn't attract any unwelcome attention or questions.

He wove through the outskirts of the village, circling the grounds and studying his options. He would start the day by observing the guards and getting as close to the castle as he could without raising questions. Tonight, he would secure a room at the inn with some sort of excuse for why he had to stay overnight. Then, under the cover of darkness, while most slept, he would attempt to access the castle. While daylight remained, he explored the streets closest to the castle, trying to look disinterested, sniffing out possible routes to get inside. As he walked, he would periodically let out a low whistle. He knew it was futile, but he did it anyway in the hope that Cytherea might hear him and at least know that he was near.

You're not alone, Cyth. I'm coming.

29

The pink light of day trickled across the horizon outside the window. A dark figure lounged in the corner, focused on the pages on his desk. A guard slipped into the chamber, head bowed.

"What now?" The figure didn't lift his gaze.

"Your Highness—"

"What do you want?" he snarled, his voice echoing across the large chamber. He pushed away from his desk and stood to face the intruder. He pounded the table, and the guard cringed.

"Your Highness, sir, a new prisoner was brought in—"

"Why are you bothering me about a prisoner?" the man asked impatiently. "We get new prisoners daily."

"My lord, this one is different."

Intrigued, he lowered his voice. "Who is this prisoner, and what makes them any different from the others?"

"We don't know who she is, my lord. She was found alone in the forest," the guard continued with more confidence. "His Majesty ordered her brought to him in the throne room for questioning."

"A girl? What kind of questions did my father ask her?"

"His Majesty asked who she was and where she was from."

"And?" he prodded, growing impatient with the guard.

"She said she was just a farm girl from Cowe who got lost."

"I don't have time for games, guard! Why are you bothering me about this?"

The guard shrank back, fumbling in his pocket and withdrawing a small golden trinket. "She had this ring, Your Highness, and her eyes are very similar to yours. I . . . I thought I should tell you."

Derian grabbed the ring from the guard's shaking hands and held it next to the one on his finger. *They are identical! How can that be? Who is this girl?* He tapped his fingers thoughtfully against the polished surface of his desk. "Take me to her."

"Right away, Your Highness."

Cytherea heard a key in the lock again, and she squinted toward the door. It was likely another servant bringing her food. She leaped to her feet, sliding one hand along the pockmarked wall until she stood next to the door and waited for it to open. She had only one thing on her mind.

I must escape.

She had been locked in there for a few days, expecting death to come with every meal. If Ailmar knew who she was, why was he keeping her alive?

The door slowly opened, and she tensed, ready to rush past the servant as soon as they bent down to lay her bread on the floor. However, instead of a servant, someone else stood in her doorway. She shrank back. This man's posture and clothing were not that of a servant but of royalty. Broad shoulders, custom-tailored clothes, and a vaguely familiar, sharp nose. The dim light from the corridor shifted across his eyes—green—and her head began to spin.

Everard?

She closed her eyes and tried to steady herself. She bit back a sob. Could this be her brother? Was he alive? Why was he *here*, dressed like one of Ailmar's noble pets? Was this some sort of cruel trick?

She opened her eyes and whispered, "Everard?"

The man turned to her from inside the door, obviously uncomfortable in the dungeon. He lifted a hand, and someone behind handed him a lantern, its flames illuminating flecks of auburn and gold in his brown hair. The lines of his face brightened into sharp contrast against the darkness.

Cytherea swallowed, her back still pressed against the wall.

"My name is Derian, Prince of the Dark Realm, and I am to be addressed as 'Your Highness' by you, girl," he demanded. "Who are you?" He sneered as he studied her dirt-covered clothing and matted hair.

Tears welled up in Cytherea's eyes. "Look at my face. Can you not see the resemblance? And my eyes, can't you see your own eyes in mine?" She took a breath to steady herself. "You are my brother, Everard."

Derian's laughter echoed off the walls. "You have been deceived by your own mind, girl. I have no sister, and my name is not Everard."

Cytherea took a tentative step forward. "But you are my brother, I am sure of it. You were kidnapped during our escape from Phoxnay, before it was destroyed by Ailmar." She took another small step toward him.

"Don't get any closer to me, girl," he said, his own green eyes narrowing. "You are likely a witch, and I want no part of your dark magic."

A single guard stood beneath the sconce in the hallway directly behind him, his armor gleaming menacingly.

"Everyone thought you had been killed." She frowned. "Are you OK? Have they hurt you?"

"How I am is not your concern." Derian shifted his weight,

and his brow furrowed. "What I want to know is, who are you, and where did you get this ring?" He held up the golden, emerald-encrusted token.

"My ring!" She reached to take it from his hand, but he snatched it away.

"Answer me!" he snapped, and his sudden fury made her shrink back again.

Ailmar has hidden his true heritage from him! He doesn't know who he really is!

"I am your sister, Cytherea," she whispered. "The day Ailmar captured you, I managed to escape with the help of others." She hoped her whispers would keep the guards from hearing.

A bark of raucous laughter once again burst from his lips. "You *are* mad! My father doesn't have any other children, and I have never been captured by anyone!" He waved dismissively and turned to leave.

Confused, Cytherea said, "Our father was King Edmond. Who do you think your father is?"

Derian rounded on her. "Stupid girl. Ailmar is my father." The door slammed closed behind him.

Cytherea's eyes stared into the darkness that surrounded her for a long moment. The silence was swallowed by the ringing in her ears. Her knees began shaking, and she collapsed to the ground.

~

Derian stormed up the passage, the heavy clang of Cytherea's cell door echoing behind him. "If anyone hears of this," he growled to the guard, "I will kill you myself. Do you understand?"

"Yes, Your Highness," the guard responded, his head bowed.

~

The day passed in a fog for Cytherea.

Ailmar is his father?

How could Everard think he was Ailmar's son? Kenric had tried to prepare her for what Everard might be like if he was alive and had been living in the Dark Realm, but nothing could have prepared her for the fact that Ailmar had made Everard believe he was his son. *How can I get him to see the truth?* The question tumbled through her head as she circled her cell.

The distant sound of children crying seeped into her dark cell once again, and she tried to push Everard from her mind. If Ailmar wanted to torture her with mind games instead of killing her outright, she would use that to her advantage. She would play his game until she found a way out of his castle, and then she would return to rescue all the children held captive there.

Sleep, eat, gather information, plan my escape.

After some time, her meager meal was tossed on the floor before her, and she leaned forward to retrieve it before one of the rats beat her to it. The delivery of her food was the only way she could track the passage of time. The bread seemed to stick in Cytherea's throat as she tried to hold down the pit of fear. The isolation and constant darkness produced such despair that it threatened to overwhelm her. She focused on her breathing to quiet her emotions and ground herself in the present. As she inhaled, the stench of evil mixed with damp moss and dead leaves that permeated the dungeon made her stomach turn, but she knew she had to eat. Her chance to escape would come, and when it did, she had to be ready.

Derian returned to his bedchamber that night after a meal with his father. He didn't mention his dealings with the girl earlier that day. It was the first time he had ever kept something from his father, and he didn't know why he did it now.

Derian sensed something peculiar about her but couldn't quite understand what it was.

Throughout the meal, his father had ranted about her, telling Derian that they had a girl in the dungeon who was a witch and that he was not to go near her for any reason. His father had never been so distressed about a prisoner. In fact, he usually didn't give prisoners much thought at all. But this girl was different, and Derian wanted to find out why. At one point in his rantings, his father had let her name slip as he vowed to kill her. *Cytherea.*

Derian latched on to the name. She hadn't been lying about that, at least.

Now, as he readied himself for the night, her name kept echoing through his head.

Cytherea. Was she a witch that had cast a spell over him? Why couldn't he get her out of his head? Why was his father so bothered by this girl?

Derian lay on his bed, holding her ring next to the one on his finger. They were identical. It wasn't out of the question that the jeweler who had made his ring had made others just like it. Yet his father had told him that his ring was one of a kind, made just for him. If this were true, the jeweler would have jeopardized his life by making another, and no ring was worth that. Derian sighed in frustration.

I must talk to her again tomorrow. Despite his father's command, Derian could not abandon this matter yet. He had too many questions. He studied the ring for a moment longer. The moon caught the emerald inset in the gold band as he laid it on the table beside his bed and sank into the feather mattress.

⁓

Derian could see the rings clearly now. A young girl laughed behind him. Something tugged on his arm, so he turned.

Cytherea.

She released him and darted away. As she did so, he caught a glimmer out of the corner of his eye. He turned toward it. The sun's rays glinted off the emeralds in two rings that hung on a chain around a woman's neck. The woman's expression was kind, smiling, and her voice soothed him. Contentment—oddly—pulsed in his heart.

Derian sat up, half expecting the woman to be standing in his chamber.

Just another dream.

He had had this dream before and thought nothing more of it; however, this time, the girl in the dream had a name.

Cytherea.

He threw back the thick bed coverings and dressed in haste.

My father is going to kill her, but I can't let that happen until I figure out who she really is.

He swept her ring from his table and hurried toward the dungeon. He had to talk to her one more time.

30

Roused from an uneasy sleep by the creak of her door in the muted silence of the dungeon, Cytherea bolted to her feet. The dim light from the torches in the corridor leaked in, drowning in the blackness of her cell. She looked up, and a dark figure loomed over her. The face was obscured in the thick shadows. She braced herself as the figure walked toward her.

When his face drew close to hers, she exclaimed, "Everard!"

"Quiet! Stupid girl," Everard hissed, glancing over his shoulder. No guard stood in the hallway this time.

"Why are you here?" Cytherea asked with a hushed voice.

Everard hesitated and looked at her in confusion. Cytherea realized he wasn't even entirely sure why he was there.

Cytherea took the chance. "I know you have questions. Please let me answer them."

"I am here only to satisfy my own curiosity," Everard stated coldly. "You won't leave this place alive. My father has ordered your execution."

The blunt statement terrified her, but she strengthened her resolve and drew in a slow breath, steadying herself. "I will tell you what you wish to know, but first, promise you will help me escape safely out of the castle and beyond the walls."

Everard was silent.

Cytherea steeled her voice as she repeated her demands. "Get me to the other side of the castle walls, and I give you my word that I will answer all of your questions truthfully."

Everard eyed her as if trying to decide whether she was bluffing. Silence stretched, and Cytherea breathed evenly, her stomach tight. If he refused . . .

"I give you my word." A slight smile appeared on his lips. "I'll help you if you answer my questions, but not before."

"Very well," Cytherea agreed, unsure if his word meant anything.

Grasping her arm, Everard took her out of the dungeon, leading her to a chamber where he said they could talk freely. He casually waved off any guards they passed along the way.

Once safely in the empty chamber, Cytherea told Everard the story of his life as she knew it, ending with his abduction. Everard listened restlessly, pacing as she spoke, and Cytherea saw that he was wrestling with the information. When she finished speaking, silence settled over the room. Everard stared out the window.

Cytherea waited without moving for what seemed like an eternity.

Finally, Everard spun around stiffly to face her. "How do I know that this isn't just some fantasy you created to escape my father's grasp?"

"Ailmar is not your father," Cytherea replied softly.

"Enough!" Everard boomed. "Answer my question! What proof do you have that I am not who I believe I am?"

"I have had the same dream over and over again my entire life, and I am staking my life on the fact that you have had it too."

"How would you know my dreams unless you are a witch?" He leaned in close to her face.

Cytherea instinctively recoiled before regaining her composure. "We are small children playing in a garden."

Everard turned his back to her, listening intently.

"A woman sits on the grass playing with us. She has two rings on a chain around her neck, and she is laughing."

He spun around and glared at her but remained silent.

She pressed on. "The woman is our mother, and the rings around her neck are the same as the one on your finger and the one taken from me." She paused again, watching her brother's face turn pale. "If you believe Ailmar is your father, who then do you think is your mother?"

"My mother was a woman from my father's court who died giving birth to me. She was unimportant to my life beyond my birth," Everard stated coldly.

He turned away from her again and resumed his pacing.

"Your birthmark—"

"What birthmark?" he interrupted impatiently.

"The birthmark on the back of your neck. It is of a dragon."

"So what? That's no secret." Everard was annoyed.

"I have one just like it," she said, lifting her hair and turning so he could see her nape.

He took in a quick breath when he saw it, but otherwise, he remained silent.

She slowly pivoted back around to face him. After a few moments, she continued. "The birthmark and the rings are my proof. These rings were around our mother's neck when we were children."

Everard looked at the ring he held in his hand, rolling it over his fingers before thrusting it toward her.

She wrapped her hand around it tightly, relief sweeping over her. "You can't deny the birthmarks." He winced at her last few words, so she didn't say anything else. When she glanced up at his face again, Cytherea thought she saw the glimmer of a tear beginning to form in one eye.

Everard whispered, "It's as if I can feel the rings from inside me."

Cytherea studied his expressions as he grappled with what he was feeling and remembering. Confusion, anger, denial, and belief fought for dominance on his face. While Everard struggled, Cytherea stood motionless, afraid that any movement might erase the memories his mind was trying to reclaim.

"I will get you out of the castle, but that is all I will do for you," Everard said sternly. It was obvious that he was working hard to swallow the emotion that had risen in his voice.

Cytherea smiled for the first time in days as she observed him. "Thank you, Everard! You will understand it all soon. I am sure of it! And when you do, I'll be waiting for you."

"Stay quiet before someone hears you!" He glanced toward the door. "We must move quickly before the change of guards at dawn," Everard said, stepping toward the chamber door.

Cytherea hesitated momentarily.

"Now!" Everard snarled impatiently.

Cytherea obediently followed him. Everard led her through yet another maze of corridors.

As soon as Cytherea began to wonder if he was leading her to her death instead of freedom, he stopped and pointed. "That door leads you to a pathway through the village toward the castle wall. It's up to you to get to the other side of the walls, but the guard changes at the rising of the sun. That will be your best chance."

"But you said you would get me to safety," Cytherea said frantically. "How will I get past the guards at the gate unnoticed?"

Everard faced Cytherea. "This is as far as I am willing to help you." A darkness fell across his face before he turned away, retreating the way they had come.

She realized then that Ailmar still had a strong hold over him. It would take more than one dream to pull Everard away from here. "If you ever want to know the truth, come find me."

Everard kept walking, so Cytherea set her jaw. *He got me here, so I'd better get myself out.* She shifted her thoughts to the task of getting past the guards at the gate.

She hurried out the door and into the night. As she headed down a dark path behind what looked to be stables, her ears caught a familiar sound moving on the wind, which brought her to a sudden stop.

It can't be. She held her breath, listening intently. After a few agonizing minutes, she heard it again.

Kenric!

She resisted the urge to run toward the sound and instead moved methodically through the shadows, stopping periodically to listen for it again. It seemed to be moving farther away, and panic gripped her. She had to find him. Kenric had tried to teach her his whistle when they were young, and she never was very good at it, but she had no choice but to try.

Cytherea concentrated on what she could remember of his technique and then gently blew until a low whistle finally escaped her lips. She quickly cut it off. The sound was deafening in the hushed streets, and she feared being discovered.

Another twittering whistle echoed in the distance.

He seemed to be whistling at regular intervals. So she waited for the next one. As soon as she heard it, she tried again to imitate it, only louder this time, and then waited. Kenric sounded closer the next time, and she whistled in reply. Now he was much closer. After she let out another whistle, she heard boots running toward her.

For one frantic moment, she wondered if she had alerted nearby guards to her presence, but before Cytherea had time to react, Kenric appeared through the darkness. He barreled into her and threw his arms around her, lifting her into the air. She returned his tight embrace, and tears of relief flowed from her eyes.

"You're OK. You're OK," he whispered like a mantra.

"What happened to Aherne?" she whispered, her throat tight.

He shook his head with a grin at the fact that Aherne was her first thought. "He's all right. Recovering in Haight."

Her fear and grief over Aherne drained out of her. "Thank goodness." She rested her head on his tunic. "Ew. You smell like manure."

She felt Kenric stifle a chuckle. After a moment, he slowly let go of her. Removing his cloak, he put it around her and led her through the village toward the inn where he had a room.

After closing the door to his room, they spoke in hushed tones.

"How did you escape the castle?" Kenric asked. "I have been trying to find a way all day and couldn't find any opening that isn't heavily guarded."

"Everard," Cytherea responded.

"Everard? Do you mean Everard, your brother? You saw him?"

"Yes. And he is alive, Kenric!" Excitement coursed through her. "He is the one who helped me escape the castle."

"But how? Where is he now?" Kenric stammered as he processed the news. "And if he knows how to get out, then why is he still there?"

"He showed me the way out through a doorway that led to the alley near where you found me."

"But there were guards there. I checked earlier. How did you get past the guards?"

"Everard sent the guards away." She flipped her hair over her shoulder and paced before him. "He has apparently been raised as Ailmar's son and—"

"He what?" Kenric's voice raised before he caught himself and brought it back to a terse whisper. "What do you mean he was 'raised as Ailmar's son'? How do you know it was really him, and that this isn't a trap?"

She stopped pacing and turned to face him, narrowing her eyes. "I know my brother, Kenric. I'm not some silly child making up a story."

"I'm sorry, Cyth. I know that. This is all just so hard to believe."

"I know. But he has my eyes, my face, the exact same dragon birthmark, and he has a ring identical to mine. It is Everard."

"OK. Then where is he now? Why didn't he escape with you?"

"He doesn't think he needs to escape. He actually believes that he is Ailmar's son, and that his real name is Derian."

"Wait." Kenric's eyes grew wide. "Are you talking about Derian, Prince of the Dark Realm?"

"That's what he said his name is, but I know that he is Everard."

Kenric stared at her in disbelief. "Have you lost your mind, Cytherea?" His voice strained to stay in a whisper. "Prince Derian? A man whose evil and ruthlessness is second only to his father, Ailmar? That is who you think is Everard?"

"I don't 'think.' I know it is him, Kenric." She looked up at him. "You must believe me."

"That might explain why Prince Derian is rarely seen beyond the castle walls, if he looks a lot like you." He shook his head. "But I can't believe that he is actually Everard."

"I know, but he will prove himself in time. And when you see him yourself, you will know."

Kenric was silent for a moment before asking, "If he believes he is Prince Derian, then why did he help you escape?"

"I'm not sure, Kenric," Cytherea sat on the bed and shook her head. "I think he remembers something of our childhood, but it will take time for him to understand who he really is."

"How can we be sure he didn't have guards follow us here and that your escape wasn't some sort of trick?" Kenric strode across the room and peered into the dark night beyond the window.

"Because he's my brother, and no matter how long we have been apart, the bond is still there. He is simply confused right now, but he will come around. I know he will."

Kenric walked back toward her. "I hope you are right."

Cytherea told him about her meeting with Ailmar, how she met Everard, and the crying children in the dungeon. She also recounted, as best she could, the route she took to escape the castle. When she finished, Kenric told her how he got through the gate but became frustrated trying to find a way into the well-fortified castle. Their stories were brief, because they both knew that even though she was out of the castle, they still had to find a way out of the castle walls before Ailmar discovered she was gone.

"Don't worry, I've got a plan," Kenric said, grinning.

Cytherea beamed, utterly relieved.

31

As the morning sun lightened the sky, Cytherea and Kenric crept back to the alley near where he had hidden the cloth merchant's cart. They watched the other merchants arrive and set up for the day. Cytherea waited in the shadows while Kenric retrieved the cart and moved it to the darkened path.

He removed the cloth, and she scrambled into the cart. Once she was settled, he replaced the fabric on top of her, burying her beneath the colorful layers until there was no sign of her.

Cytherea forced herself to be calm as the cart bumped across the cobbles toward the main gate. She knew that Kenric was focused on trying to appear casual while still keeping a brisk pace. She could hear more voices and sensed an increase in activity around the cart. They must be nearing the gate. No one was looking for Kenric, but if Ailmar had already discovered that Cytherea had escaped, he would have notified the gate guards by now, and they would likely search the cart.

The soldiers at the gate were only mildly concerned when Kenric approached.

"Why are you leaving so soon?" one guard asked. "The market has only just opened."

"Hey, I didn't see you come in with the others today," another chimed in.

"Yes, I stayed at the inn last night," Kenric responded calmly.

Cytherea held her breath in the cart.

"I must have eaten some bad meat," Kenric continued, "because I was ill all night. I am just trying to get home, where I can rest." Cytherea was impressed with his improvisation. "I'll be back to sell tomorrow."

Movement jostled Cytherea; the guards had waved him through. When the cart finally bounced from the wooden drawbridge onto the dirt road heading away from the castle, Cytherea and Kenric both breathed a sigh of relief.

While the cart rolled along the road, she thought about the castle village and how life was inside the Dark Realm. There was a heaviness in the thick, grayish air even when the sun was overhead. When she and Fenia had gone to the market in Ceka, there was a fair-like atmosphere, but in the Dark Realm, it felt solemn and stifled, with only the occasional buyer dully bartering for goods. In Ceka, there was lively chatter and boisterous voices haggling over prices—it felt alive. In contrast, the Dark Realm was full of people existing but never truly living. Cytherea found it hard to shake the feeling of gloom that had crept inside as soon as she had crossed into the Dark Realm.

It suddenly occurred to Cytherea that she never saw any children in the marketplace. No sounds of children's laughter echoed through the streets of the Dark Realm, only the melancholic calls of villagers and smug soldiers.

Where were all the children? The fear she had in the pit of her stomach since her capture began to wane, and in its place, the seed of contempt and resentment grew.

After some time, Cytherea felt the cart round a wide bend in the road, and she knew that they were at last beyond the prying eyes of the castle guards. Before long, Kenric slowed and then turned off the road and into the trees that once again lined the road.

Weariness made Cytherea's limbs tremble. When Kenric stopped in the forest to help her out of her hiding place, the aches and pains she had suffered over the last few days flared with every movement, causing her to wince.

"You're injured," Kenric said with his brows knitted together.

"No. Just bumps and bruises," Cytherea reassured him. "It will all heal soon enough."

"We will have a healer tend to you when we get to Gregor's." Kenric's tone told Cytherea that there would be no argument.

She followed him as he pushed the cart back onto the road and they made their way back to the quaint village of Belmis and Gregor's horse.

"Is this Haight? Is Aherne here?" Cytherea asked. "I was so afraid he was dead."

"This is Belmis, and it will take more than a Dark Realm soldier to kill that horse." Kenric smiled broadly. "He had a nasty gash to one of his legs, which made it difficult for him to walk."

Pain lanced through Cytherea, and her eyes filled with tears.

"He is safe, though," Kenric said hurriedly. "Gregor is caring for him. Haight is the next village over, an afternoon's ride. You will see him for yourself when we get there later today."

"And the sword? Is it safe?"

"Yes, thankfully, the sword is safe."

After paying for the horse's board and paying the stable owner to return the handcart and wares to the old woman, Kenric mounted and pulled Cytherea up behind him. They were both anxious to get to Gregor's, but they rode at a slower pace due to the burden of two people on the horse's back, unlike the Dark Realm soldiers that pushed their poor beasts well beyond reason. But even at this sluggish pace, they reached Haight before the midday meal.

32

Derian wandered back to his chamber in a haze. His mind was a storm of questions and vague memories that fought to resurface. He pushed the memories back while he struggled with everything the girl had said. He couldn't deny that their eyes were identical, as were their rings and birthmarks, but what about his life? What about the only father he had ever known? Was it really all a lie? Prisoners destined for execution would say a lot of things if it might give them a chance to escape, but Cytherea's words seemed to elicit strange memories in his mind. Once he entered his chamber, he slammed the door behind him and began pacing the floor.

After a time, his confusion hardened to anger, and it burned through the pain. It had all been a trick, of course. How idiotic he had been to believe her! Cytherea was not his sister from a past he didn't remember. She was a witch who had cast a spell over his mind.

"How could I let her get away?" he shouted to the walls.

He flung wide the door, letting it thud against the interior wall, and marched out of his chamber, determined to meet with his father and confess his failings. His frantic gait, fueled by anger, slowed when he reached his father's wing of the castle. His fury dissipated. He halted as long-buried memories flashed through his mind, growing clearer until they overwhelmed him.

He turned toward a window, and the sun was warm on his face . . .

~

Sunlight shone overhead as Derian ran and hid behind a bush in the garden. He was laughing. The smell of flowers and cut grass filled the air around him, and his hands felt the smooth green leaves of the bush that pressed against him. He tried to hold still as he heard her calling.

"Everard! Where are you?" the woman called playfully. "Cytherea, help me find your brother."

He giggled again and pressed harder into the bush, when suddenly a bird flew from within, startling him and making him fall backward. He landed hard on his bottom and began to cry. Almost immediately, he was surrounded by arms and silk. The woman's arms around him made him feel secure, and the silk of her dress was soft against his skin. His tears soon stopped, and he blinked up at her. Her eyes were smiling down at him. He reached up to hold the rings that hung around her neck.

"Mother is here. There is nothing to fear," she said.

~

His mother's face was suddenly gone, and Derian blinked, reeling as he once again stared down the dark passage. The woman in the vision looked so much like the girl, Cytherea, and him. And she'd called him "Everard." He tried to shake the thought from his mind.

"Is everything all right, Your Highness?" a guard inquired.

"Yes. I'm fine," Derian answered gruffly.

As he continued walking, Derian absently twisted his own ring around his finger. His father had told him that his ring was one of a kind, that he'd had it made specifically for him as a gift for his birthday.

How does she have an identical one? And why did these rings keep appearing in his mind like flashes of memory? He stopped again. The smell of hay and horses filled his senses.

Derian sat astride a horse, and a pair of large, strong hands held him in the saddle. He reached forward to grab the horse's mane in his hands. The horse shifted its weight, and Derian cried out in fear, but the hands around him kept him secure.

He heard a boisterous laugh and then a powerful yet gentle voice. "Easy, son, it's OK. Your father's got you."

Derian turned to look at who was speaking. It was not his father, Ailmar. His gaze moved up to the man's eyes—they were emerald green!

Derian stumbled, breaking his reverie and bringing him back to the present. He caught himself with his hand against the passage wall.

A guard walking by lunged forward to keep Derian from falling. "Your Highness! Are you ill?"

"I'm . . . I'm not feeling very well," Derian stammered. "Please help me back to my bedchamber."

"Yes, Your Highness, of course. Shall I have a servant appointed to care for you?"

"No need. I think I merely need to lie down. I must be overly tired. I didn't sleep well last night."

"Are you certain, Your Highness?"

"Yes, I'm certain. I'll be fine after some sleep. Tell my father that I will not be at dinner tonight."

"Yes, Your Highness."

In his bedchamber, Derian dismissed the guard. His mind swirled with the chaos of emotions and memories. He counted and recounted his steps from one end of the bedchamber to the other, trying to make sense of everything until he finally lay down on his bed and fell into a fitful sleep.

Derian was running, pulling the little girl called Cytherea along behind him as they played hide-and-seek in the garden. He rounded a tree and glanced behind, failing to notice the pond. They both fell in, water splashing everywhere. It was shallow, and they easily made their way back to the grass, where they sat and laughed.

The dream jumped, and he and Cytherea stood inside a castle, both dripping wet.

The man with the green eyes tried unsuccessfully to be stern and tell them that they could have been hurt. However, when their mother entered the room, she burst into giggles. Their father could not hold his own laughter any longer, and his guffaws mixed with their mother's musical giggling. Chuckles bubbled up from Derian's throat.

When Derian woke in the morning, his clothes were damp with sweat from a night of dreams, nightmares, and memories. He changed into fresh clothes and called out to the guard outside his door.

"Yes, Your Highness?"

"Have my stallion saddled and readied for a journey."

"Right away, Your Highness."

While the guard hurried off to relay the message to the royal grooms, Derian packed some clothes into a bag and rushed down the hall. He would find this witch, Cytherea, and demand that she remove this curse of false memories from his mind. For what else could they be?

33

Cytherea's clothes were filthy. Combined with her unkempt hair, she knew she looked frightful as they walked up to the pleasant little cottage across from the forge. She attempted to smooth her hair and tunic before Kenric opened the door, but it was futile.

He smirked at her. "I can't believe you are worried about how you look."

"I've never met them, and I am supposed to be the heir to the throne of Phoxnay," she snapped, glancing down at her torn breeches. "I certainly don't look like much right now."

"They won't care," Kenric reassured her. "They'll just be happy that you're still alive." With that, he slowly opened the door.

A giant man immediately jumped up from his meal and met them at the door. "You made it!" he boomed, giving Kenric a hardy slap on the back. Kenric caught himself with a staggering step, his lips lifting in what the man probably thought was a smile but Cytherea knew was a grimace. "Anna and I were beginning to lose hope."

"Not me!" chimed in a young boy that looked to be about eight years of age. "I knew you would be OK, Kenric!"

The man laughed as he looked down at the boy. "Looks like

you have quite a fan here, Kenric." To Cytherea, he said, "I am Gregor, and this is my son, Brockton."

A petite woman rose from the table as well. She performed an awkward curtsy before Cytherea. "I am Anna, and we are so grateful to have you in our home."

Cytherea shifted uncomfortably as Kenric responded, "This is Cytherea, daughter to our late king and queen."

"There is no need for any formalities," Cytherea said. "I'm just someone who is trying to help."

"You must be hungry," Anna said. "We've only just started our meal. Please eat, and then you can get settled."

Cytherea's stomach rumbled, reminding her of how little she had eaten recently. The aromas from Anna's table made her mouth water. "Thank you. It smells wonderful."

Cytherea took in her surroundings. The cottage felt like a warm hug, much like their cottage back home. It was small but well kept. The main room and the table where they ate were at the front, and doorways led to two small rooms in the back where she assumed the family slept. A low loft over the main room appeared to be mainly used for supplies for Anna's cooking. The scent of moss from the earthen walls mingled pleasantly with the herbs, spices, and meats from past meals that had soaked into them. A hearth fire blazed, warming the room as well as the pot that Anna used for preparing their meals. There were three chairs arranged in a semicircle to one side of the hearth, and the table where Cytherea now sat was positioned on the other side so that both areas received plenty of warmth.

She was given a hearty portion of meat and bread, and the conversation flowed easily as they ate, Brockton chattering on about how he had been caring for the horses. It was evident that hospitality was a cornerstone of their way of life. The evening stirred fond memories of meals at their cottage growing up. It was a reprieve from the horrors of the last few days, and for that, Cytherea was grateful.

She studied Gregor and Anna as they laughed at their son's tales. The two were opposite but complementary figures. Where Gregor was large and gruff, his wife was petite and gentle. However, despite his imposing figure, he was quick to heed his wife, Cytherea noticed with a smile. She felt the love that flowed through this little family and laughed while Kenric joined in Brockton's enthusiasm. The warm food filled her and allowed her to set aside her worries about Ailmar and Everard and all the evil around them for a moment.

Once they had all eaten, Brockton was excited to show Kenric and Cytherea how well he had cared for the horses. She was anxious to see Aherne, and they all followed the boy as he ran toward the barn. The moment Cytherea entered, Aherne began stomping and bobbing his head.

"I see that Aherne is back to normal," she said, laughing as she went to his side to check his wound.

"I have been applying the salve that Sir Kenric left with me," Brockton announced proudly.

"Sir Kenric?" Cytherea questioned, quirking one eyebrow at Kenric, who tried to hide his smile.

"And I brushed them twice a day while telling them stories of how brave Princess Cytherea and Sir Kenric were."

"Princess," Kenric whispered in Cytherea's ear, grinning. They carefully checked their horses for any other injuries that might have been missed.

"It looks like both horses have been well cared for and thoroughly spoiled," Cytherea proclaimed. She placed her hand on the boy's shoulder. "Well done, Sir Brockton."

Brockton beamed at her approval and his new title. After giving the horses a few oats, they left the barn and returned to the cottage.

"Gregor will fetch you some water so you can get cleaned up and rest," Anna said. "Brockton will sleep in our room, Cytherea, so you can have his room, and, Kenric, if you don't mind moving some things around up there, you can sleep in the loft."

"We don't want to intrude on your family. We can get rooms at the inn," Kenric insisted.

"Don't even think of it," responded Gregor firmly. "You will stay here. We have a lot to discuss, and I feel safer having Cytherea here instead of an inn where strangers come and go."

Cytherea smiled up at him. "Thank you." She turned to Brockton. "And thank you, Sir Brockton, for letting me sleep in your room."

He turned pink, pleased with her favor. "It is my honor, Princess Cytherea," he said with a bow.

Cytherea smiled and didn't chastise him for his formality.

"We are getting reports that the Dark Realm soldiers' activities have increased recently," Gregor said, briefing Cytherea and Kenric once they were cleaned up and settled in the main room. Anna was cleaning up after their meal. "There has not been any mention yet of them looking for Cytherea, but that could change at any time."

"Tell me about the loyalists, Gregor," Cytherea requested. "Where do they get their information and how accurate is it?"

"I don't know all of their sources, but these are men that have kept track of everything the Dark Realm has done since the fall of Phoxnay. They have also been watching over you." His eyes darkened. "We're still not sure how none of us knew in advance that they had found you at your farm."

"Do you think someone is no longer loyal to us?" Kenric asked.

Gregor grimaced. "I hate to believe it could be true, but it's also the only likely explanation." He glanced over at Cytherea. "Some of these loyalists are second generation. Their love and loyalty for Phoxnay were passed down from their fathers. Over the years, their numbers have increased and now spread across the land to Klobyn and even kingdoms beyond. The likelihood of someone turning against us is low, but not impossible. Kenric, what can you tell me about the castle? Did you find a way we could get into the castle proper once we are inside the outer walls?"

"Without your help, I doubt I would have been able to get through the outer gate of the wall. I searched for most of a day and night trying to find a weakness in the castle, and I couldn't find anything. The only openings were all heavily guarded."

"We've been trying to get operatives into the castle for years, so I'm not surprised. But Cytherea's escape may draw Ailmar out into open battle."

"Would that be . . . a good idea?" Cytherea asked.

Gregor nodded. "The castle is his stronghold. Easy to defend, and he's undoubtedly stockpiled food and provisions there that could last for months, at least. We don't have the resources or weaponry for an extended siege, but if we draw his army out, we might stand a chance."

"What do you know about Ailmar's staff?" Cytherea asked.

"Only tales." Gregor eyed Cytherea. "What do you know about it?"

"She saw it," Kenric interjected. "She actually spoke to Ailmar."

Gregor's eyes widened. "You are lucky to still be alive. Your escape is sounding more and more like a miracle."

It was Everard, Cytherea wanted to say, but she held her tongue. "The staff seems to operate under some kind of dark magic."

"Why do you say that?" Gregor leaned in, curious.

"There is black smoke, or what seems like smoke, that emanates from the black orb that sits at the top of the staff. Only, it isn't really smoke." Cytherea struggled to find the words to describe it. "It was more just darkness. Thick and penetrating. I can't explain it."

Gregor sat back, stroking his beard as he thought. "Do you think that Ailmar's magic actually comes from the staff, or does the staff get its magic from Ailmar?"

"I don't know for sure, but the feeling I got was that the magic came from the staff, but that is only a feeling. My exchange with Ailmar was very brief, even though it seemed like an eternity at the time."

"I can only imagine." Gregor thought for a moment longer. "Do you think he knows who you are?"

"Yes."

"Why do you think that, Cytherea?" Kenric's tone divulged his horror at the thought of Ailmar knowing who Cytherea was.

"I gave him a false name and story, but when he was finished with questioning me, he looked at me—or more like he looked inside me—and called me 'princess.'"

Anna gasped from across the room.

Kenric stood abruptly. "We have to get you out of here now!"

"Hold on, Kenric." Gregor placed his hand firmly on Kenric's shoulder, easing him back into the chair. "If he knows who she is, then that is all the more reason for her to stay and fight him."

"Yes, you mentioned that my escape might lead Ailmar out of his castle. How do you know the loyalists would stand a chance in open battle?" Cytherea asked, ignoring Kenric's worried look.

"It would be a better chance than attacking him in his castle. But before we get any further with a plan, tell us everything you found out about Ailmar, the castle, and anything else that might be helpful for us to know."

The rest of that day was spent exchanging information. Gregor told them about the Dark Realm activities from the recent reports, and Cytherea shared her experiences inside Ailmar's castle, including her meetings with Everard and Ailmar. Gregor was also taken aback and struggling to believe that Prince

Derian was Everard, and he agreed with Kenric that he could not be trusted, but there was little they could do now except be prepared. The day passed quickly, but by the end, Cytherea's mind was turning as they began planning an attack on the Dark Realm.

After the evening meal, Gregor was curious and asked, "What about the sword? Have you found the Sword of Phoxnay?"

Without answering, Cytherea got up and crossed the room to where her belongings were and pulled the great sword from its sheath. The gemstone immediately began glowing, and it illuminated the dark room.

Gregor and Anna both gasped at the sight.

Brockton's eyes were huge, and his mouth was agape.

Cytherea held it out for them all to see. She smiled when she realized that this was the first time the young boy was speechless.

Brockton quickly found his words again. "Can I hold it?" he asked with awe in his voice.

"No, son," Gregor said.

But Cytherea smiled and sat next to Brockton. "It's OK. You can touch the hilt. Just be careful of the blade."

Brockton tried to wrap his small hand around the hilt, but it was far too big for him, so he used both hands and tried to lift it. The glow stopped.

"Easy, son." Gregor reached forward to help him steady it.

"What happened to the glow?" Brockton asked, a quizzical look on his face.

"Cytherea isn't holding it anymore," Kenric responded. "Hand it back to her for a minute."

Cytherea took the sword from Brockton, and the gemstone began to glow again. This time, both Brockton and Gregor had wide eyes and open mouths. She handed it back to Brockton, and the glow stopped.

"I've heard stories of the magic of the great sword, but I never knew how many of them were true," Gregor said solemnly.

"Magic?" A perplexed look crossed the boy's face as he scanned the sword.

"Yes, son. The Sword of Phoxnay possesses a kind of magic."

"Is Princess Cytherea magic too?"

Laughing, Kenric answered, "Yes, Sir Brockton, Princess Cytherea is magic, in a way."

Cytherea gave him a disapproving look.

"It is said," Gregor began, "that the great Sword of Phoxnay has the power to defeat evil. In fact, it is the only thing that can defeat Ailmar. However, the magic only works if the sword is wielded by a direct heir to the throne of Phoxnay and of the Sainte-d'Agneaux bloodline."

"And that's Princess Cytherea!" Brockton exclaimed.

"That's right, son."

"It's late," Anna's gentle voice interjected, "and I think Princess Cytherea needs some rest, as does Sir Brockton." She smiled.

Cytherea stretched, suddenly realizing how tired she was. "Thank you, Anna. I think I will try to get some sleep." After she got up, she took the sword from Brockton. He smiled broadly as the glow of the gemstone returned.

34

Cytherea sat up and looked out the small window by her bed. It was still dark, so she lay back down, happy to have some time to process all that had happened. The quiet of the cottage was occasionally pierced with loud snores she suspected were coming from Gregor. She smiled and gently touched the ring that was once again around her neck, thanks to a chain borrowed from Anna. Cytherea allowed the memories of her mother to flow over her. Those memories felt as comfortable and calm as her memories of growing up with Tarquin and Fenia. She was grateful to have been raised by loving guardians. Did Everard feel loved? An evil man had raised him, but could an evil man still love?

Cytherea became restless at the thought of Everard and Ailmar, so she quietly got up, dressed, and headed out to the barn to see Aherne. As she crossed the small road in front of the cottage, the village was silent, except for the crow of a rooster telling her that the sun would soon be rising.

When she entered the small barn, Aherne wandered over and nuzzled her. His horsey scent wafted over Cytherea, and she rubbed his soft muzzle until he pulled away from her hand to search her for treats. After giving both horses a treat, Cytherea began absently braiding Aherne's mane as she pondered her past.

"Aherne needs some flowers in his mane." Kenric chuckled, and Cytherea jumped. "I'd ask what you were thinking so hard about, but I probably already know the answer." He stopped, and his tone grew serious as he chastised her. "You can't just leave the cottage alone, Cyth. Ailmar will soon discover that you are gone, and then there will be soldiers everywhere looking for you."

"Well, apparently, I have my own guard following me every-where," she said gently.

"I'm serious. If I hadn't heard you leaving, you would be out here alone."

"I know. I promise I won't do it again." She paused. "Do you think we will ever get back to the cottage and Fenia?" She continued braiding Aherne's mane.

"I do. And you will go back to daydreaming under the big tree in the wildflower field."

"I don't think it will ever be like before. With everything that has happened."

Kenric tilted his chin, his eyes piercing. "You know different things about the world, but who you are inside will always be the same."

"Do you think that is true of Everard? Is he still good inside?"

"I don't trust him," Kenric admitted. "But if he didn't have something good still inside him, he would not have helped you escape."

Hope bubbled up inside Cytherea at Kenric's admission. "We have the same blood running through us, so there has to be some good in him. If we can get him away from Ailmar, then I have to believe he will see the truth!"

"Let's hope so." Kenric sounded skeptical. "In the meantime, I'm hungry. Let's get the morning meal started."

Cytherea finished braiding Aherne's mane and gave him a final pat. She followed Kenric back to the cottage. He was ever the practical one, taking life one day at a time, or at least one meal at a time. Cytherea chuckled at the thought.

That evening, Anna was mending some of Gregor's breeches while Gregor and Brockton headed out to the forge to finish up the day's work. Earlier in the day, Gregor had begun teaching Cytherea about battle strategy, training, and anything else that might help her lead them against Ailmar. Gregor had also sent out messages to ask some of the loyalists to gather for a meeting. But while they waited for their arrival for the most part, they continued to go about their daily lives so as not to raise any suspicion. Cytherea and Kenric became restless with nothing to do except stay out of Anna's way while she prepared their meals.

"Why don't we take the horses out to the small paddock behind the barn and let them get some exercise?" Cytherea suggested.

Kenric hesitated. "I don't want people to see you or the horses."

"It's dark out now. Besides, it's right behind Gregor's barn. It isn't visible from the main road. You can't expect Aherne and Tredan to stay cooped up in a barn all the time."

Kenric sighed. "All right, but can you at least wear the long cloak with the hood covering your head?"

Cytherea wrinkled her nose. "All right, if it will get me outside for a little while."

They only saw a few friendly-looking villagers moving about as they crossed to the barn, so they were not overly concerned by the sound of hoofbeats coming around the bend. Even so, Kenric hurried Cytherea into the barn to wait until they had passed. When the horse and rider came into view, Cytherea gasped and started toward them.

"Hey!" Kenric hissed, but she was already back on the road.

As he caught up to her, Cytherea heard Kenric draw in a sharp breath. Kenric had never seen Prince Derian in person, and the resemblance to Cytherea was impossible to deny. However, his garments denoted that he was indeed the prince of the Dark Realm.

Kenric stepped in front of Cytherea.

"Everard," she said cautiously while trying to get around Kenric. "How did you find me?" She wasn't sure if she should be nervous or happy that he was there, but she wanted to believe the best of him.

"It would seem that you found me," Everard replied slowly. "I was searching for you in the villages nearest the castle."

"For what?" Kenric growled and repositioned himself between the two.

Cytherea shot him an angry look. *He's abandoned Ailmar. Maybe he wants to join us!* Her heart soared with hope.

Everard dismounted and smiled darkly in Kenric's direction. "We have not been properly introduced, but you are right to be suspicious." He tried to look casual. "I am not here to capture or harm her. You have my word."

Kenric looked at him blankly. "Your word means nothing."

Still smiling, Everard guided his horse closer to Kenric and extended his hand. "Your caution is admirable, but I offer you a handshake as a gesture of my sincerity."

Kenric glared at Everard's hand, making no move to respond to the gesture. Undaunted, Everard shifted his gaze to Cytherea. "I have come to strike a bargain with you, *sister*." He said the last word with some difficulty.

Cytherea pushed Kenric aside and took Everard's hand herself. "I will accept your word, and I will listen to this bargain you wish to discuss." She ignored the doubt pushing its way to the front of her mind. *This is my brother. He can't be evil ... can he?*

"Very good." Everard shook her hand.

"Cytherea, what are you doing?" Kenric asked angrily.

"I am taking my brother at his word," she said.

"You don't know anything about him. He's Ailmar's son! He likely has a regiment of soldiers close behind him, on their way to take you back to Ailmar, where you will be killed! How can you trust him?"

Everard grinned as he watched them argue.

"He is my brother!" she shot back. "And he came here of his own free will."

"He's your brother by blood only," Kenric snarled. "Everything else about him is evil."

"If he has the same blood, then he must have good inside him."

"You are wrong," Kenric said softly, and then he leaned closer to Everard. "If you betray her, I will make sure it is the last thing you ever do."

"Threats are unnecessary, Kenric," Cytherea said resolutely.

"Yes, Kenric," Everard spat out his name and sneered. "Threats are unnecessary." Turning back to Cytherea with a less haughty look, he said, "It's getting late. I will get a room at the inn. We can meet there in the morning to discuss the bargain I mentioned."

Kenric opened his mouth, but Cytherea shot him a stern look. Instead, he headed back into the barn.

Cytherea gave her brother an apologetic look as Everard cast one last glance over his shoulder at her. She thought she saw his expression darken. Then he mounted his horse and headed toward the inn. She shook her head against her doubts and turned to follow Kenric.

Cytherea placed herself directly in Kenric's path to the small paddock. "Why are you acting like this?"

Kenric crossed his arms. Tredan was saddled and standing behind him. "You mean distrusting Ailmar's son? A man who was raised to be complicit in the Dark Realm's slaughter? The son of the man who rips small children from their mother's arms and throws them into dungeons? The man who was raised to believe that all these things are right and justified? I think that *my* actions are quite reasonable!"

"So *I* am acting unreasonably?" Cytherea snapped. Blood rushed up the back of her neck.

"He is Ailmar's son!" Kenric repeated again.

Matching his tone, Cytherea hissed, "Are you insinuating that my brother is evil?"

"I am insinuating that he is no longer your brother." Kenric led Tredan around Cytherea, who stared after him, open-mouthed.

"How dare you," she said, unmoving.

"He stopped being your brother the minute he started believing he was Ailmar's son."

Cytherea let Kenric walk away, then she went to get Aherne. Her teardrops fell into the dirt.

35

Ailmar absently examined his cuticles, leaning back against the broad polished stone of his throne. "Guard!" he shouted.

The guard rushed forward, bowed his head, and knelt before his lord. He trembled slightly.

"I wish to interrogate the girl prisoner further. Bring her to me." Ailmar waved off the guard before him.

The guard remained on the ground with his head bowed low. He swallowed before speaking. "Forgive me, Your Majesty, but I have been informed that the girl managed to escape." This last word tapered off as fear gripped his voice.

Ailmar straightened. His blink of disbelief hardened into a glare at the terrified guard. "Escaped? No one escapes my dungeon!" He curled a fist under his chin and lowered his voice. "Bring me the head of the guard on duty during the escape—and the heads of each person in his family—before nightfall, or I will have your head in their place."

"Yes, Your Majesty." The guard stood and hurried out of Ailmar's presence.

Ailmar paced the full width of the throne room, unable to

contain his anger. He caught the eye of another of his guards and shouted, "Get me Prince Derian!"

The guard bowed his head. "Your Majesty, His Highness was seen visiting the female prisoner prior to her escape, and he has not been seen since."

Silence gripped the chamber. Ailmar spun to glower at the guard bowed before him, his cloak rippling through the air. His grip tightened on his staff. "Do you dare suggest that my son had something to do with a prisoner's escape?" His voice came out a growl.

"N-no, Y-Your Majesty." The guard's bow deepened.

"Then what *do* you think?"

"Y-Your M-Majesty, my concern is for the s-safety of H-His Highness. There are rumors that this girl is a witch and can control people's minds. I fear that p-perhaps she cast such a s-spell over His Highness before her escape or that perhaps he has been c-captured by her accomplices during his m-morning ride." The guard bowed so low that he was almost entirely prostrate.

Ailmar struck the man's head with the end of his staff. "Rally my men and go find him and bring him home."

Without another word, the guard fled the throne room. Once the guard was gone, Ailmar tapped his staff in rhythm with his frantic pace up and down the chamber once again.

When he estimated the guard had relayed his orders, he stopped before a window and looked out. The castle grounds erupted in hurried movement, a large contingent of Dark Realm soldiers rushing to the stables to ready their horses. Muffled shouts and the clattering of hooves on the cobblestones wafted through the window.

"Where is Derian?" Ailmar mumbled to himself as he monitored the activity below him. "She couldn't have taken him from me so easily. I raised him as my own. He must still be loyal to me."

He marched from window to window, unaware of his

remaining guards listening and observing him. "Where *is* he?" he shouted in frustration. "Once they find him and bring him back, I will kill the girl!"

A slow smile broke through his angry scowl and then faded away. "Find Prince Derian!" he shouted, suddenly rushing from the chamber into the corridor. "Find him!"

36

That night, Cytherea had barely fallen asleep when she woke to a hand covering her mouth. Her eyes flew open.

Soldiers, Kenric mouthed, and released her.

She shook off her dreams and pulled on her boots. Kenric's sword glinted when he moved fluidly to the window, pointing. Cytherea reached for the hilt of her sword in the darkness and slid her fingers over the gemstone, covering its glow. She peered out the window, following his finger with her eyes and squinting into the moonlit street.

The trees at the edge of the village swayed against the wind, and she drew in a slow breath, marveling at Kenric's perception. Had he been keeping watch at his window all night? Backing away from the window and using a whisper that was barely audible, she said, "We have to warn Everard."

Kenric's eyes narrowed, but he jerked his head toward the window. "He already knows. I saw him in the street when I went out to get a better look. He's outside." Grinding his teeth, Kenric added, "I hope you are right about him."

As soon as the words left his mouth, the peaceful night was shattered by thunderous hooves and shouts.

The soldiers of the Dark Realm had come.

They rode in unison, their dark armor gleaming with an eerie light as it swallowed up the moonlight. They numbered about thirty, but they blended with the darkness around them, making them difficult to count. The horses' eyes pierced the air before them, and the dust from their movement swirled around them. The whole scene was nightmarish and made Cytherea's stomach churn.

Kenric and Cytherea ran to the front room of the cottage where Gregor stood with his body pressed against the door. Anna was already hiding with Brockton in their room. They listened intently to one soldier shouting orders.

"Release all boys under the age of ten for the honor of serving in the Dark Realm's army. You will bring them out to us, or we will take them by force!" The soldier scowled as faces began to appear in windows. "We are also looking for a girl, a stranger to you, with unusual green eyes. If you have seen her, tell us where she is, and we will leave your children."

Riders leaped from their horses and stood in front of the quaint cottages that lined the street.

The soldier who had spoken stood gazing at the homes around him. "I see no one has information for us. Very well." He nodded to the other soldiers with him. "Seize the boys!"

Cytherea shot a panicked look at Kenric, and the blood drained from her face. "They can't!"

Kenric's answer was swallowed by the screams of mothers and the wails of their children. Cytherea wouldn't stand there and watch. She had to do something! She turned to run out of the room, but Gregor's massive hand grasped her arm before she ever took a step.

"You can't go out there!" he whisper-shouted. "They will only capture you and return you to Ailmar." He turned back toward the window, his fingers tightening on her arm. "I can't let that happen, no matter what."

"We can't just sit here and do nothing while they take all the children," she said as loud as she dared.

"We have no choice," Kenric said bluntly.

"What do you mean? I have a choice, and I am going out there to stop this madness." She yanked on her arm, but Gregor's grip only tightened more. "Let go of me!" she whisper-shouted, trying to free herself from his grasp. "How can you be so heartless? Can't you hear that?"

Kenric turned toward her, his eyes like steel. "Cytherea, you cannot do anyone any good in Ailmar's dungeon, or worse, dead. We will save the children, but we can't do it now. You are the only hope we have of defeating Ailmar and the Dark Realm! Think rationally and not out of emotion. You were born to rule the people of this land. You must survive to step up and lead them out of this darkness."

She stared at him incredulously. "How can I learn to lead if you never listen to me? If you never let me step in to save my people? Just because my parents were king and queen doesn't mean—"

Frantic banging on the back door interrupted them, and Everard burst into the room. Anna screamed, likely thinking the soldiers were breaking in.

"Get Cytherea out of here!" Everard shouted.

Kenric was already pulling Cytherea toward the door Everard had come through. "Everard, distract the soldiers so we can get away from here, or they'll kill your sister!" Everard shot a look at Cytherea and then back at Kenric, who prodded his chest. "Do it now! Prove that she is right about you."

Everard met Cytherea's terrified gaze, then he bolted past them and around the side of the cottage toward the street.

"Keep her safe, Kenric." Gregor clasped Kenric's shoulder.

Kenric nodded at the big man. Then he grabbed Cytherea's hand, and they ran together down the back path, heading for the forest. She glanced back at her brother.

Before he exited the shadows between cottages, Everard stopped, composed himself, and strode calmly into the road amid the chaos.

Cytherea allowed herself to be pulled along. Could Everard stop them?

The cacophony came to an abrupt halt, and in the distance, an unfamiliar voice said, "Your Highness! His Majesty, your father, was concerned when you did not come home last night. The rumors said a girl used her witchcraft and took you."

Everard laughed a bit too loudly. "I am fine. I simply wanted some time to myself away from the castle. I should have informed my father. I didn't mean to cause all this commotion."

"What about the girl that escaped the dungeon?" the soldier asked.

Kenric continued to run. He pulled Cytherea farther from the soldiers, and she couldn't hear Everard's response. She and Kenric ran behind the cottages and shops of the village, and the screams of the women and children lent them speed as the duo raced toward the cover of the trees. They could hear the soldiers making their way through the village, and the yelling and screams were suddenly close behind them. Between the shops, Cytherea caught sight of men who fought to protect their sons but were struck down by the more powerful Dark Realm soldiers. Cytherea was horrified, but she couldn't stop because Kenric's grip was locked on her hand as he dragged her away from the dreadful scene.

They had almost reached the safety of the forest as they turned a final corner that would take them through the back of the village wall. It was more to designate the village's boundaries than for protection, and Cytherea could easily leap over it. However, she unexpectedly collided with Kenric's back. He released his grip and steadied her, reaching behind him with one hand while rapidly pulling his sword above his head with his other hand. Cytherea staggered backward to avoid getting in the way, and then she saw the soldiers running toward them.

She grabbed for her sword, but Kenric shouted, "No! Run. Run now!"

He slashed at the first soldier, who fell with a gurgle.

Cytherea hesitated. How could she leave him? Kenric said that he had pledged his life to protect her, but this was the first time she understood that he was ready to give his life for her. She could not let him do that, so she pushed down her fear and turned to fight.

37

Cytherea raised her sword, lunging toward the soldiers attacking Kenric. She engaged one while Kenric fought off the other two. The clang of blades filled the air. After engaging the soldiers for a few moments, the muscles in her arms began to burn. These soldiers had trained their whole lives to fight, and she had not. Her intermittent training with a sword was child's play in comparison. Her blows weakened, and soon the soldier's sword sliced through her defenses and nicked her arm. She let out a shout of pain.

"Cytherea!" Kenric called frantically. His distraction gave his opponents the chance they needed. A blade caught him deep in the leg. Kenric screamed and fell, his sword clattering helplessly to the ground.

Cytherea inhaled to summon the strength she had left and charged. The hilt of the Sword of Phoxnay was hot in her hand, its gemstone lighting her path. She plunged her sword through the knee of her attacker, and as he fell, shrieking, adrenaline coursed through her. She jumped over him with her sword raised again and landed a slicing blow to the nearest soldier's neck. He toppled with blood spurting from his wound.

She leaped toward the remaining soldier as he raised his sword to land a deadly blow on Kenric, and she thrust her blade through a gap in his armor, deep into his stomach. She grunted, pushing the blade in as hard as she could, the light from the gemstone momentarily blinding her. The final soldier fell with a snarl, and his sword caught Kenric as he tried to roll out of its path. Cytherea lost her grip on her sword, which was still inside the soldier, and it was pulled from her hands when the soldier collapsed. Her arms trembled, and she stared at the soldier's unmoving body.

I killed him. She glanced toward the other soldier whose eyes stared blankly ahead. *I killed both of them.* Her vision narrowed to the soldier's face at her feet, and she could only hear the deafening ringing in her ears. Kenric's moaning snapped her back to the present, and she forced her eyes off the dead soldier.

"Kenric!"

Blood was everywhere. She couldn't tell if it belonged to him or the soldiers. Kenric's eyes were closed, and his painful moans continued. Cytherea tried unsuccessfully to drag him out of the street before another soldier could find him and finish him off. Her fight with the soldiers had left her arms too weak, but she couldn't leave him there. So she gathered her strength, locked her arms under his, and began to pull with all her might. It was then that she felt two strong arms wrap over her shoulders.

She spun in fear, only to sigh in relief. "Everard!"

"Let me help," Everard murmured.

Cytherea retrieved her sword from the slain soldier. She forced herself to swallow the bile that rose in her throat. Everard lifted Kenric effortlessly and carried him back to Gregor and Anna's cottage. He grabbed the door handle, then hesitated and released it before leaning a delirious Kenric against the cottage wall. Everard gestured for Cytherea to go ahead inside. Then he ducked around the corner.

Cytherea hurried after him. "Everard, stop!"

He paused, meeting her eye.

"You can't go with them after what they've done."

"The soldiers know I'm here. If I don't return with them, my father . . . Ailmar"—he shook his head—"I will lead them away from you."

"What about the children? Make them let the children go!"

"I can't do that."

"Why? Why can't you?" Tears trickled down her face.

"We did not have time to discuss our bargain."

"Bargain? You are bargaining with the lives of children? What do you want?"

"You have cursed me with your magic. I will return the children if you release me from the curse and take away the dreams you have put in my head."

"I can't do that, Everard," she said, frantically wiping away the tears. "I didn't put anything in your head. Those are your memories. I have no magic and—"

"How can you say you have no magic? I saw what you did with that sword of yours. Release the curse, and I'll release these children." He smiled coldly at her.

"Please believe me," she pleaded. "I have not cursed you. Make them let the children go."

Kenric moaned, and Cytherea glanced back. When she did, Everard abruptly turned and ran up the street to join the soldiers of the Dark Realm. Cytherea leaned against the cottage, sobbing and confused.

The sound of the soldiers' horses eventually faded, but the cries of broken families were embedded permanently in her heart.

Kenric moaned again. Cytherea wiped her tears and rushed around the corner to his side.

"It's going to be all right, Kenric." She opened the door to the cottage.

"Get out!" Gregor snarled, lunging forward with a sword in hand.

"Gregor!" Cytherea shouted as she dodged his blade. She looked up. His eyes were wild with fury. "Gregor!"

"Cytherea!" His eyes softened slightly and dropped to the blood on her arm. He lowered his sword. "Are you hurt? Where is Kenric?"

"It's just a small cut, but we need to get Kenric inside."

Gregor rushed past her and soon had Kenric on the bed in Brockton's room. "I will fetch the healer." He hesitated as he shot Cytherea a questioning look.

"What is it?"

"Why did a Dark Realm soldier help you?" Gregor asked slowly.

"He is my brother," Cytherea said flatly.

Gregor's hand tightened on his sword.

"He is my twin, but it seems that we are not really the same." She straightened and faced Gregor fully. "He will not hurt any of you. You have my word."

"Your word is too late." Rage laced his voice and flickered in his eyes. He moved toward the door.

"What do you mean?" Worry gripped her.

In the other room, Anna sobbed.

"Gregor!" Cytherea stopped him before he left. "What happened? Are Anna and Brockton hurt?"

"They've taken him." Gregor glanced back, and fury returned to his eyes. "The soldiers took Brockton." He smashed his hand against the door, and it slammed into the wall as he stormed out to find the healer.

Cytherea sucked in a breath, unable to comprehend what he had said. *They've taken Brockton?* Her heart was torn in two, and her mind was spinning. Her movements became stiff as she absently wrapped Kenric's wound with rags she made from her torn clothes still sitting by the bed. Once she had done all she could for Kenric, she went to find Anna. When Cytherea had entered the cottage just moments before, she had been focused on Kenric, and only now she saw the aftermath of the struggle that had happened there. The table was broken, chairs were strewn all around, and Cytherea's mind flashed to the scene back home after the soldiers had killed Tarquin. She could only imagine the fight Gregor had put up trying to save his son. She followed a fresh wave of sobs from Anna and soon found her huddled in her bedchamber with her face on the floor.

Cytherea had no words that could soften her pain, so she collapsed on the floor, wrapped her tightly in her arms, and wept with her.

38

Gregor returned with the local healer, who took out her supplies and began to minister to Kenric. The healer silently applied herbal salves and poultices to Kenric's wounds before she looked up at Cytherea.

"He's lost a lot of blood and will need a lot of rest. He may not be awake again until tomorrow," she explained.

Cytherea's voice was stolen by the tears that she tried to choke back in vain. *Will he live?* She couldn't bring herself to ask the question aloud for fear of the answer. He had been there with her for as long as she could remember. She wasn't sure she could face her destiny and the army of the Dark Realm without Kenric by her side. He had *always* been there.

The healer wiped Cytherea's tears with her apron and looked deeply into her eyes for a few moments before speaking. "You have greater strength than you believe. Hold on to that. Your destiny draws near."

"What do you mean?"

"I only know what I see. I do not always know what it means, but I think you do." The healer turned her gaze back to Kenric and continued her work.

For a time, Cytherea observed the healer moving her hands gently over Kenric's wounds and mumbling words Cytherea didn't understand. Gregor held Anna, who still quietly wept as they stood in the doorway to the small room, hoping that Kenric would survive.

"Will he be all right?" Cytherea was finally able to ask when the healer paused in her work.

"I believe so, after some rest. I will be back to apply more salve later." She rummaged through her things and pulled out a small vial. She gave it to Cytherea with instructions to give him the potion as soon as he was able to drink. Then the healer gathered her things and rushed out to help others who had been wounded that night.

Once the healer was gone, Anna went to the front room to find the other ingredients the healer had given them for the potion. Silence descended except for the sounds of Anna picking up chairs and cleaning up broken items from the floor.

"Is she going to be all right?" Cytherea quietly asked Gregor.

"She is giving herself a purpose," he replied. "If she keeps herself busy, she will be all right until we get our boy back. You will get him back, won't you?"

"Yes," she answered without hesitation. "You have my word." After a few moments, Cytherea stood. "I'm going to check on the horses. Please let me know if he wakes up."

Crossing the front room, she met Anna's gaze as she picked up the pieces of a small vase that had been broken in the fight. Cytherea thought better of interrupting and headed outside. When she opened the door, the crisp night air washed over her face, and she allowed it to dry her tears before she pulled the hood of her cloak over her head and walked briskly to the barn. She needed room to think and to get control of all the emotions rushing through her as the events of the last several days washed over her.

She gave the horses some oats. Then she began braiding

Aherne's mane to give her hands something to do while she tried to get a grasp on what had happened and what she needed to do next. First was her capture. The sound of those crying children was something she couldn't get out of her mind. Now Brockton was in that horrible place. The thought was almost unbearable. At the same time, she was haunted by the faces of the two soldiers she had killed. She knew that she would have to use her sword in battle, but actually killing someone, even someone evil, was hard for her to process.

Then there was Everard—the brother she hadn't even known existed until just days before. Now that she had met him, she was left more confused than ever. Cytherea wanted to believe there was good inside him, but she was starting to wonder.

He let the soldiers take the children. He had the power to stop it, but he didn't. Why? And he accused her of being a witch and for cursing him somehow. How could he think that?

Was Ailmar's magic so strong that he could turn someone good completely evil? She wanted to hold on to the hope that Everard had some good still inside him. He had helped her escape the castle and then helped Kenric tonight, but it was all too confusing.

Cytherea felt like her circumstances and the people around her were pushing and pulling her into decisions. It was time to change that. It was time for her to gain some control over the chaos happening both inside her and around her. When she'd turned to fight the soldiers with Kenric, it had felt like the first time she had done something to try and stop Ailmar. It had felt right, and she knew that it was time for her to start fighting back. She had to save the children and the people of Phoxnay. *My people.*

Now she just needed to figure out how.

After she finished braiding Aherne's mane, she crossed back toward the house with a renewed sense of purpose. Multiple shadows flickered in the glow of the hearth fire inside the cottage. When Cytherea approached the door, she heard men's voices. She gripped her sword and silently pushed open the door.

Instead of enemy soldiers, however, she found a small group of men talking quietly with Gregor. She stepped inside. They quieted and turned toward her. She studied them, her hand still clutching her sword, unsure of who they were.

A tall, lanky man took a step toward her. He was about the age Cytherea's parents would have been if they were still alive. "So I hear you're looking for an army to fight the Dark Realm."

Cytherea glanced at Gregor, who nodded as if to encourage her to speak. "Yes," she admitted, "but who are you?"

"This is your army," Gregor said, stepping forward. "Many families have lost their children to the Dark Realm, including these men here. For that, we will fight, and others will fight too. We will fight for our children and their future."

"Th-thank you all." She glanced down as she stumbled over her words, uncomfortable speaking to a group of strangers. "I never imagined I would have an army this quickly, but I will be honored to lead you, with the help of Gregor and others who have trained in matters of war. However, we will need much more than a few men to defeat the army of the Dark Realm."

"We know. This is Drake, the commander of Phoxnay's former army." Gregor casually gestured at the tall man. "I'll let him explain."

Drake. The name tickled a memory until Cytherea recalled Tarquin's voice: *Drake and Edmond had been friends since childhood, and the king trusted him with his life.* Her eyes shot to Drake's. This man had known her parents well. She had so many questions, but this wasn't the time, so she pushed them aside in her mind.

"How can we be sure this is Cytherea and not an impostor?" asked a man in the back of the group.

Gregor swept a thick, hairy arm toward Cytherea, agitated. "You know there have been loyalists watching her for all these years. She can't be an impostor."

"True. But she was captured and put in Ailmar's dungeon. No one has ever escaped Ailmar's dungeon alive," the man continued. "How do we know that Ailmar didn't work his dark magic and somehow send an impostor back to trick us all?"

"Tarquin's son, Kenric, was raised with her, and he knows her. He is lying in the back room recovering from wounds he received while trying to protect her." Gregor's impatience with this man's questions was evident in his stance. "Besides, look at her! She is the very image of her mother, and the eyes—you can see her eyes. Even Ailmar's magic couldn't duplicate all of that."

"Gregor is right," Drake interjected. "She is the mirror likeness of Queen Lisel in both appearance and mannerisms. No magic can duplicate that."

"But we don't know how powerful Ailmar's magic really is. How can we be sure?" another man asked.

Tired of being ignored and talked about like she wasn't there, Cytherea took a step toward them hesitantly, then steeled herself and said, "I am Cytherea, daughter of King Edmond and Queen Lisel, of the house of Sainte-d'Agneaux, heir to the throne of Phoxnay, and I carry my father's sword." She raised her sword, and the gemstone, which had been concealed by her cloak, sent its light to the four corners of the room.

The men all gasped and fell to one knee with heads bowed.

"Please . . . please stand," she said, her voice revealing her discomfort. "I understand your questions, but I ask that you trust those you know—Gregor, Kenric, Drake, and others—that I am who I say that I am. We have all lost much at Ailmar's hand, and I would consider it an honor to fight him with you."

They all stood silently.

"Now, if we are finished debating my identity"—Cytherea turned toward Drake—"please explain where we might find an army."

"Your Highness—"

"Cytherea is fine," she interrupted. "Please dispense with all formality until I have a throne to claim." The words felt odd to say. Her royal lineage had always been a distant concept, but now it was becoming reality.

"Of course," Drake began again. "The people in this room represent just a few of those that are still loyal to the Phoxnay crown. They all know the tale of your escape and have been told stories of your life in Ceka. However, for many of them, your presence here is still much like seeing a character from a dream or a childhood tale come to life. For me, it is a day I have been waiting many years to see."

Cytherea sheathed her sword. "I think everyone, myself included, is trying to grasp all that has come to pass in recent days. But for now, I think we should concentrate on the matters at hand. How many fighting men are in this village and in the surrounding villages that are within a couple of days' ride?"

"Not enough to fight the Dark Realm," Drake answered flatly. "And if there were enough loyalists, we wouldn't be an army. Ailmar's men train their whole lives for battle. The men here are just farmers and merchants. Phoxnay's army was either killed, captured, or dispersed throughout the countryside."

Cytherea paused to consider that information. "Tell me more about the loyalists. How many are they?"

"I do not have an exact number, as many have been in hiding, but it is not a small number, perhaps as many as one thousand. I am also confident that those numbers will increase once word spreads that we are building an army to defeat Ailmar."

"What about other kingdoms? Gregor has told me that Klobyn is loyal, but are there others?"

"I believe so, Your—Cytherea," Drake corrected himself. "Others that are sympathetic to our plight haven't yet been willing to turn Ailmar's wrath in their own direction. However, we believe they will help us when they see we have a chance at defeating Ailmar's army with you and the Sword of Phoxnay."

Hope welled up in Cytherea's heart. This was a start. It would take time—*probably more time than we have*—to raise an army. But this was the seed she needed. "Can the loyalists send word to the villages throughout what was once Phoxnay and to any other kingdoms that might be willing to join with us? Discreetly?"

"Yes, I can do that," Drake answered.

Cytherea began to pace, trying to determine how long it would take to accomplish this. She was hopeful that Everard would be on her side, however, a part of her knew there was a chance that he could be leading the Dark Realm army to them even now.

"What is bothering you, Cytherea?" Gregor asked, brows knit together.

"I don't know if we will have enough time to gather the army we need," she answered uneasily.

"Why is that?"

"My brother, Everard."

"Your brother is alive?" Drake asked incredulously.

"Yes, he came to see me when I was held prisoner in Ailmar's castle and—"

"What do you mean he came to see you?" Drake interrupted.

"It seems that after he was kidnapped during our escape, Everard was raised as Ailmar's son," she finished, and looked around at their faces.

"Are you saying that the prince of the Dark Realm is your brother, Everard?" Drake asked.

"Yes." Cytherea heard gasps from those in the room.

"Derian is the son of Ailmar, and a dangerous force." Drake's eyes narrowed.

"He was here last night, and he knows that Cytherea is here," Gregor said.

The room became quiet, and Cytherea watched the faces of the men as they took in the information. Gregor remained silent and refused to defend Cytherea this time. He didn't like her connection to Ailmar's son.

Drake was the first to break the silence. "We were told that one of the heirs of Phoxnay had been captured by Ailmar the night of your escape from Phoxnay, but we assumed that the child had been killed. It is also known that Prince Derian is rarely seen outside the castle walls, so very few people know what he looks like. But what makes you think he is your brother?"

"I have seen him, and so have Kenric and Gregor." Cytherea hesitated, unsure how to explain all that had happened between her and Everard. "There is no mistaking our likeness. He also has the birthmark, and other things that prove he is truly my brother. Not only that, he helped me escape Ailmar's dungeon."

"So he is on our side?"

"No! He is not on our side," snapped Gregor suddenly, causing Cytherea to jump. "He helped the men that took our boy!"

"It appears that his allegiance is still to Ailmar," Cytherea said, trying to stay calm and ignoring Gregor's outburst, "but he has helped me more than once."

"Did your brother lead the raid on this village?"

"No, Everard came to talk to me. The soldiers were looking for both of us when they raided the town. My brother is only beginning to remember his childhood, but he has already shown some loyalty to me." Her voice was more confident than she felt.

"Are you sure they were looking for him?" asked Gregor. "Or did he lead them here and find you by accident?"

Could Everard be deceiving me? Cytherea wondered. Did her brother bring the soldiers here? She didn't know, but she couldn't show that uncertainty here. "If that was the case, Gregor," she replied firmly, "he would have seized me then. He had many opportunities. But he didn't. Ailmar may have brainwashed Everard, but he doesn't control him. There is hope for him yet."

39

"Father," Derian called calmly as he strode into Ailmar's throne room.

Ailmar was not so calm. "Where have you been?" he asked as he stood, his wooden chair sliding back from the table.

"I was bored and wanted to go for a long ride."

"Don't lie to me, Derian!" Ailmar shouted, slamming his fist on the table in front of him. "You have been gone for two days. That is much more than a long ride to alleviate boredom." Ailmar's face was red, and his eyes blackened as he lowered his voice. "Don't think that I won't kill you for betraying me just because you are my son."

Derian tried to still the fear rising inside him as he shared the false story he had devised, but he wondered why he felt the need to lie to his father, and why he felt compelled to protect this girl he had just met.

"You are worried for nothing, Father. I simply went for a ride in the countryside, and my horse began limping, so I decided to let it rest awhile in a nearby village."

"Why did you leave without telling me or taking your

guards?" Ailmar stepped around the table, moving directly in front of Derian.

Derian instinctively took a step back. "It was a simple ride. I didn't think I needed guards, and I didn't want to bother you with something so mundane."

"You were seen with the girl in the dungeon before she escaped." Ailmar leaned toward Derian until he stood nearly on top of him. Spittle that smelled of rotted meat fell on Derian's face when his father spoke again. "Did you help that girl escape?"

More nervous now, Derian steadied himself under the piercing glare of his father. He should tell his father the truth, that the girl was a witch and had cast some sort of spell over him, but he wanted to learn more about her and who she really was.

"Of course not! When some guards told me that you had captured a girl, I went to see her just out of simple curiosity. I was there only a few minutes before I realized that she was obviously unwell, telling wild, fantastical tales, so I left with little conversation between us. I didn't even realize that she had escaped. That must have happened after I left on my ride. I trust you found her and returned her to her cell?"

Ailmar spun around and stalked across the room. "No, we have not, and I expect you to join the others as they search the surrounding villages until she is found and brought back!" His anger echoed through the high ceilings of the chamber and startled Derian, who had seen his father's wrath on many occasions.

"Of course, Father. I will head out at dawn."

"Bring her back to me, Derian! And if she carries a weapon with her, bring it directly to me. Am I clear?"

Derian stood with his head cocked in curiosity, studying his father as he paced in rage. "What type of weapon do you think a girl would carry? A dagger, perhaps?"

Ailmar hesitated before answering. "It's a sword, and it is extremely valuable. Bring me the girl and her sword, and then I will give you the honor of killing her."

A slight smile crossed Derian's lips. He had seen that sword and the glow of its gemstone in Cytherea's hand. If his father was interested in it, then it must have more than just monetary value. And now he was determined to discover what made the girl's sword so important.

Ailmar stopped pacing and turned to look at Derian, who was distracted by the thought of this new information.

"You may leave me," Ailmar said with a dismissive wave of his hand.

Derian hurried from his father's presence.

His hands shook as he headed down the corridor toward his chambers. He ignored bowing servants and focused only on the words of his father. Ailmar was set on killing this strange girl with the green eyes, but Derian wasn't through with her yet. His treacherous mind kept bringing up memories of a life he didn't know, and she was certainly to blame. Ailmar had cared for him and given him everything he could want. *He wouldn't have lied to me about where I came from—would he?*

But even if his father had lied, did it really matter? *How can I even be questioning my father?* Cytherea was a witch, and she had cast some sort of curse on him. He had to keep her away from his father long enough to discover why Ailmar was so concerned about her and her sword.

Derian closed the door to his chambers and leaned against it. He would aid in the search, yes, and would keep the searching soldiers away from Haight for now. In the meantime, he would work to overcome the curse and the foreign feelings and memories until his mind became clear once again. His father would find her eventually, but at least Derian would have time to decide whether or not he wanted her dead. If so, perhaps he'd take her sword for himself and figure out why his father was so interested in it.

40

Cytherea stretched out the aches in her joints and muscles after sleeping on the floor by Kenric's side. Anna had made her a pallet from the extra blankets she could find, but it was still the floor. Cytherea pulled on her boots, hooked her scabbard around her waist, and stepped gently into the front room, attempting to avoid making any sound. She pulled her cloak over her head and then opened the door to step outside, her body braced against the chill. The cold sharpened her senses and cleared her mind, allowing her thoughts to gain clarity after a restless night.

She and the men had been up late trying to figure out how many fighting men they could gather and how quickly. The network of loyalists was already on the move, riding on the fastest horses to spread the word. An army was gathering, but would they be ready in time?

Her thoughts eventually drifted to Everard. If she fought the Dark Realm, would Everard aid her, or was he using her for his own purpose? At first, she had been so sure that he would have a good heart despite being raised by Ailmar, but she couldn't ignore his conflicting actions or everyone else's distrust of him.

She shook her head to rid herself of that thought. He was her brother. He'd helped her escape Ailmar's castle, and he'd helped Kenric. But what was this bizarre bargain he'd tried to make with her? *Why does he think I am a witch?* Most of all, why wouldn't he stop his own soldiers from taking the children from the arms of their mothers in Haight?

Her heart and mind were both confused on what to think about Everard, but for now, she needed to focus on other things. She would discover Everard's true character in time. Meanwhile, she and the loyalists had to come up with a plan to defeat Ailmar's army.

She reentered the cottage and passed through the kitchen, where Anna was already awake and preparing the morning meal. Anna looked up briefly before she turned back to her work. Her pain was evident in every movement, even though her tears were likely spent. Cytherea drew close and put a hand on her shoulder. Anna peered up at her dully.

"I'm sorry," Cytherea whispered hoarsely as tears welled in her own eyes.

Anna laid a hand on top of Cytherea's. "You cannot take responsibility for things done by those ruled by evil." She let out a sigh. "You did not take my child from me. Ailmar's soldiers did that."

"But they came here looking for—"

"It doesn't matter why they came, only that they came here with evil intent. Evil men did this. Not you."

Cytherea dried her eyes and held Anna's gaze. "I will bring him back to you. You have my word."

"I know you will." Anna smiled at Cytherea before a haunted looked came over her face. "I can't bear to think about what they might be doing to Brockton even now."

"When I was in the dungeon, I could hear the children crying all around me, but they were not being hurt physically, just alone and afraid. Kenric told me that Ailmar left them alone for a while as the first step toward his brainwashing, so we have a little time."

Anna stopped her work for a moment and took a deep breath, taking in the information from Cytherea.

"Brockton is stronger and wiser than his age," Cytherea added. "He will survive, and I will bring him back and place him in your arms once again."

Anna went back to her cooking, and Cytherea watched her. She knew that Anna's excessive cooking and cleaning over the last day had kept her mind off things she couldn't bear, so Cytherea left her alone and went back to check on Kenric.

Cytherea picked up the small stool in the corner, placed it next to Kenric's bed, and sat down, squashing the feeling of helplessness that gripped her throat. Anna seemed so sure that Cytherea would succeed, but maybe that was because she was the only hope Anna had of seeing Brockton again one day. Regardless of Anna's reasons for believing, Cytherea had given her word, and she would bring Brockton home or die trying.

Cytherea shifted her focus to Kenric, whose face seemed more relaxed. His forehead was no longer beaded with feverish sweat. She dipped a rag in the bucket Gregor kept filled with water by the bed and gently wiped Kenric's face. The healer's potion seemed to be working, because his sleep seemed more restful. She watched him and tried to match her breathing to his, hoping it would help her relax.

She couldn't shake the thought that he might have died trying to protect her. And now she was going to lead an army of old soldiers, farmers, and craftsmen to risk their lives fighting the trained soldiers of the Dark Realm? How many more would die by following her into battle? But then again, many more would die or be condemned to a life of slavery if they didn't stop Ailmar. She knew in her heart that they had to try, but more than that, they had to succeed. She had to stop allowing herself to doubt. Those who would follow her needed to see her strength and resolve without a hint of uncertainty.

Leading her people against Ailmar was her destiny. It was

what her parents had fought and died for, and she would do the same, guided by the power of the sword that her father had wielded years ago. Cytherea closed her eyes and drew in a long breath. Her mind reached into the past, and she once again heard Tarquin's voice: "When you are older and the time is right, you will return to take your rightful place as queen."

Ailmar had destroyed her home and murdered Tarquin, and he had done the same to the homes of the people of Phoxnay and many of their loved ones so many years ago. They had lived with their loss much longer than she had. It was time for Ailmar to pay. She knew that now was the time, and her destiny was calling her to follow in her father's steps. It was time to allow the Sword of Phoxnay to fully empower her so she could lead her people and destroy the evil that had taken so much from them.

Kenric shifted, forcing Cytherea from her thoughts.

"Kenric? Can you hear me?" she asked gently.

His body stilled.

"Kenric?" she tried again. "Please wake up." She paused, searching his face, but he didn't stir again. "Kenric? Please wake up."

"You are getting bossy these days," he mumbled with his eyes still closed.

Cytherea shook his shoulder gently, unable to hide her excitement. "How do you feel?"

"Like I've been kicked in the head by a horse. And my leg doesn't feel much better."

"The healer said her potion might make your head ache but that it would pass. As for your leg, it looks a lot better than it did yesterday."

"Yesterday?" he said, opening his eyes. He tried to sit up, winced, and lay back down, cradling his head in both hands. "What happened? Where is Everard?"

"Everard went back to Ailmar's castle and—"

"I knew it!" Kenric interrupted. "I knew he would betray you!"

"He helped me save you."

Kenric's eyes narrowed. "What do you mean?"

"He showed up after the attack and helped carry you back here."

"What did he want?"

"What do you mean? He was helping you."

"I don't believe Everard would do anything without demanding something in return." Kenric looked up at her. "So what did he want? What was the bargain he wanted to make with you?"

"He didn't want anything." Cytherea couldn't tell Kenric about their conversation before he left with the soldiers—at least for now.

"You don't think it's convenient that he *happened* to show up to help after we were attacked by some of *his* soldiers?"

"I don't know what to think right now, Kenric, except to focus on raising an army. I'll have to figure Everard out later."

As they spoke, Anna ducked into the room and set a plate of food on the small table next to the bed. "Welcome back, Kenric!" She started to walk to the other side of the bed, but before she did, she rested her hand on Cytherea's shoulder. "Cytherea, please have something to eat. You will need all your strength in the days to come."

Cytherea reached over and picked up the plate. Anna was right. Cytherea couldn't fight if she were weak. She tried to eat while Anna checked Kenric's wounds and applied more of the healer's salve.

After tending to Kenric and convincing him he was hungry, Anna left to get him some food. While she was out of the room, Cytherea took the opportunity to tell Kenric about Brockton.

"I need to tell you something, but you have to promise me that you will stay calm," Cytherea began.

"What's wrong?" This time, Kenric forced himself to sit up, ignoring his pounding head. "Tell me." Kenric grew impatient.

"Quiet." Cytherea glanced in Anna's direction, but she was busy and not paying attention to them.

"Tell me, Cyth." He remained quiet, but his tone was full of frustration.

"The soldiers . . ." She had a hard time making herself say it out loud. She took a deep breath and tried again. "The soldiers took Brockton."

"No!" he shouted, but then shot a look toward Anna, who glanced through the door at his outburst and then turned back to her stew. He lowered his voice. "How is Anna dealing with this so well?"

"She's not. I think she has blocked it from her mind and is focused on doing what she can to help us get Brockton back to her."

"I'll help." Kenric tried to move his legs over the side of the bed with a grimace.

Cytherea put her hand on his shoulder. "There's nothing you can do right now. We will meet with some of the loyalists here later this morning. Until then, lie down. The best thing you can do is rest for a little more."

After Kenric finished off two helpings of stew, Cytherea made him promise he would rest. Then she took up her sword and went out to the paddock behind the barn to practice some drills. When she passed Gregor's forge, he was already busy turning any scraps of metal he had into something sharp that could be used as a weapon. They would not be much to look at, but they would cut and stab, and that was all that mattered.

Upon Cytherea entering the barn, the horses perked up their ears, and Aherne's head began to bob as usual. She released the horses into the paddock to get some air and decided to do her drills in the barn instead while Aherne and Tredan periodically poked their heads in to check on her.

After an hour of working with her father's sword, her arms burned, and she kept missing her mark on the barn post.

Frustrated, she threw the sword to the ground and sat in the dirt, glaring sullenly out at the horses, who were dozing in the bit of sunlight that peeked between the ever-present clouds. As she watched them, Cytherea was reminded again of the farm.

Home.

Ailmar's men had destroyed her home and killed Tarquin. Ailmar had to be stopped.

"But how can I stop him if I can't even use a sword?" she shouted to the empty barn.

Aherne raised his head abruptly at her voice, ears swiveling, searching for danger. No one was there, so he relaxed and watched Cytherea with heavy eyelids.

Cytherea stood and circled the barn, continuing her solitary conversation. "Why would anyone follow me into battle against the Dark Realm? Who do I think I am?" She plopped back down in the dirt, frustration coursing through her body.

Aherne clopped up behind her. His breath on the back of her neck reassured her, and she turned to pet his soft muzzle. Playfully, he shoved his head against her back.

"Aherne!" Cytherea gently scolded. "I am not in the mood to play. Leave me alone."

But he kept pushing her until she finally stood up.

"There! I'm up! Are you happy?"

Ignoring her, Aherne moved to her sword on the ground and stood next to it, turning his massive head back toward Cytherea.

"What are you doing?"

He tossed his head and pranced around her, bumping her with his shoulder toward the sword.

"What, are you my trainer now?" Annoyed, she stomped over to the sword and picked it up. "How can I bear my father's sword? I'm not worthy of it."

Aherne stomped his hooves, and Cytherea turned and stared at him.

"What are you trying to tell me, Aherne?"

His massive head bobbed up and down. He hopped from fore-hoof to forehoof, raising dirt and dust until the air around them was thick with it and the daylight was momentarily dimmed. In that cloud of dust, the gem in the hilt glowed even more fiercely.

She looked back up at Aherne as the dust settled. "All right. You win. I'll keep practicing until I get it right." Seemingly satisfied, Aherne sauntered back out into the paddock and settled himself for another nap. Cytherea raised the sword to continue until it was time to meet again with the loyalists.

41

Cytherea, Kenric, Gregor, and Drake sat at a small table inside the village inn, which was crowded with loyalists. They were mostly men, but a few women mingled among them. Cytherea could feel their questioning eyes piercing her as they sat waiting for the meeting to begin. Her hands began to sweat and her confidence began to falter again. Kenric laid a hand on her shoulder, and she glanced at Gregor, who gave her a nod of encouragement.

Cytherea forced herself to her feet, preparing to address them. She looked around the room and realized that most of the men there dwarfed her, even seated. Her voice seemed to stick in her throat, and silently, she wished that Kenric would stand up and take over, but he couldn't. She knew she had to stand on her own now. Only through the power of the Sword of Phoxnay could Ailmar be defeated, and it was her destiny as the heir to the Phoxnay throne to wield it. The responsibility weighed heavily on her. The loyalists had waited so long for her to lead them, to reclaim what was theirs. Her bloodline was required for them to defeat the evil that had taken everything from them, and it was time for her to take her rightful place now. Her eyes went back to

Kenric, Gregor, and Drake. Once again, Gregor simply nodded, a silent nudge.

"Thank you all for coming," she said. "I—"

"I thought we were here to talk about fighting the Dark Realm, Gregor," one man interrupted, "so why is this girl here?"

Others murmured in agreement.

Cytherea clenched her fists. Gregor seemed to be worried that she might bolt from the room at any moment, because he put his arm out behind her and gently pushed her forward.

"Let her speak!" Gregor boomed. "Cytherea is our sovereign, and as such, she deserves your respect."

"How do we know she is who she claims?" another man questioned.

Several voices answered.

"Look at her face—she looks like Queen Lisel."

"She has the eyes."

"Tarquin's son was entrusted with her safety—who are we to doubt him?"

"Cytherea?" Gregor looked at her and then shifted his glance to her sword.

Cytherea flinched slightly but then straightened her back, lifted her chin, and stepped forward on her own this time, drawing her sword as she repeated what she had told the smaller group the night before, calmly and clearly.

"I am Cytherea, daughter of King Edmond and Queen Lisel, of the house of Sainte-d'Agneaux, heir to the throne of Phoxnay, and I carry my father's sword." She raised the sword, and the gemstone blazed.

All those in the room gasped, even those who had seen it the night prior. When no one challenged her further, she slid her sword back into its scabbard and began the meeting.

"Ailmar and his men have taken your children, and they almost killed Kenric, Tarquin's son and my defender, during this last raid. The Dark Realm must be stopped, and all your children returned to their homes." She took a breath. "I will fight them alone if I must, but I am asking you to join me." She glanced around at each face, and her heart raced. Blank faces watched her.

In the silence, Gregor rose from his seat, turned toward Cytherea, and knelt before her. "I pledge my loyalty to Princess Cytherea, rightful heir to the throne of Phoxnay. I will follow you into battle against the Dark Realm." He bowed his head.

She stared at him. Kenric immediately did the same, despite the pain etched in his face as he bent his wounded leg. Gradually, each man and woman followed Gregor's lead until all of them knelt before her.

Cytherea was stunned, the true force and truth of her heritage making her numb. *What should I do now?* She stood before them at a loss.

Eventually, Gregor raised his head. "These people have pledged themselves to your service, Your Highness."

Say something.

"Th-Thank you," she stammered awkwardly. "Let's raise an army!" Her cheeks felt hot, and she swallowed her embarrassment.

Gregor unsuccessfully stifled a laugh. The other men looked at her in confusion. Cytherea shot Gregor a pleading look, and he finally stood up. "You heard her, men! Let's raise an army!"

They all sat back down at the tables.

Cytherea, trying to sound confident, relayed the information from her discussions with Gregor, Drake, and others, "Some of the loyalists are riding to bring the others here. We will become an army by gathering all those who are currently dispersed. With your help, we will turn farmers and merchants into soldiers. We will begin training today with those that are here and then with the others as they arrive." Her eyes flitted from face to face around the room as she thought back to Gregor's and Drake's instructions last night about what roles she needed to appoint while waiting for the other loyalists to arrive. "Are there any former soldiers among us today?"

One man near the back of the room stood. His hair was gray, but he still looked healthy and robust.

Cytherea addressed him. "What's your name, sir?"

"Marcus, Your Highness."

"Marcus, you, Drake, and Kenric will head up the training. Gather any other former soldiers to help you as they arrive. You will need to train in hand-to-hand combat." She paused. "Be mindful of the fact that our weapons will be whatever each man has available—axes, daggers, farming tools, farrier's tools, and the like. Anything that can be sharpened can be a weapon. Gregor has offered the use of his forge for any that need their weapons sharpened or to turn other items into weapons." She surveyed the room. "Is there anyone here that can run the forge? I need Gregor with me, because I'm appointing him as my second-in-command."

Anna stood. "Gregor taught me how to use everything in his shop, and I can train others that are not able to fight." Gregor beamed at her with pride.

Cytherea smiled. "Thank you, Anna." Then she turned back to the others. "Ailmar knows I'm alive, and it is only a matter of time before more soldiers come looking for me. When his spies tell him that we are gathering here and that we are raising an army, he will muster the soldiers of the Dark Realm against us. Time is short. Every person must do their part."

The room became loud as those present began talking among themselves. They seemed eager to get started. Despite the support of those in the room, her confidence faltered. She took a moment to herself, grasped the sword's hilt, and closed her eyes. The heat from the gemstone gave her courage, and it was almost as if she could hear the voices of those who had held it before her giving her the courage she needed in the moment. She took a few minutes to breathe in the sword's power the way Kenric had taught her to do whenever her mind was unfocused or unsure. The sword's hilt pulsed within her grip, and she felt her mind calm. After a few moments, she opened her eyes and began quieting everyone before continuing.

"Those that can't fight, follow Anna to help with the weapons. Those that can fight, gather anything that can be used as a weapon and meet in the pastures beyond the village for drills and training. Those familiar with the area surrounding this village, remain here to discuss where the village's defenses need to be fortified and where we can use natural defenses."

As they headed out, Cytherea raised her voice over them again. "We can't let Ailmar and his evil continue to rule our land, and we can't let him take our children. We will fight and we will win!" She drew and raised her sword, and the others raised their own weapons in reply, a spattering of farm-made tools, heirloom swords, and clenched fists. "For Phoxnay!" she shouted.

"For Phoxnay!" the others shouted in unison.

The gem in the Sword of Phoxnay radiated brilliance, bathing all those in the room with its glow as they headed out.

42

Marcus and Kenric found two additional former Phoxnay soldiers in a nearby village, and they met with the men who assembled for training in a large group. When more soldiers arrived, they would be able to break into smaller groups for more specific training. The village men were strong from working on their farms and at their various trades; as a result, their fighting skills improved quickly.

Each morning, the men would assemble outside of the village in the large open fields, which were normally used for the village horses and sheep to graze. The lush grasses and vibrant wildflowers were soon trampled under the feet of men and horses. Makeshift tents were hastily erected within the tree line surrounding the field to house Cytherea's growing army. The drills began well before dawn and ended long after night took hold.

Work on fortifying Haight's wall also progressed ahead of schedule, and Gregor's forge burned bright all through the day and night, creating and sharpening weapons. Loyalist agents monitored the activity of Ailmar's forces, and shockingly, their search parties were keeping away from Haight for the time being.

Their luck wouldn't last forever, and they had to use every minute to prepare before Ailmar discovered them and mustered his army against them.

In the following days, more men arrived, bringing news that additional riders had been sent out to reach the loyalists in villages in the farthest reaches. Cytherea was shocked by the number of men who were enlisting. *But will they all get here in time?* She wanted to believe in Everard, but she knew that he was still loyal to Ailmar, and he might lead him to her any day. A small part of her hoped he was keeping the searches away from Haight on purpose. Every day that passed meant another day closer to the return of Ailmar's soldiers.

As Kenric's health improved, he was able to help for more extended periods each day to train and plan. One morning, he and Cytherea walked through the makeshift campsites that were spread as far as she could see along the edges of the forest. She stopped to thank those she passed while Kenric went to help Marcus with the day's training.

After a little while, Cytherea headed onto the training fields. Several people were already there sparring together and warming up. When she got closer, she stopped and stared in bewilderment. Some of those loyalists sparring had long braids down their backs and wore dresses that had been hastily modified into breeches.

"Surprised?" Gregor startled her when he came up from behind.

"A little. Are they here to fight?" Cytherea asked and continued watching the women spar.

"Yes. They want their children back, and they will follow the hand that wields the sword. They'll fight with you."

Cytherea smiled. The young women wielded their weapons with remarkable skill. "Even though Tarquin taught me some fighting skills, I hadn't considered that women would join with us to fight. Their bravery inspires me. And they'll give us an unexpected increase in numbers."

"Yes, they will," Gregor answered. "Many more wanted to join us, but some have been assigned to stay behind and care for the farms and the children still remaining."

"Those women back home serve as warriors as much as those that fight."

"Yes, they do." After a pause, Gregor raised his voice for all to hear. "All right, everyone! Form ranks! Let's get started!"

Cytherea hurried to join the others in fighting tactics and battle maneuvers. She was surprised to find how quickly the men and women learned the basic and even advanced fighting techniques. They had not fought before, but the hard work in their daily lives had given them the strength of seasoned soldiers. Cytherea was relieved, because that meant they only needed to learn how to use their strength in battle. When she tired from the strenuous training sessions, she looked to those around her to find the resolve to keep going and push her limitations.

After another exhausting day, the sun set over the village, wrapping it in silent shadows. She put Aherne back in the barn to rest for the night, deciding to walk back to the training field after she ate.

She stopped in at the forge to see how things were going in there before heading to the small cottage she had quickly come to love. She blinked at the dark sky and marveled at the myriad of stars she could see on this cloudless night. How could something as evil as the Dark Realm exist in a world that contained such beauty? Her sore arms shifted her attention down to her sword. Her father's sword. The Sword of Phoxnay. She raised it to eye level and rubbed the dirt off the gemstones. The main stone began to glimmer, but the smaller stones remained unlit. Would they ever glow one day? She had so many questions about this sword, but no one was left to answer them. She sighed and continued into the cottage.

She set her sword on the table and sidled toward the fire. Anna was there cooking for any who came in hungry.

"The stew is ready. Sit down and have some," Anna said.

Too tired to speak, Cytherea strode toward the table and sat down.

"Have you gotten any sleep in the past few days?"

"Not much." Cytherea smiled up at her. "Have you?"

Anna gave her a tired smile.

The cottage door opened again. Kenric shouldered in, bringing an armful of wood for the fire. Cytherea was so relieved to see him up and about and taking on some routine tasks, nearly healed after such a frightening wound.

"It's about time you started contributing to the work around here," Cytherea teased.

He leaned against the doorframe and smiled at her. "You have quite an army building out there."

"More keep coming every day. And did you see the women, Kenric? The women are coming to fight, too!" she exclaimed breathlessly.

"Women? Fighting?" Anna asked in shock.

"Yes, they say if I can fight, then they can fight! They are here to save their children!" Despite her exhaustion, Cytherea struggled to keep from dancing across the room. "They are all here to fight for Phoxnay!"

Kenric laughed at her enthusiasm. "You did it, Cyth. You've raised yourself an army!" He limped to the hearth and laid the wood by the fire. The small limp was all that remained of his wound.

"Don't overdo things, Kenric," Anna warned him. "You are still healing."

Nodding in obedience, Kenric sat next to Cytherea at the table.

Anna continued, "I must take some food to Gregor, or he will never eat. Can one of you watch the fire?"

"Yes. One of us will. Gregor is at the training fields," Cytherea told her.

After Anna slipped out the door, Kenric turned to Cytherea with a grim look on his face. "I need to discuss something with you."

"Of course. Is something wrong?"

"I want to take some of the men and try to rescue Brockton and the others."

"We can't spare any men, Kenric." Her voice was on the verge of cracking. "And I can't spare you." Cytherea panicked at the thought of going into battle without Kenric.

"Marcus is fully capable of training our people. And we received word that the king of Klobyn is sending men to help."

"Klobyn is several days away."

"I know, but they are already on their way. I can head them off and take some of their men with me toward Ailmar's castle. I won't take any men from those already here."

"Then what?" Cytherea asked curtly. "You've seen how impossible it is to get into that castle, and you can't walk a regiment of soldiers through the front gate."

"We won't. We will wait and watch. You know Ailmar will get word of your growing army, but you don't know when. We will watch and send word when we see signs that he is readying his men, which will give you time to be prepared before they reach you." He paused, trying to read her expression, but she kept her emotions off her face. "Then, while some of his soldiers are away, we will overtake any guards left behind and free the children."

"You are assuming that Ailmar will leave his castle virtually empty of soldiers."

"It is our best chance. You know it, Cytherea! We have to try."

"Fine." She relented with a long sigh. Kenric was right, but she dreaded not having him close by. He had always been there for her, for as long as she could remember, but she had given her word that she would bring those children home, especially Brockton. Letting Kenric go was her best chance of that.

"Thank you!" Kenric clasped his hands. "We will bring those boys home again."

Cytherea took a deep breath. *This could be a death wish, Kenric.* But she couldn't bring herself to say it. Instead, she said, "You can leave tonight, but first, brief me on our numbers so far."

Relief flashed in Kenric's eyes at the change in topic. He began, "We had a large group arrive this morning, maybe as many as one hundred, and another, at least as large, was just arriving when I left to come here."

"How many do you think we have in total now?" She dared to hope for a positive report.

"I don't know exactly with so many arriving. Maybe nearly one thousand fighting men, with more coming throughout the day and night. Gregor will get a count in the morning from each village leader."

"The Dark Realm likely has many times that number." Her stomach dropped with this realization. "Am I leading these people to their death? We don't have enough people to match Ailmar's army, and I don't know how much more time we have to train."

"Winning a battle isn't always about numbers, Cytherea," Kenric reassured, taking her hand. "War is more about the mind. It's the smartest opponent that will win"—he squeezed her hand for reassurance—"and our army is smarter."

Cytherea nodded, holding back the tears that threatened to escape.

"And anyway, we have the healers. Ailmar banned them from his service before your parents' time because he feared their magic. They did an incredible job on my leg. That means that our wounded will heal, but theirs will not."

He was right. They could heal most deadly wounds in a few

days, and many minor wounds in an afternoon. Cytherea smiled, feeling more confident.

Kenric went on. "Many Dark Realm soldiers have been so brainwashed that they are likely unable to have an independent thought, especially in battle. That means they can only follow orders from their commanders or Ailmar. They don't have the ability to adapt to a change in battle tactics from us, which is why we are training our fighters to be able to adapt quickly and easily."

"What do we do about those soldiers that aren't brainwashed and fight with Ailmar of their own free will?"

"I believe there are fewer of those, and we will be able to fight them off." He paused. "But the entire Dark Realm army is under whatever kind of dark magic Ailmar possesses."

"And how do we fight that?"

He stood and picked up her sword. "We get you and your sword to Ailmar."

"So we have a chance?"

"Yes, we do. A good chance, I believe, and all these men and women are coming here because they believe that too."

"It's just so much responsibility."

"Better get used to it, my future queen."

43

A courier sprinted through the dim corridors of Ailmar's castle. The dust from a long ride billowed from the tails of his cloak. He pushed past guards that tried to slow him as he drew near to Ailmar's chambers.

"I must speak to His Majesty immediately," the messenger insisted when he was blocked from reaching the door. "This cannot wait until morning!"

"His Majesty is sleeping. Are you certain this can't wait?" the guard growled, pushing the intruder back. "We will both feel His Majesty's wrath if you wake him with something trivial."

The messenger did not relent, even after the guard's somber warning. "I have to speak to His Majesty now!" he shouted, shifting from foot to foot. Sweat spilled down his forehead.

"Very well." The guard pushed on the door, which creaked open slowly.

The messenger pushed his way through. "Your Majesty! I have urgent news for you!"

The last few words woke Ailmar, who angrily rose from his bed, pulling on his night cloak and moving swiftly toward the messenger and the guard in the doorway. "What is the meaning of this intrusion?"

Both men fell to their knees in fear.

"Your Majesty! Forgive me, but I would not have disturbed you if I did not have extremely urgent news." His voice was trembling.

"What is it, then? Tell me before I have you killed or taken to the dungeon and tortured!"

With nothing to lose, the man stood. "The people in the villages of Phoxnay are amassing an army."

"Bah! Urgent news?" Ailmar's laugh echoed through the corridor. "A peasant army! They are no threat to me." More guards arrived to investigate the commotion. "Take this man to the dungeon," Ailmar commanded and turned back into his chamber.

"But, Your Majesty!" the messenger shouted as he was dragged away, "Their army is growing daily, and their leader claims to be an heir to the throne of Phoxnay!"

Ailmar clenched his fist, wrenching the door fully open. "Phoxnay does not exist! If this man speaks any more treasonous lies, kill him!" After the hysterical man's pleas for mercy faded around a corner, Ailmar pointed at a remaining guard. "Bring Prince Derian to me immediately."

Moments later, Derian burst into Ailmar's bedchamber, still adjusting his uniform. "What is it, Father? Are you unwell?"

Ailmar clasped his hands behind his back, staring out his window into the darkness. "What did the female prisoner tell you when you spoke to her?"

Derian's heart stopped. He swallowed. "Why do you ask me

about a prisoner in the middle of the night? I barely spoke to her. She only spoke with the ramblings of a witch."

Ailmar whipped around, eyes alight with rage. "Don't deceive me! I have reports that you were seen in the corridors with her before she escaped. You told me she was mad. Then you left for a two-day jaunt." He inched closer until Derian caught the full pungent scent of his breath, and he had to force himself not to retch at the putrid odor. "And now she cannot be found despite your efforts—with half my men?" Ailmar's eyes burned into his son.

Derian pressed his lips together and lifted his chin.

"I ask you again. What do you know about the *girl*?" The last word came with such force that Derian took a step back.

His mouth had dried. His heart was racing, and his mind was a storm of confusion. He had scoured the countryside for a glimmer of truth among the rumors but had been unable to verify Cytherea's claims. He was ill-equipped to deal with his father's wrath. His hesitation sent the fire of Ailmar's hand across his face. Derian stumbled and dropped to one knee.

"Stand up, you fool!" Ailmar spat. "Tell me what the girl told you!"

Derian struggled to regain his feet and forced his voice to work. "Nothing! I swear it, Father!"

Again, Ailmar sent him to the ground with another blow, but this time, Derian managed to scramble to his feet.

"You are my son! How dare you lie to me!"

"Father, I would never l-lie to you," Derian stammered, even though that was exactly what he was doing. "She only rambled on about a bizarre story. As I told you before, she was mad. She says that I am her brother and that you are not my father, but I told her she was wrong! Your men and I have been searching all the villages. There's no sign of her—"

"What did you say?" The blood drained from Ailmar's face. "What *exactly* did she say?" Ailmar stepped closer.

Derian curled his hands into fists to keep them from shaking. "She thinks that I am her brother, but I told her that she was wrong, Father. Her similar features are an oddity of nature."

Ailmar felt his face turn hot. "Return to your chambers. Don't come out until I ask for you."

"I have done nothing to deserve this treatment," Derian pleaded.

"You have kept secrets from me, Derian, and you've lost my trust. You must prove your allegiance is to me alone."

"We are father and son. My allegiance is to you only!" He raised his fist to his chest. "Do *you* know who this girl is?"

"I know exactly who she is," Ailmar sneered quietly. To Derian, he said, "You will have to prove your loyalty to me after your deception."

"But how, Father? I will do anything." His green eyes pleaded.

"You will get your chance soon enough." Ailmar turned to the guard. "Take my son to his chambers and set someone at his door day and night. He is not to leave for any reason. Is that clear?"

"Yes, Your Majesty." The guard bowed low, taking Derian by the arm and leading him out of Ailmar's chambers.

As soon as Derian was gone, Ailmar called for another guard. "Bring me Commander Yon immediately."

"Yes, Your Majesty."

Ailmar burst into Derian's chamber days later. The room's foul odor stopped his father just inside the doorway.

"Get up! It is time for you to prove your loyalty to me."

"Of course, Father." Derian scrambled to get dressed. "How?"

"We are going to battle, and you will ride with me."

"Battle? Who are we fighting?" They had no enemies that he knew of powerful enough to come against their army.

"The girl and the minuscule army she is bringing against me."

"But why do you and I need to go? She is no threat to us." Derian ran a hand through his greasy hair. "This should be something one regiment could take care of for you, Father."

"No, she is turning the peasants against me, so she must be taught a lesson. The girl and her peasants will feel the full force of the Dark Realm army." He paused, his lip curling at a tray of half-eaten food. "And you, my son, will have the honor of removing her head and placing it on a stake for all to see." Ailmar sniffed the air around his son. "After you bathe. I'll send the servants."

Ailmar turned on his heel and stalked out of the room. Derian felt the blood drain from his face. He sank back onto his rumpled four-poster bed, and his head began spinning with questions. *Who is this girl that my father would summon his entire army against her? What if these dreams are true and she really is my sister? What if she is lying?*

He shook his head, trying to rid himself of the turmoil inside. "It doesn't matter," he said aloud to the empty room. "I must prove myself to my father, and to do that, *I must kill Cytherea.*" With renewed energy, Derian readied himself for battle.

44

After traveling for two days, Kenric slowed Tredan to a stop and peered through the branches of the forest around him at the movement on the trail up the hill. That should be the Klobyn army, but he didn't want to show himself until he was sure. His muscles tense, he nudged Tredan forward for a better view of the road.

The first horse and rider rounded the curve in the road just ahead. Kenric relaxed. The horse and rider proudly displayed the emblem of the house of Klobyn, and Kenric eased Tredan out from the trees onto the road to intersect the path of the Klobyn army. The soldiers drew their swords and signaled to those behind to halt.

"Identify yourself and clear the way for the army of Klobyn!" the first soldier grunted.

"I am Kenric Feydeau, sent to speak to King Aldegunde on behalf of Princess Cytherea of the house of Sainte-d'Agneaux, the rightful heir of the kingdom of Phoxnay!" He opened his hands to show they did not hold a weapon.

"Stay where you are while we relay the message."

Within seconds, a large man approached. He had a wild head

full of long red tresses that fell well beyond his shoulders. His stern face was ruddy from a life in the wind and sun, and his eyes belied a sense of humor behind the grizzled outer shell.

"Kenric Feydeau!" King Aldegunde said. His stern expression turned kind. "You are certainly your father's son. The resemblance is amazing. I was sorry to hear of your father's passing. I know that Edmond trusted him with his very life."

"Thank you." Kenric cleared his throat in an attempt to hold back his emotions.

"I pray you are not here to tell us we are too late."

"No. Ailmar has yet to attack, but we expect it any day now. Our army is growing quickly, and I am sure it will not go unnoticed for much longer."

"Then what message do you bring?"

"Her Highness, Cytherea, has asked me to travel to the Dark Realm to alert her when Ailmar and his army heads out and then to rescue the boys that are currently imprisoned there while Ailmar and his army are fighting. However, our army is so small we couldn't spare any men to help with the rescue. It is my hope that some of your men could be spared to help with this endeavor. I don't know what we will encounter there, but it is our best chance to bring the children back to their families."

"Lagos!" King Aldegunde shouted, and a young man on horseback approached. "Ask Lucan to move his platoon forward to help with this rescue." He turned back to Kenric. "It will take a short time for them to gather provisions to take with you. In the meantime, tell me about Edmond's daughter, Cytherea. Does she have the sword?"

"She does. Cytherea is strong and brave despite her young age. She is passionate about serving the people of Phoxnay."

King Aldegunde smiled. "Much like her father was before her." He leaned in closer. "Has she learned the magic of the sword?"

"She is learning, but she didn't know of the sword's existence until the day my father was killed, and even I know very little of what its powers are."

"In the hands of the Sainte-d'Agneaux bloodline, it holds the power to lead, and it's the only power strong enough to defeat the evil of Ailmar and the Dark Realm, which is what is needed for the battle ahead. However, the power of the Sword of Phoxnay goes much deeper. The sword will teach her as she grows."

They were interrupted by the third platoon, all on horseback, assembling just ahead of them on the road.

"These men will serve you well, Kenric." King Aldegunde stated proudly as he waved his hand toward them.

"I have no doubt, Your Majesty."

After brief orders from their king, the small group broke away and headed toward the Dark Realm while the rest of the Klobyn army continued their path to join Cytherea and her new army.

After a hard day's ride, Kenric and his men entered the Dark Realm. They continued through much of the night until they stopped near the edge of the forest that faced Ailmar's castle. They rested the horses and set up a watch schedule so the others could sleep while they waited for signs that Ailmar's army was on the move.

Kenric felt like he had just closed his eyes when a hand touched his shoulder. He sat up, and the sun hit his eyes as it filtered through the leaves above him. He judged it to be late afternoon.

"The castle gate is being opened, and we have seen a lot of movement just within the walls beyond the gate," the Klobyn soldier informed him.

Kenric stood and sheathed his sword, which he'd kept ready

while he'd slept. "Let the others sleep until we are sure the army is leaving. Then we will watch until they are well on their way before we start making our way to the castle."

He followed the lookout to the tree line and watched. By then, the gate was fully open, and a mass of dark figures moved just inside the castle wall. He wished he could get a closer look, but there was nothing but open fields between the tree line and the castle. He would be easily spotted by any lookouts that might be on top of the castle wall. He had to bide his time until they left.

Within an hour, Kenric heard distant shouting and then the thrum of the soldiers' feet. A black mass spilled from the castle gate and crossed the wooden bridge onto the road leading to Haight. His heart dropped at the reminder that these soldiers were headed toward Cytherea, and he fought against the urge to abandon his mission and return to protect her. He had to reassure himself that Cytherea was not the little girl he used to protect growing up. Now she had the Sword of Phoxnay and was leading an army against Ailmar. He had to push aside his worry about her and focus on rescuing the boys.

Kenric waved Lagos to him. "Take the fastest horse and get the message to Princess Cytherea that Ailmar and his army are on their way. You must get there ahead of Ailmar to give them time to ready themselves. Understood?"

"Yes, sir! I will ride like the wind, sir!"

The young soldier ran into the trees behind and disappeared from his sight.

45

Cytherea woke to Aherne's distant neighing. She rolled herself off the bed, pulled on her riding boots, and grabbed her sword. She ran toward the door and called Gregor's name.

"What is it?" Gregor leaped into the room, dressing as he followed her.

"Something's wrong."

She flew out the door and raced across to the barn. Aherne was kicking at the barn doors, so Cytherea flung them open wide. He bolted past her, nearly knocking over Gregor, who was rounding the corner. After Aherne slid to a stop outside, he bobbed his head toward the road. At the same time, thunderous hoofbeats warned of a horse approaching at a full gallop moments before he appeared out of the darkness.

"They're coming!" the rider shouted.

While she didn't immediately recognize the colors of his riding tunic, Cytherea knew the man was an ally.

One of Kenric's men.

His horse's sides were lathered. Aherne pranced and snorted. The messenger's horse sank onto its hindquarters and came to a sudden halt, nostrils flared.

"Who?" Cytherea shouted, grabbing Aherne's halter to prevent him from further rattling the rider's horse.

The rider tumbled out of the saddle with his head bowed, clearly recognizing her. "Your Highness, Kenric sent me to warn you. The armies of the Dark Realm are heading this way."

"How long do we have?"

"They'll be here by dawn."

Cytherea's face hardened, and she snapped into action. "Gregor, wake the village and the camps! Prepare for war!"

Gregor sprinted into the barn. Within minutes, he emerged bareback on his stallion and galloped past Cytherea without pausing. He rode through the village toward the training fields, shouting, "Prepare for war!" as he went.

"Rest your horse here," she said to the exhausted rider. "And come with me. What is your name?"

"Lagos, Your Highness." He bowed his head again.

"Lagos, you can eat and rest briefly before joining the others."

After taking care of his horse, they entered the cottage. Anna, who had heard Gregor and Cytherea rush out earlier, was already up, putting food together for her and Gregor to eat. Anna's frightened eyes stared at Cytherea and Kenric's messenger.

"Anna, please feed Lagos and let him rest for a time. He will join us later."

Anna nodded, her eyes still wide. The platter she held trembled as she began loading it with food.

Cytherea strode over to her and put a hand on her shoulder. Anna stopped her work and wiped her tearstained face with a corner of her apron. "I will bring them both home to you, Anna. Until then, stay strong."

Anna nodded again, emotions choking off her words. While Anna tended to Lagos, Cytherea tightened the sheath around her waist and drew her sword. She looked at it briefly before closing her eyes.

Cytherea inhaled, and the sword grew warmer in her hand. When she exhaled, the chaos in her mind began to calm.

She inhaled and felt her mother's and father's love surround her. She exhaled, and she was filled with love for the people of Phoxnay.

She inhaled and felt the power of the sword flow from her hand and into her entire being. When she exhaled, she opened her eyes, ready to defend the honor of Phoxnay and all her people.

She slid the sword into its sheath and confidently headed back out the door.

Aherne was waiting for her outside, his head bobbing in anticipation. He had been born after Cytherea had escaped Phoxnay, so he had never been to war, but it was in his blood, and he pranced anxiously. He would soon fulfill his duty and the legacy of his own heritage. He seemed to know what was coming and was ready to carry her into battle. His muscles twitched, revealing his struggle to remain still long enough for her to saddle him and jump on his back. As soon as she was seated, he sprang to life, galloping toward the training fields before Cytherea could give him a command.

As Aherne thundered through the village streets, they passed others readying themselves to join her. Men and some women rushed to saddle their horses or headed out on foot, bidding loved ones goodbye. They all paused to look up when Cytherea passed them. The responsibility of their lives rested heavily on her shoulders.

I will not let them down.

By the time Cytherea reached the edge of the village, the sky had faded from dark blue to pink with the approach of dawn. She passed one of the sentries getting into position to guard the village, and she slowed Aherne. The road sloped down to the training fields, where there was a flurry of activity. From this distance, even the occasional shout was muffled. Her heart swelled with pride as those brave men and women readied themselves to face a mighty army that far outnumbered them. She was proud to be leading them. The burden of leading them was beginning to feel more natural to her, and her confidence grew stronger each minute.

Ailmar, your cruel reign is about to end.

Cytherea tapped Aherne's flanks, and he burst into a full gallop once again.

Her mind turned to Kenric. She wished he was by her side. She had to catch herself from turning to look for him beside her as he had always been. She forced her mind away from Kenric and back to the people in front of her. These people—her people, the people of Phoxnay—believed in her and the legacy that her parents had left behind. Her heart swelled as she raced to join the controlled chaos below.

At the training field, Cytherea was enveloped by the activity of the newly formed army of Phoxnay. Horses were cinched into saddles, provisions were set up in designated tents, weapons were given a final sharpening, and the freshly named leaders shouted orders. Aherne pranced in exhilaration beneath her. He was excited by all the commotion and the anticipation that hung in the air around them.

Cytherea nodded to a group of archers stringing their bows. Older boys, not quite of fighting age, ran around her massive horse on errands for their commanders. She was thankful that these few boys had escaped Ailmar's grasp, but she worried about them being so close to the battle and to Ailmar. She was brought out of her thoughts when one of these boys was in such a hurry that he stumbled right into Aherne's shoulder. Cytherea looked down to make sure the boy was not hurt.

He blinked at her with fear in his eyes. "I'm sorry, Princess Cytherea! I didn't know it was you."

"It's all right. Aherne's a big horse. You didn't hurt him," she said with a reassuring smile. She no longer corrected those that used her title. Kenric and Gregor had convinced her that it was a sign of respect and added to an air of authority, so she'd relented.

"Thank you, Your Highness." He gave a quick nod before he moved around Aherne and ran off to complete his task.

She nudged Aherne forward. One of the scouts galloped up beside her on an exhausted mule. "They are close. Ailmar's army will make it to the village if we don't stop them," he reported between gasping breaths.

"Very well. It is time. Care for your mule and then join us." Cytherea urged Aherne into a trot to find Gregor, who she had appointed as commander of her army. The soldiers parted to give her a clear path toward the command tent in the center of the encampment.

"Gregor!" she shouted over the noise. Lifting her hand, she balled it in a fist.

He met her gaze, eyes flicking from her face to her outstretched arm, and then he turned, his voice booming across the once-peaceful pasture. "Form ranks! We attack now!" Swinging into his own saddle that was now secured to the back of his stallion, he lifted his axe. "For Phoxnay!"

"For Phoxnay!" they all shouted in unison.

The cheer echoed throughout the camp amid the squeak of leather saddles being tightened, the dull thud of nervous hooves, and the shouts of last-minute orders. The activity helped drown out the fear that had begun to creep slowly through Cytherea's veins. Pushing the fear aside, she trotted Aherne to the lead of those on horseback. As the sun rose over the horizon, she led her army toward the growing darkness beyond.

46

Kenric and his men stayed deep within the tree line as the Dark Realm army passed by on the road to Haight. The soldiers were so close to where they were hiding that they could see their vacant eyes beyond their helmet visors. Were the men they used to be left beyond the trance that Ailmar held over them? Kenric shook off his growing sadness and refocused on freeing the boys that were held in the dark dungeon ahead from suffering the same fate.

Soon a feeling of dread rose within him, and the now-bright sun began to dim, the unnatural darkness enveloping them. The men beside him shifted uncomfortably, and even the most seasoned soldiers had to resist the urge to flee. Ailmar and his dark cloud of magic was passing them.

Kenric lowered his head and hoped that whatever magic Ailmar had was focused ahead and not toward them hiding so close. His breath caught as he again thought of Cytherea face-to-face with such vile power, even though he knew she had the power of the Sword of Phoxnay protecting her. She was his sovereign now and leading an army into battle. Nevertheless, his father had taught him his whole life that their purpose was to protect her. Kenric always would.

The blackness gradually slid past them, and the sound of the Dark Realm soldiers' boots began to fade. Kenric motioned for his platoon to stay down until he was sure the army was a safe distance beyond them. Then they moved to the edge of the trees. Kenric and two of the Klobyn scouts scoured the pastures in front of them, searching for any movement beyond the gate and through the sentry openings in the wall. Nothing.

Kenric spoke in hushed tones. "We won't be sure that the guards are truly gone until we expose ourselves beyond the protection of the tree line."

The hand of one Klobyn soldier was quickly raised. "I volunteer to go first."

Another man stood. "And I will go with him."

The two men were soon stepping into the clearing, first hesitantly and then gradually more confidently. They hurried toward the towering walls before them. Soon they were entering the gate, where they turned and signaled the others that it was safe to proceed.

The Dark Realm guards could be waiting for the rest of them to appear in order to ambush them, but they had no choice but to try. Kenric pulled himself onto Tredan and signaled his men to move. They all kept their weapons at the ready and watched for any movement from the castle walls. However, they made it to the gates without incident. The gates were closed but unexpectedly unguarded. After several men managed to open the gates, they walked into the walls surrounding Ailmar's castle. The air was thick. An eerie silence hung over them, muting the clatter of their horses's hooves on the stone street. The small village inside the castle walls appeared to be abandoned, and Kenric sent some of his men out to check the sentry stations. They reported back that they were all empty.

It appeared that Ailmar had taken every soldier with him to fight Cytherea and had left his castle completely defenseless. But of course, who would be reckless enough to break into Ailmar's castle?

Kenric chuckled.

Lucan, the Klobyn regiment leader, tilted his head. "What's funny?"

"Ailmar left his castle unguarded because it never occurred to him that anyone would try to break into it."

"His arrogance is our good fortune!"

"Yes, it is. Although it could be a trap. Everyone stay alert," Kenric ordered. "Let's hurry up and find the boys. The sooner we are out of here, the better."

Kenric was familiar with the outside of the castle from his time there previously, and Cytherea's directions for inside the castle led them quickly to the area where the boys were being held. The men paused briefly to allow their eyes to acclimate to the darkness. Quiet sobs came from behind some of the thick wooden doors that lined a long corridor. The despair Kenric heard went straight through his soul, and he urged them all forward.

"We are here to free you, not harm you!" Kenric's voice echoed against the stone walls. "We come in the name of the kingdom of Phoxnay, and we are taking you home."

The muffled sounds of movement were joined by small hands pounding on the inside of the doors to let their rescuers know they were there. Kenric was afraid they would harm themselves in their desperation. He ordered some of the men to spread out along the doors to try to calm those inside while the others worked to break open the locks one by one. Each door was sealed with a thick bolt, but a few strikes with an axe broke them free, the noise causing the young boys beyond to shriek in fear.

Still uneasy, Kenric kept a lookout at the top of the steps that descended to the dungeon in case the noise roused any soldiers that might have been left behind. His men worked quickly, and they soon had all the children freed. Brockton ran and hugged Kenric in a tight grip. He returned the embrace, grateful the young boy seemed unharmed and was now safe.

Lucan pulled Kenric aside. "They are severely malnourished and traumatized. I'm not sure they can make the journey back to Haight."

"We will get to the safety of the forest and give them food and water there," Kenric replied. "Then, for the journey to Haight, we will carry as many as we can on our horses. We can walk and lead the horses if necessary." Once he got the children to the safety of the forest, they could travel the rest of the way more slowly hidden within the woods, but they needed a way to move them quickly now. "We can find a wagon in the village and put them in there," he told Lucan. "We can have a couple of horses pull that. Any others can ride behind us on our horses."

Lucan nodded. "Very good. I will send a few men out to find a wagon and get the horses ready."

Kenric nodded and went back to helping the boys out of the darkness and into the light of day.

47

Ailmar watched from a hillside as legions of his army marched past him. The soldiers of the Dark Realm army stared ahead, emotionless, sweat rolling down their faces unnoticed. They had been marching through the night but were unaffected by any sense of exhaustion. Without feeling or concern about their fate. They were under the complete control of Ailmar's dark magic.

Their armor was adorned with thick ebony plates that covered their bodies like scales and gave off a distorted reflection of the world around them. They were being pressed into a relentless pace, and the rhythmic clanging of the armor announced their approach to those in their path. The thunderous stomping of their boots echoed off the hills before them and throughout the valley behind. It drowned out all other sound. Birds and other creatures scattered before the massive army, attempting to remain out of its grasp.

A slight sneer broke across Ailmar's face, mirroring the dark heart that beat within his chest. His grip on his staff tightened. A putrid smoke billowed out from the onyx orb affixed on top and filled the sky above the soldiers, leaving them in a stifling darkness.

He was pleased with the army he had spent years creating. He analyzed their faces, and a feeling of satisfaction swept over him. He had taken their carefree smiles and turned them into soldiers. His masterful sorcery had taken over their very souls until they were his to command. He chuckled smugly to himself as his army pressed forward.

~

The army of the Dark Realm rolled like smoke down the hills into the valley, immense and deadly. Cytherea paused and looked behind her at the men and women of Phoxnay's army. Most of them were on foot, carrying homemade weapons fashioned from axes and farm tools. Those that had armor had divided it up to share it as best they could with others. Many had bits and pieces of armor sewn together to cover the vital parts of their bodies. Their eyes, though full of fear, were trained forward, and their faces were set with determination as they moved toward their approaching enemy.

Cytherea convinced herself that it didn't matter what they were wearing or the weapons they carried. What mattered was what was in their hearts, and she was impressed with the army they had created in such a short time. She wanted to believe that Kenric was right about battles not being won by numbers, but as she wheeled Aherne toward the oncoming Dark Realm army, her heart faltered. Either way, it didn't matter now. She had to focus on the goal of taking back the kingdom of Phoxnay, saving her people's children, and destroying the evil of Ailmar.

Where is Everard in that mass of darkness?

Gregor rode up next to her, and he, too, searched the shadows before them. He moved his horse around Aherne, looking for something within the smoky clouds until he stopped and narrowed his eyes. He turned toward her.

"What is it?" Cytherea asked, trying to steady her voice to match her physical stature with her chin held high.

"Ailmar is with them."

"How do you know?" She peered deeper into the darkness.

Gregor's gaze was steely. "The dark magic he possesses is what keeps them shrouded in shadows." He gave her a half-smile. "You should feel honored that he came personally. It means he considers you a real threat."

Cytherea shifted uneasily in her saddle at the thought of seeing Ailmar again. Aherne sidestepped uneasily, sensing her tension. She drew up her reins and placed a hand on his neck to calm him. "We knew of his magic, but what concerns me is that no one seems to know how much or what type he actually wields."

"That is true, and it may only be enough to create this murky canopy, but whatever magic he has, I feel certain that he will display it all soon enough."

"Yes, we—"

Cytherea's words were cut off by a deep rumbling beneath them, which grew until they were being shaken by the trembling earth.

She struggled to hold Aherne as his hooves danced, trying to find steady ground. "What is that?"

"I don't know," Gregor answered, struggling with his own horse. "But it has happened before and has the animals in the forest restless and tense."

"It must be what caused the strange behavior of the animals Kenric and I crossed on our journey here from Ceka, although we didn't feel the ground move or hear any rumbling."

"Animals are more sensitive to it. They likely felt it even when you didn't."

"What is it?"

"He is conjuring something." The voice behind Cytherea and Gregor startled them, and they turned to face who was speaking.

It was one of the older loyalists, who had moved up to the front lines despite Cytherea's attempt to protect him near the back. "Ailmar. He is trying to conjure something."

"What do you mean?" Gregor asked.

"Ailmar has a powerful magic in his grasp, but he hasn't become strong enough to wield it yet. He is attempting to conjure something with it."

"What?" Cytherea asked, glancing back at the oncoming army.

"That I don't know, but I do know that we need to defeat him before he gains enough strength to accomplish whatever he is trying to do."

Her confidence began to falter.

Gregor's stubbled face turned toward her. "Don't forget. There is powerful magic in your family line as well."

"Maybe, but I don't have any magic powers," she said.

"Your sword seems to disagree with you."

Cytherea put her hand on her sword's hilt. The gemstone warmed at her touch. "I hadn't considered that to be magic."

"If that isn't magic, I don't know what is." Gregor smiled before becoming solemn. "Cytherea, I believe there are a great many things you do not yet know about yourself."

Unsure of what to say, she chose not to respond. Instead, she steadied Aherne beneath her. "Are we ready?" she asked.

"Yes, Your Highness."

"Very well, then." With that, she drew her sword. Aherne spun and galloped down the formed ranks of her army. "For Phoxnay!" she shouted, leading her army into the darkness. *To victory or death.*

As they moved forward, Ailmar's cloud swirled around them, darkening the area but not entirely blocking out the sun. The horses snorted when they breathed in the vile thickness. Cytherea struggled to inhale, and she slowed Aherne to get her bearings. Thrusting her sword into the air, she looked up at the disappearing blue sky and then at her sword and its glowing gem.

It was bright but not bright enough to cut through the unnatural darkness. *How can we fight if we can't see our enemies?*

Even as the question ran through Cytherea's mind, she felt a vibration coming from the sword hilt and through her hand. It surged up her arm and rushed through her body. The other gems on the Sword of Phoxnay flashed in a spectacular rainbow of colors, beaming in all directions and piercing the dark evil around them.

Cytherea shielded her eyes and smiled broadly. She felt the weight of the malevolent cloud lift from her.

When she glanced beside her, Gregor's mouth was fully agape in shock. As the thick clouds were forced back and the muffled silence thinned, the men and women behind Cytherea cheered with renewed confidence.

Her smile soon faded. The thunder of hooves and armored feet grew louder. The army of the Dark Realm raced toward them. But before she could act, the infantry of Phoxnay had already run past her, ready to meet their enemy. The riders were right behind. Cytherea urged Aherne onward to join them.

Her blade joined the clamor of metal hitting metal as they met their enemy. Cytherea and Aherne lunged forward, and the Sword of Phoxnay scraped the armor of a Dark Realm soldier, causing an unholy shriek. She was reminded of the soldier Kenric had killed in the barn back home. These soldiers had on armor that was darker than onyx, and the mirror-like reflection was both disorienting and distracting in battle when she was surrounded by it. Seeing her own reflection in the grim mirrors was unsettling. Yet she kept on.

Weapons clashed, and many of her soldiers, once disarmed, grappled with their adversaries hand-to-hand. Aherne's hooves maneuvered over a ground littered with weapons, bodies, and blood. Cytherea steeled herself against the death and dying around her. There would be a time to grieve later, but now it was time to fight. Someone screamed, and the flat of a broadsword slapped against her arm. Aherne reared, kicking and almost throwing her from the saddle. She slashed blindly at the foe attacking her, but her blade never found its mark. When Cytherea raised her eyes to see the fighting around her, the Dark Realm soldiers seemed invincible. Farther back in the throng of murderous soldiers, the swirling cloud was darkest.

Ailmar must be there.

She urged Aherne straight toward it. She fought off or evaded the Dark Realm soldiers that were in her path.

If I kill him, this ends. We will be victorious.

Gregor, still astride his mount, appeared at her side.

"I have to get to Ailmar!" she shouted to him over the din. "We cannot defeat them as long as he can wield his magic."

Gregor lifted his axe. "I am behind you."

Cytherea spurred Aherne deeper into the blackness.

Gregor shouted at the fighters around him. "To me!"

The infantry roared, following Gregor and Cytherea valiantly into what she believed would be certain death. All sound was vanquished until she only heard the beastly, murderous breaths of the enemy surrounding her.

Legions of soldiers seemed to stand between them and Ailmar, and he appeared to move farther away with every soldier they cut down. Her enemy had trained his army well. They were desperate to protect him, and their numbers were unfathomable. As time wore on, Gregor and those that had followed Cytherea were slowing in their attack. The cloud of darkness tried to encircle them whenever she and the Sword of Phoxnay moved too far ahead of them. The farther away from her army she moved, the less her sword was able to keep the darkness back from them. Several men had been forced to retreat, and Gregor's axe was swinging wildly, with less control than before. The look in his eyes was savage as he fought to get through the lines of soldiers in front of him.

"Cytherea!" Gregor shouted by her side. "We are dangerously

deep inside their lines. We must fall back before we are completely cut off from our ranks."

Cytherea hesitated.

"Watch—!"

A sharp blade pierced her side. She instinctively swung her sword in her foe's direction, and this time, she felt the blade meet the black armor. The soldier screamed. Cytherea leaned in as her blade, unbelievably, melted into the armor. She put all her weight behind it and pushed. The blade flowed fluidly into the soldier's now lifeless body until he slumped off his horse and landed on the ground, grotesquely contorted.

She looked aghast at the soldier and then at her sword, unaware of her own injury. She could not have pierced that soldier's armor with her own strength.

When she remained frozen, Gregor grabbed Aherne's reins and turned the massive steed, leading them out of the battle and into the tree line. Gregor took the Sword of Phoxnay from her so it wouldn't slip from her slack hand. The jeweled hilt immediately dimmed, and the darkness began to close in, aiding them in their escape from the fighting. As the last of the sword's light waned, several of the Phoxnay men blocked the Dark Realm soldiers, allowing Gregor and Cytherea to slip away. Her head spun and her vision blurred. Sensing that his rider needed to get to safety, Aherne eased into a gallop. Curled over toward her left side, Cytherea only saw a blur of steel, horses, and faces through the trees.

"Stay awake!" Gregor bellowed.

Cytherea shook her head, willing herself awake, but she was losing the fight. A different kind of darkness began closing in. Sorrow overwhelmed her as she cried for her people dying on the battlefield.

I failed.

48

"No!" Cytherea cried out while trying to sit up. She found herself under a makeshift tent with Anna leaning over her. The sun had risen high in the sky, and the sounds of battle were distant. "What happened?"

Anna gently checked the bandages at Cytherea's waist. "Shh. You were wounded. You'll be all right."

Cytherea tried to sit up again, but Anna gently held her down. "You must rest a little while longer."

"I need to get back out and fight," she protested, struggling. "Where is my sword?"

"Here." Anna pointed to the weapon, which lay dark beside her. "It is ready when you are."

Cytherea quit struggling and steeled her voice. "I'm ready."

"You have had a powerful healer working on you, and your wound is healing." She looked at Cytherea's wound. "You seemed to mostly be overcome by exhaustion. Your body is struggling to keep up with the power of the sword, but you should be able to return to the battle soon."

"I need to find Gregor."

"You need to rest. He returned to the battle right after

bringing you to me." Anna laid a plate of food next to her. "Eat. You need your strength."

Cytherea sat up and winced. She immediately scarfed down the food before throwing the blanket off and standing slowly. The world spun around her, but she planted her feet and steadied herself until it passed.

Anna waved a nearby healer over and said, "It seems we can't keep her here any longer. Please give her whatever she will need before she returns to the battle."

The healer applied a salve to the wound while Cytherea fidgeted, anxious to get back into the fight. She didn't like leaving her people to face the Dark Realm without her.

"My lady," the healer said, "we healed your wound, but your body is not fully recovered, so please be careful. You cannot be killed while you have the sword's protection, but your body can wear down because you are not used to the exertion of its magic."

"Thank you," Cytherea said as the healer secured her bandages. "I will be careful."

Once the healer had completed her application, Cytherea found Aherne waiting outside the tent. Ignoring the pain in her side, she mounted, and they galloped back into the fray.

Cytherea soon found Gregor. "We need to try to get to Ailmar again."

Gregor looked at her with a grim face. "I can't let you risk your life like that again. You can lead from behind the lines where you will be protected."

"Gregor," she said, her voice firm, "the Sword of Phoxnay protects me. The men and women fighting with us will need its light and inspiration in front of them. It is also the only way to stop Ailmar."

Gregor nodded curtly, resigning himself to her logic.

Cytherea faced the battle, speaking over her shoulder to him. "Thank you for getting me out of there safely."

He bowed his head. "It is my duty to protect my sovereign."

Cytherea changed the subject. "How is the battle going? How many people have we lost?"

"Ailmar's men are strong and ruthless. We are little match for them. However, our people are fiercely devoted to the cause, and no one is willing to back down. We will keep fighting until the end."

Cytherea was silent for several heartbeats. "The only path to victory is for me to get to Ailmar and stop him. I must find a way."

"Well, not the way we tried earlier. We must find a way to reach him discreetly, without him seeing us. If he knows we are coming, then he will keep moving to protect himself."

"You are right. But how do we do that?" She paused. "Any word from Kenric and those attacking the castle?"

Gregor shook his head. "Nothing yet, but it would be difficult to get a messenger to us now. Kenric is strong and smart. I believe he will succeed.

"I want to believe that too."

The battle continued to rage, and Cytherea took account of her army. The battlefield was littered with bodies of the dead and dying. Each face belonged to a farmer, villager, father, son, mother, and daughter that had believed Cytherea when she told them they could defeat Ailmar's evil. She felt the sting of tears threatening to spill over, but she forced them back. What remained of the army of Phoxnay was weary, and their numbers were dwindling, but she couldn't let them see her crying. Not now in the middle of the battle.

The healers that had gathered to help were overwhelmed by the numbers that required their care, yet they continued to heal as many as they could. A feeling of despair washed over Cytherea. The army of the Dark Realm seemed to increase and grow stronger as they ravaged what was left of the people of Phoxnay.

Cytherea's thoughts turned to her father and mother. She

knew that they too must have felt a wave of helplessness as Ailmar's army had annihilated their people and destroyed their land before ultimately killing them as well.

What would my father do at this moment?

Part of her wanted to give up, but she knew she couldn't. She wouldn't. The legacy of her heritage forced her to continue. She understood now why her parents had stayed to fight instead of escaping to safety with her. The part of Tarquin's story that had made her cry as a child now filled her with pride. Her parents' legacy was to protect and fight for the people of Phoxnay. This realization flooded Cytherea's soul with an unexpected power. At that moment, her heart began to beat stronger, and her mind began to push away the feelings of doubt and defeat.

She took a deep breath and whispered, "I may die today, but not before I kill Ailmar."

Cytherea moved Aherne forward, and Gregor followed. She was searching for a way to get to Ailmar unseen when suddenly a large cloud of dust flooded the hills to the west. Cytherea's heart fell once again.

No!

Ailmar's soldiers had flanked them. She watched helplessly as the cloud rapidly advanced toward them. She looked toward the peaceful village that she had called home these past few weeks, and her heart broke at the realization that it was about to be overrun by evil.

I failed. The thought came again unbidden. *I can't fail!* She took a breath to refocus and urged Aherne into a gallop behind their fighting lines, heading toward the tree line. Gregor followed, shouting orders to some of the men to reform ranks right behind her.

I'll approach Ailmar from the tree line and hope it conceals us until we reach his position.

Her only goal now was to kill Ailmar before he could kill her and to do it before those trying to flank her army reached them.

As she neared the trees, she couldn't shake the feeling of doom that washed over her. She glanced behind her to make sure that Gregor was close. She pulled Aherne to an abrupt stop when she noticed a lone rider racing toward them from the village. She turned into the rider's path with Gregor beside her. The rider galloped closer and pulled his horse to a stop when Cytherea blocked his path.

"I am looking for Princess Cytherea," the rider said breathlessly.

"I am Cytherea. What is it? Are you here about Kenric?" she asked, hoping that Kenric was still alive.

The messenger shook his head. "Kenric's forces have made it to the castle, and it was virtually empty, except for a few guards and servants, but that is all I have heard so far."

"Ailmar, in his arrogance, apparently never expected anyone to attack his castle," Gregor said. "Cytherea, he has brought his entire army down on you."

Cytherea looked at him for a moment before the messenger spoke again.

"I am here to bring you news from Klobyn," the rider continued.

"Save your news. Instead, get a fresh horse and head out to find those trying to rescue the children. Tell them that the Dark Realm army has come around the west side to flank us, and they should not return here—"

"Forgive me, Your Highness," the boy interrupted with his head bowed, "but that will not be necessary."

"What do you mean? I gave you an order," Cytherea said sharply. She didn't have time to be questioned by a messenger.

Gregor looked at her, surprised at her uncharacteristic tone. The pressure was wearing on her, but her question needed answering. "Let him speak, Cytherea."

She nodded for the young messenger to continue.

"Your Highness, those are not soldiers of the Dark Realm

coming across the hills from the west. That is the army of Klobyn."

Her eyes widened, and her heart soared. Hope renewed within her. She glanced over and met Gregor's eye. "Then we still have a chance."

Gregor thrust his fist in the air with a joyous hoot.

Cytherea smiled at him. "We need to regroup with a new plan of attack." She turned back to the messenger. "How many are there in Klobyn's army?"

"The number that was sent is about five thousand. Others had to stay behind to ensure the kingdom remained protected. They have sent word to the kingdoms beyond Klobyn as well, and they will be sending some of their men."

Gregor slapped the messenger on the back, nearly sending him to the ground in his enthusiasm. "Well done, lad! You and your horse need food and rest. Head to camp and rest there as long as you need before returning."

Cytherea looked up to the western hills. The Klobyn army moved swiftly toward their camp. "We will meet with the commanders of the Klobyn army now and lay out our battle formations for him so they can join the fight."

49

Cytherea and Gregor met briefly with King Aldegunde and the commanders of the army of Klobyn, and a new battle plan was devised. They decided that the Klobyn army would mount a quick and boisterous attack on the west side of the battlefield to turn Ailmar's attention in their direction. In the meantime, Cytherea, Gregor, and a few others would carefully make their way through the forest on the east side to come up behind Ailmar while he was hopefully still distracted by the Klobyn soldiers. Cytherea's gamble was that Ailmar, in his arrogance, might not consider a second attack coming from behind. She hoped that would give her the chance to kill him.

As word filtered through Phoxnay's battle lines that the Klobyn soldiers had arrived and increased their numbers significantly, the army of Phoxnay gained a renewed energy and sense of hope. Once the battle plan was drawn, Cytherea and Gregor scanned the battlefield, hunting for Ailmar. The malevolent darkness that lingered over him seemed to move constantly, making it nearly impossible to pinpoint his location. But Cytherea was determined to find him, kill him, and end this horrible battle.

"There!" Gregor pointed his new spear—a replacement for his

broken axe—toward the east side. "Near the middle of the Dark Realm soldiers. The black mist looks thicker there. That has to be Ailmar."

Cytherea peered across the sea of soldiers until her eyes landed on the spot Gregor indicated. "I see it. Let's head to the forest and make our way toward him. I'll send a messenger to let the Klobyn army know when to begin their surge on the west side."

After sending the messenger off, she nodded to Gregor.

"With me!" he shouted to those around him. He thrust his spear into the air, and the small regiment soon disappeared into the trees.

Gregor and Cytherea peered through the branches, trying to keep their eyes on Ailmar's location from inside the dense forest. Their progress was slow without a clear trail, but Ailmar had not moved.

It worked! He doesn't know we're coming.

Nearing his position, Cytherea heard the shouts of the Klobyn army from the opposite side of the battle, and Ailmar's position shifted slightly. Gregor turned toward Cytherea and nodded. They urged their horses to move faster and were soon directly in line with the darkness that marked Ailmar. They rode as swiftly as they could to the edge of the trees. Encouraged by the fighters with her, Cytherea pulled out her sword, and they burst from the cover of the trees.

The gem on the hilt of Cytherea's sword glowed brightly as the blade melted the steel of enemy armor and tore through the flesh of many of Ailmar's men. Instead of waning, her strength seemed to renew with each swing of the mighty blade, allowing her to fight long beyond her physical ability.

The sun hung low in the sky, and the Sword of Phoxnay dripped with blood. But Cytherea continued fighting, trying to reach Ailmar even though the darkness that hovered over him once again seemed to keep moving farther away. After she felled another soldier, Aherne suddenly balked, shying to the side and rearing suddenly. When his front legs returned to the ground, Cytherea stiffened.

Ailmar.

In one hand, the evil king held the staff Cytherea had seen in his throne room, its black orb gleaming. She watched, momentarily mesmerized, as it swallowed the surrounding light, leaving only shadows behind. It wasn't creating dark clouds; instead, it was somehow creating an absence of light. She forced her eyes away from it and examined his other hand. She was surprised that he held no visible weapon, except the staff. His horse, its eyes wide with terror, pranced erratically as if ready to bolt at any second. Ailmar sat atop him in the same abominable armor that his army wore, the blood of his victims slowly dripping down the mirrored sections like grotesque art. Oddly, he had left his head unprotected, as if mocking those that opposed him.

Ailmar's eyes locked on her, and a sneer formed on his lips.

What arrogance! Cytherea gritted her teeth beneath her helmet. *He believes he is untouchable.*

"Did you, a simple farm girl, think that you could possibly defeat me?" he shouted over the din of battle.

His laughter crawled down her skin. Aherne remained motionless under her, ears flat against his head. The stallion snorted, and his muscles tensed, ready to charge, but Cytherea held him back. The echo of the fighting around her faded into a dark fog as Ailmar's black eyes bored into her. Confusion began to muddle her thoughts, and she tried in vain to clear her mind of the gloom that threatened to take over. A voice in her mind repeated that she really was just a simple farm girl trying to defeat the entire army of the Dark Realm. Her confidence wavered until a familiar voice cut through the haze.

"Your dark magic won't save you this time, Ailmar." It was Gregor.

Cytherea had momentarily forgotten he was beside her. His

stallion plunged forward, forcing Ailmar's steed back, and Gregor thrust his spear toward Ailmar's neck. Aherne danced, but Cytherea remained dazed under Ailmar's magic and was unable to react when another Dark Realm soldier approached through the pall around them. Without warning, the second rider unhorsed Gregor with his lance. Gregor's stallion stood defiantly over his beloved master, snapping and kicking, but when the horse reared, the dark soldier plunged the jagged lance into his heart. The great steed let out a piercing sound before his body dropped lifeless to the ground.

Gregor let out a gasp, rolling clear of his fallen steed before rising on a wave of fury and lunging toward the soldier. The dark soldier's horse instantly reared and landed its massive hoof to the side of Gregor's face, sending blood everywhere. Gregor's body went limp, and he fell to the bloodied ground. Cytherea screamed as panic swept over her.

Ailmar laughed. He jumped from his horse with his staff raised above his head and strode toward Gregor. Cytherea flinched at the sight of the barbaric spear on the end of it.

He is going to kill Gregor!

"No!" Cytherea screamed, forcing her mind to clear. She jumped from Aherne with her sword raised above her head just as Ailmar placed a booted foot on Gregor's chest and plunged the wicked spear through his eye.

Rage fueled Cytherea. She charged forward, her sword's gem nearly blinding her as she swung at Ailmar. Her blade met his armor, and a bolt of light pierced the darkness that clung to the evil king. The blade melted through Ailmar's armor, entered his flesh, and sliced through his bowels.

Darkness spewed from the staff that still protruded from Gregor's eye. Ailmar's scream echoed all around her until it gradually weakened and eventually stopped altogether. Emotionlessly, Cytherea watched Ailmar's body collapse.

She pulled back the Sword of Phoxnay, now dripping with

Ailmar's blood. The shadow that hung over the battlefield began to dissipate. Ailmar's spell had been broken, and he lay powerless on the ground next to Gregor. She stared in disbelief at the man who had helped her find confidence in herself.

"Father!" cried the soldier that had attacked Gregor, jumping from his horse.

Cytherea's eyes moved to follow the soldier, who removed his helmet and threw it to the ground. Her breath caught in her throat.

"Everard!" she shouted.

Her brother flung himself down next to Ailmar, wrenching at his armor and sobbing. Her thoughts returned to Gregor. She hurried to his side, tearing off pieces of her tunic to use to try and stop his bleeding. Aherne paced next to them.

Voices shouted all around her, and soon there were others pressing torn clothing into Gregor's wounds. The fighting began to shudder to a stop as the soldiers on both sides watched the darkness, the symbol of Ailmar's power, dissolve into the wind. Cytherea knelt next to Gregor, one hand still holding her sword. She viewed the scene before her.

Bodies littered the ground.

Some Dark Realm soldiers pulled their helmets off, looking disoriented, unsure of what to do next. Others ran toward the forest to escape, their minds now free of Ailmar's grip. However, many soldiers still held their positions. Ailmar's darkness had taken a permanent place within them. Those soldiers nearest to them were focused on Everard, who still knelt over Ailmar's body. Her brother screamed.

"He's dead! You killed my father!" Everard jumped up and rushed toward Cytherea.

Another loyalist that had been with Cytherea and Gregor moved to step between them, but Cytherea stood and stepped in front of him.

"Everard, stop!" Cytherea raised her sword, the gems of power still glowing brightly. "I am your sister!"

Everard's brow furrowed. He stumbled, stopping within steps of her. "You are not my sister! I am not Everard! I am Derian, Prince of the Dark Realm, son of Ailmar!"

Taken aback by his cutting words, Cytherea lowered her sword.

Everard's gaze shifted back and forth between Ailmar's body and Cytherea.

"I am your sister, Everard. Join me. Let's rebuild our parents' kingdom together." Cytherea offered her hand to him, but he only glared back at her.

Abruptly, Everard turned, pulled Ailmar's staff roughly from Gregor's eye, and sounded the retreat. What was left of the Dark Realm army fled back toward Ailmar's castle with Everard leading them.

Cytherea thought she saw a slight shadow rise again from the staff's orb before Everard disappeared over the hill beyond.

50

Cytherea, still numb from shock, headed back toward camp, leading another soldier's horse that carried Gregor's body. His wounds had been too severe, and it was too late for the healers to help him. He was gone.

The cheers and shouts of victory from Phoxnay's army began to subside when Cytherea approached. Several others joined the solemn group heading toward the healers' tents in search of Anna.

Cytherea ran her hands over Aherne to ensure he was not hurt, but miraculously, he only had a few minor wounds that would mend quickly with the healers' ointment. Relief and sadness washed over her, and she was unable to hold back the rush of tears. She glanced behind her again, where the remnants of the Dark Realm army had disappeared on their way back to Ailmar's castle.

The castle!

She gasped and repeated the thought aloud, "The castle!" She wiped away her tears. "What about Kenric and the children? We need to warn them that the Dark Realm soldiers are headed back." Cytherea was frantic. If Kenric was still in the castle, then Everard and his army would soon discover them. Kenric would be trapped.

A man next to her started to turn toward the village. "I'll send our fastest rider!"

However, someone near the back of the crowd alerted her to a horse racing toward them from the edge of the camp. "A rider!" they shouted.

Cytherea braced herself for the news they were bringing.

She urged Aherne slightly ahead and then waited, heedless of the voices around her, as the rider neared. Soon she recognized the rider's blond hair and lanky form as well as the warhorse beneath him. Emotions overwhelmed her.

Kenric!

She jumped from Aherne and ran toward Kenric. Tredan slid to a stop.

"How—" Cytherea started to speak but was startled into silence when Brockton poked his face out from behind Kenric. "Brockton!"

"Sir Kenric saved me!" the young boy said.

Cytherea grabbed him in her arms, and the tears began to flow again.

Brockton leaned back to look at her. "Why are you crying, Princess Cytherea?"

"They are tears of happiness, Brockton. I'm just so happy you are back and safe." She was unable to tell him about his father at that moment.

Kenric slid from his saddle and scrutinized Cytherea's face. "What is it, Cyth?"

She gave him a look that made Kenric cock his head in confusion, and then she smiled at Brockton while she wiped away her tears. "Marcus," she called to a nearby soldier. "Can you take Brockton to Anna?"

"Certainly, Your Highness." He nodded before lifting the boy onto his saddle.

Before Marcus left, Cytherea leaned in and whispered to him, "Not a word until we arrive."

"Understood, Your Highness." He mounted his horse with Brockton securely in front of him and galloped toward the tents to find Anna.

Kenric took Cytherea by the shoulders, "What has happened, Cytherea?"

Cytherea forced a smile, ignoring his question. "Thank you for bringing him home, Kenric. Where are the other children?"

He understood her first concern was the safety of the children. "They're with the Klobyn men coming behind me. We avoided the road and took them through the forest, so we didn't inadvertently run into any Dark Realm soldiers. If the battle went badly, we planned to turn toward Klobyn and get them to safety. A scout informed us that the Dark Realm army was retreating, so we headed straight here. I rode ahead with Brockton instead of sending a messenger to inform you." Kenric's eyes clouded as they examined Cytherea. "Are you injured? Let me get you to a healer. You are covered in blood. Where are you hurt?"

"I'm OK," Cytherea reassured him.

"What happened?"

"Ailmar's dead," she answered, her voice flat from the shock of it all.

Kenric paused briefly, taking in the news. "Did you kill him?"

"Yes." Cytherea's voice didn't even sound like hers because she was so detached from the statement.

"And Everard?"

"He led the Dark Realm army back to the castle." She stopped and took a breath. "There's something I need to tell you." She hesitated.

"What is it? What has happened?" He looked around. "Where is Gregor?"

She lowered her head. Grief poured through her again, momentarily stealing her voice.

"Is Gregor wounded?"

"Gregor is dead," she whispered. Her tears began to flow unchecked.

Kenric looked around frantically, searching for Gregor. "How can that be?"

The crowd of soldiers that had been accompanying her from the battlefield had formed a screen to hide Gregor's body from Brockton. They now separated for Kenric to see. He gasped when he saw the man's massive body limp across the back of a horse.

Cytherea took Kenric's arm. They moved closer to the lifeless form of the man they had both grown to love. "He died protecting me, Kenric." She struggled against the sorrow that tried to drown her. "I would be dead if it weren't for him."

"How? What happened?" Kenric's expression vacillated between disbelief and confusion.

"There's a lot I need to tell you, and I'll answer all your questions. But first, we must take Gregor to Anna."

Kenric agreed. "There will be plenty of time for explanations, but Anna and Brockton must be told."

The following afternoon, Kenric strode quietly into the barn and watched Cytherea braid Aherne's mane. He knew it soothed her in some way to do something that she had done so often as a young girl. A time when Ailmar and the Dark Realm were just stories his father told her. A time when her life was easy and her cares were few. It wasn't that long ago, and yet it seemed like it was a lifetime away.

He sighed. "I thought I would find you here."

Cytherea turned. "I couldn't stay in there, drowning in their grief. I had to find a place to breathe. The sound of Anna's and Brockton's cries pierce my soul."

Kenric fed Aherne and Tredan a handful of oats. "They will get past this, Cyth. We all will. It will just take some time."

Cytherea stopped braiding, sat on a small wooden bench, and put her face in her hands. "It is my fault! Anna has lost her husband and Brockton his father, and it is all my fault!" She raised her head, her face flushed red. "Everywhere I turn, there are people grieving their loved ones because of me! Tarquin, your father, is dead, and it is all because of me!"

Kenric stepped to her, took her by her shoulders, and stood her up. "Look at me, Cytherea!" He gently lifted her chin and calmed his voice. "None of this is your fault. The only person at fault is Ailmar. He did this. He destroyed families, their children, and their loved ones. Ailmar is the one who is to blame for the death of Gregor, my father, your parents, and everyone else that died in this battle and in all the years since the fall of Phoxnay. You are the one that has saved them from Ailmar. They could never have defeated him without you and the power of your sword. We will mourn the dead, but then we will honor them by rebuilding the kingdom of Phoxnay. Because of you, your people can finally return to their home."

Cytherea searched his face. "I don't know what to do to help ease their pain."

"You can't. But you can be there for them and point them to the future that their loved ones died to give them. You can honor those that have died by taking your rightful place on the throne of Phoxnay and leading them back to their home."

She nodded, appearing more resolved. "I will do my best to follow the example of my father and mother that I have heard from all of Tarquin's stories. I believe my mother would start by being with her people, loving them, and helping them bury their dead."

"I think that is exactly what she would do." Kenric wrapped one arm around Cytherea's shoulders and led her back to the cottage where they would start making plans for honoring the dead.

5I

The sun beamed down on Cytherea standing next to the mound of fresh dirt where Gregor had been laid to rest just a short time before. The splendid brightness forced its way into the sadness welling up inside her, and she couldn't help but smile. It was just like him to burst into her sadness and make her smile. The bright day seemed an appropriate way for nature to pay homage to the giant of a man that had brought joy and laughter to so many. She hadn't known him for long, but she couldn't image not hearing his booming laughter again while he played with Brockton or lovingly teased Anna.

"I don't know how they will get through this, Kenric." She sighed as she watched Anna and Brockton walking slowly back to town.

Kenric followed her eyes up the road. "I know, but they are both strong and have lots of people that will help them keep going." He turned back to Cytherea. "How are you, Cyth?"

Her eyes immediately filled with tears that began falling down her cheeks. She had been so focused on taking care of funerals and grieving loved ones that she hadn't stopped to think about how she was since that afternoon in the barn. It instantly over-whelmed her.

Kenric put his arms around her and let her cry. After a few minutes, she felt his tears landing softly on her hair.

He spoke quietly. "We've made and lost a lot of friends in a short time, but none have died in vain. They have all died a hero's death."

She looked up at him. "Including your father. He faithfully honored his pledge to my parents and ultimately gave his life to protect me. Without him, none of this would have been possible. I still can't believe that he is gone."

"I know. Part of me believes that we will go back to Ceka and he will be there waiting for us."

"He would want to hear every detail of what has happened." The thought brought a small smile to her face.

"Only having us pause the story occasionally for my mother's stew." Kenric chuckled and wiped away his tears.

"When Phoxnay is rebuilt, we will honor them again," vowed Cytherea. She laid one more flower on the fresh dirt before turning to walk home. Aherne and Tredan followed behind Kenric and Cytherea as they shared their stories of both Gregor and Tarquin.

Everard sat at a table in the shadows of the throne room, muttering under his breath. His head turned toward the sound of a guard entering.

"You High—" The guard stopped himself and cleared his throat. "Your Majesty."

"What is it?" Everard growled, and the guard took a step back. "I told you I wasn't to be interrupted."

"I beg your pardon, Your Majesty." The guard stumbled over his words. "But the chronicle keeper has arrived at your request."

Everard rose quickly, his chair scraping against the stone floor. "Well, what are you waiting for? Send him in!" He crossed the room and took his place on what was once his father's throne. He tapped his fingers impatiently. The movement kept him from grabbing his father's staff, which leaned against the throne.

The sound of robes dragging down the corridor preceded the chronicle keeper. He entered, and Everard suppressed a gasp. The keeper's face was shrouded under a cavernous hood, but his eyes were like orbs of fire that pierced the murkiness surrounding them. When he moved forward, it seemed as though he floated. Everard gathered himself and gazed down on the strange figure before him.

"Are you the keeper of the chronicles of ages past?" Everard asked.

"I am." The keeper remained standing.

"Bow to your sovereign ruler!"

Unflustered, the chronicle keeper responded, "I have allegiance to no one, only to the records of ages past and to the days that will soon be past."

Everard gritted his teeth, ignoring the refusal. "I must know what power my father was seeking before he was murdered by that woman."

"The power your father sought was beyond his ability to control. He would never have succeeded in his endeavors."

"Answer my question!"

"The power you seek is already within you." He raised a long, bony finger and pointed toward Everard. "But be warned: some powers should be left alone."

Everard paced impatiently before the throne. "Tell me how to access this power. If it was important to my father, then I will not rest until I have uncovered it."

The chronicle keeper responded calmly, "I will not take the

responsibility of awakening such a power. I will not help you access it."

"I will have you killed if you refuse!"

"Your powers are great, yet you hold no power over me."

"Guards!"

As the guards rushed in, the chronicle keeper calmly turned and exited the chamber.

Everard shouted behind him, "Stop him!"

The guards hesitated in fear of both Everard and the chronicle keeper, who gradually disappeared back down the corridor from where he had come.

"Go after him and throw him in the dungeon until he gives me an answer!"

The guards ran down the corridor but returned only moments later.

"H-he is g-gone, Your Majesty" one guard sputtered nervously.

"What do you mean 'gone'?"

"It's as if he just disappeared. The guards farther down the corridor say no one ever passed. He is just gone."

"You incompetent fools!" He grabbed his father's staff and lifted it in anger. A cloud of darkness rose from the onyx globe that rested on top and flashed forward until it reached the guards. They began gasping for air and then dropped to the ground, dead.

Everard's eyes were wide as the power of the staff washed over him. He hurried across the room to the desk where his father's writings were and began studying them with renewed energy. They seemed to be bizarre ramblings, but Everard now believed they were written in a way only his father understood. Everard believed that his questions could be answered right here in the writings before him, if he could only decipher what they said.

The darkness from the orb continued to fill the room. He

tightened his grip on the staff and closed his eyes in meditation. The staff began to vibrate. A rhythmic hum traveled into Everard's hand and throughout his body. He connected to the power of the staff. Soon he would discover the greater power his father had sought.

When Everard opened them once more, his emerald-green eyes turned black.

In the following days and weeks, Cytherea helped tend to the wounded that were still in need of care and visited the healers who were working with some of the Dark Realm soldiers that had managed to recover after Ailmar's power over them had ended. The loyalists had begun the process of reconnecting the soldiers to their families and supporting them as they healed from the ordeal of their time in the Dark Realm.

Anna and Brockton mourned Gregor, but Anna kept herself busy caring for the injured to avoid succumbing to despair. Brockton also gave her a reason to keep going while he found his way in the world without his father's guidance.

Their victory celebration in the weeks following the battle was subdued but joyous, and they honored those who had given their lives to achieve it. Their happiness was, in part, an homage to their sacrifice. Parents were thankful for having been reunited with their children. Soldiers shared stories from the battlefield; some of those stories were accurate, and some were a bit exaggerated, but no one minded.

One day, Kenric found Cytherea cleaning the wound of a soldier. She sighed without looking up. "There are still so many injured."

"Yes, there are," he agreed, "but there are healers who can help them, Cyth. You have other things you need to tend to."

"Of course, I lost track of time." She stood, wiping her hands on her breeches before calling a healer to take over for her.

"You always do when you are helping the wounded," Kenric chided gently. They left the cottage—one of many that had been set up as a temporary healer location.

Cytherea smiled up at him. "What else is on the schedule today?"

"A meeting with the military leaders this afternoon to officially declare you as the sovereign of Phoxnay." He grinned. "It will be a simple, less formal coronation, but as the heir to the throne of Phoxnay, you have a land to protect and a people to lead. Now is the time for you to officially take your place as their queen." Kenric paused. "Your Majesty."

Cytherea absentmindedly tucked her hair behind her ear, rested a hand on the hilt of her sword, and smiled.

ACKNOWLEDGMENTS

This book was a lifetime in the making, and it rattled in the back of my mind for years before I put the words down on paper. If I had never written this book, it would have been my one true regret at the end of my days. Because of that, "thank you" seems so inadequate to those who have helped my dream become a reality, but there seem to be no better words.

So, thank you first and foremost to my incredible husband, Gerry Wells, and my children, Caleb and Donia, for constantly nudging me to start writing it down and then encouraging me to keep writing when the task seemed overwhelming. Their love and support made me believe I could do it, and without it this story would still just be in my mind, never to be told.

Thank you also to my editors. Christi Martin helped take this book from a short, awkward story to a complete novel. Amber Helt and the Rooted in Writing team then took over and ensured that the story was consistent and that my words made sense and were spelled correctly.

I want to also thank all of my wonderful friends that listened to me talk endlessly about this book. You were all always interested and encouraging.

Thank you to God, who gave me the gift and joy of writing. Without him, I am nothing.

Finally, thank you to the man whose name I can't remember, who told me at the end of my job interview that he wouldn't hire me because God told him that I had a book in me and I should go write it. This is that book.

About the Author

Diana Kristine Wells is a born and raised Texan who loves her husband, her children, and animals of all kinds. She knew she wanted to be a writer in elementary school when she wrote her first story, took it home, illustrated it with crayons, and bound it between two pieces of cardboard held together with yarn. Since then, she has primarily written poetry, some of which has been published in anthologies. She mulled over the idea for her first novel in her head for years until her family and friends finally pushed her to put it on paper. This is that story.